C903582400

KU-783-323

ALL RIVERS RUN FREE

By Natasha Carthew

ALL RIVERS RUN FREE

Natasha Carthew

riverrun

First published in Great Britain in 2018 by riverrun

riverrun

An imprint of

Quercus Editions Limited
Carmelite House
50 Victoria Embankment
London EC4Y 0DZ

An Hachette UK company

A CIP catalogue record for this book is available
from the British Library

Hardback 978 1 78648 862 6
Trade Paperback 978 1 78648 863 3
Ebook 978 1 78648 861 9

10 9 8 7 6 5 4 3 2 1

Typeset by CC Book Production

Printed and bound in Great Britain by Clays Ltd, St Ives plc

For Evelyn

COLD ACRE CREEK

WOOLEY WOOD

CAMPSITE

TAMAR LAKES

N

S

R I V E R   T A M A R

LAUNCESTON

BODMIN
MOOR

MORWELLHAM QUAY

COTEHELE HOUSE

CALSTOCK

RIVER
LYNHER

SALTASH

PLYMOUTH

TORPOINT

KINGSAND

FREATHY CLIFF

RAME HEAD

Coast

THE FIRST TIME IT happened it was the worst of all times; the young woman told herself it was important not to forget this. The first show of red when it wasn't meant the first moment she glimpsed a chance at happiness, since then it had gotten easier. Familiarity was all; failure a used-to thing another blood-drop in the ocean.

She stood on the furthest stretch of rocks and bent to the surf to place the tiny raft into the water. Floating in the ebb tide the bit of meat didn't look like much at all, the kerosene-soaked rag made more of it than what it was what was it? Not a baby not life in any recognizable form except it came from life: this was the best she could do. The only part of her she could ever hope to leave the cove, she would set it free with fire and water same as all the other little creatures that had come before; she would help it evade the grip of that prison place.

One strike of match she flicked the flame spot on, a practised shot and she returned to the beach the fire she had lit and sat to watch the thing the solitary star be gone be burnt and washed; it was better this way better than leaving a piece of herself in the cold creek ground.

'Easy come,' said Ia. 'Easily another.' She didn't mean this she didn't know what else to say if she was respectable she would have said something sacred she wasn't.

When the last wink of light flashed out on the horizon and full dark down she waited for the cove to fill with night its shackles tight around her its weight like bog water until she could no longer breathe; she lay down and searched the sky for stars kicked her boot into the driftwood flames to make her own.

She could hear her heart beat in her ears it split the silence one atom at a time. A little wind the last of tide water the ocean taken away, this the only sound it didn't count she endured it every day.

'You come back to me,' she said. 'Bring me somethin for the baby; a gift for a gift.' She sat up and put her hands to the fire; it wasn't cold not yet but warmth meant small comfort; she caught it and put it into her hoodie pocket took it with her as she walked the short stretch of sand. She reached the cliff-path steps the short climb without light knew the place better than she knew herself; when her feet hit the stony ridge she didn't stop headed toward home a quiet place without hope it would be the quietest. What else to do but go to bed; in the morning she would forget this night like a dream she would overlook the detail of loss find a place to put it somewhere less lonely, imaginary, gone.

THE FIRST THING TO wash up on the shore next morning was a crate of oranges, just that. Tiny pools of sunlight scattered on the shingle-sand, the rock pools spread golden, happy to be tricked into summer. Ia had watched them come in from the caravan window at the sink; she had been looking at her reflection, the contrasting blonde hair black-eye bruise, she was about to contemplate worse when she saw it. A slick of colour being and then split, the oranges were one thing and then a hundred things; she wondered if the dots connected they would reveal their true meaning. She took her first pill of the day rinsed her mug and wiped the laminate sides like always each morning and kept the spectacle at the corner of her eye for as long as she could bear. This magic thing this secret moment that had drifted into the bay and Ia watching alone she was always alone.

She stretched to open the window to smell the fruit and fill the caravan with sweet notes not the usual sour and stood with the breeze pressed to her cheeks. This was colour no paint no palette could replicate; thrown against the slate grey sea the sand the bastard rocks it was the sun come down heaven fallen upon earth. The sea had listened, a hundred gifts for a gift.

'OK,' she said. 'You remain forever it's a straight swop this life I can do.'

She put on her coat and buttoned and slipped the leather journal that she was never without into her pocket and she wished for colours not the usual Cornish slate so she could record this phenomenon draw it for her sister Evie a present for when she saw her again. She stamped her wellie boots in the lean-to porch and amongst the pile of soft-maybes she found a hessian sack worthy of collecting fruit.

Outside the morning was coming good, mizzle just and a light wind threatening clouds; Ia knew they would clear on this gift-given day they had to. She went tentatively toward the western headland and stood looked down on the campsite and hoped nobody else had witnessed this apparition but as usual no folk were up the van doors shut the store by the pool still boarded; it was the same every morning. She went on toward the pathway steps and down on to the beach. Morning was her time since early days she had made it so; she cherished the calm the silent amity, thanked it each and every dawn and in return it gifted her with such delicate scent and colour she called it hers it was she alone who noticed.

She bent to the first orange and plucked it from the sand held it against her nose. An early childhood memory making juice she let the thought bathe her and become river. Oranges everywhere and each one picked and placed gently into the sack like precious stones. She found them floating in the rock pools and caught like crabs between the spurs of flint and barnacle, the skin tight the flesh firm she could feel the muscle of the thing between her fingers in her hands each one was a punch.

With the rocks and shingle combed through she sat with the bounty between her legs and wondered where she might store the oranges to keep them from him. Two more days fishing two more days until his return Ia was determined to make the most of this freedom. Do what the fuck take flight let her imagination drift before the customary anchor drop and drag, no more fruit just fish and potatoes occasionally when he bothered to barter at the campsite.

She left the sack beneath the bench and walked the cliff to where the rock stabbed furthest into the ocean, a thin split of land barely wide enough for standing and yet every morning Ia did just this like a lighthouse it was her duty. Beneath her feet the shingle-rock plunged into the water no matter what tide it towered six hundred feet above sea level the closest she would ever get to knowing liberty. She lifted her arms and dared herself to push a little further forward step off, she heard her sister's voice call out to her a memory made old through remembering too much, she sat back and dug her heels into the turf.

As far as the eye could see a serpent wind raced across the sea coming in to spoil her day. It snapped low to the ground both tail and teeth looking for a way out a way into the caves the hollow trees the spaces that had yet to be claimed. Ia watched it follow the cliff path to her right and stop dead at the bight, saw it slip and crash into the sea be returned to the bay by the rip current; nothing could escape the place, if it had asked she could have told it this. Thirteen years ago she had asked the same question, now the distance between time and memory had fallen wayside, but sometimes it felt like the first year the first day the first fist-fight minute.

Thirteen years unlucky and still Ia did not fit or something about the north coast place did not fit her. When she arrived she had been twelve years of age and all for the show she did her best to please him. She'd learnt to gut and cure fish and clean and pet the caravan into how she supposed it should be and she was happy when she reached sixteen, a new bride. Despite no ceremony no ring she'd learnt to abide had made the van her home and she kept his dream of rebuilding the surrounding ruined cottage into a worthy house give him babies whatever he wanted she would do it. Ia had found her place in things: somebody desired her she was needed. She had told herself she could do this, be a wife a mother be her own woman.

Thirteen years and the caravan he had hoisted into the ruin was still their only home, though by the bind of ivy and bracken it had morphed into the ruin walls and like them it clung to that last remaining dream. And still no babies, no fruit grew from deadwood.

On first arrival Ia had tried to make friends with the women in the neighbouring campsite, through Dad's blood they were kin all kinds of cousin but no matter she was a blonde-haired, hazel-eyed south-coast girl, they didn't like her and the men didn't like her in public, not until her curves came busting did they circle; it wasn't a bother easy money was all. If Bran had provided the way he was meant she wouldn't have split for anyone; it was a game of survival Ia had got good at enduring.

Ia Pendilly was not a woman worth bothering she was mostly left alone, a loner not by choice but by the choice of others, a girl gone over, got old before her time. She could still hear their gossip come in on the night wind; they called her names called Branner worse, but back then he had a little kindness, he took her in with nothing to her just a roaming girl his cousin's kid, bereaved and in need of fixing, he didn't touch her until fifteen.

Ten years hoping and still no full-term baby to show commitment she supposed it had taken its toll; the travelling doctor said a miracle child was what they should pray for told Branner not to waste his time on this girl go and get another. The two men had laughed and Ia too. She'd never learnt how to be opposing, never had the time the guidance, with Mum and Dad dead and sister Evie gone and the pervading dark no matter how hard she stretched for light, felt for substance, texture in the gloom. She smiled, thinking on a way to be the person she would never be but please God why not? She was twenty-five and backalong folk used to say she was a brave kid, growing up she always sought adventure put fire into Evie's sensible shoes, ready to run the risk go at things head-on colliding, she had thrown caution to the wind it had returned a storm its damage was everywhere. There was nothing much to Ia's life except oranges in that moment they were everything to her.

'CLOSE YOUR EYES,' SHE told herself. 'Remember.' She needed time away not far, a moment home, she found Evie sitting in the garden.

'What you up to?' she asked.

'Mum's photo album.' She wriggled across the blanket so Ia could join her.

'The one that ends with us as babies?' asked Ia.

Evie nodded and she pushed the open book toward her sister. 'She was beautiful weren't she?'

Ia agreed. 'Got a sparkle in her eyes; where you spose it went?'

Evie thought for a minute. 'Maybe it went into us.'

'You reckon?'

'We got em int we? Mum's eyes, most of us is Mum.'

'Where's the photos of Dad?'

'Next page, here he is with Mum, teens int they?'

Ia studied the photo and nodded. 'Can't wait till we're teenagers.'

'Next year,' said Evie. 'Tell me what then Ia?'

'I'm always tellin you.'

'Tell me again; tell me like it's a story.'

Ia sighed worked it like a hardship it wasn't it was her favourite tale.

'We'll leave here and go live in a cottage close to the beach,' she began.

'Who will?'

'Me and you and our babies and we'll have cats and a dog and a hundred hens so we int never short of eggs.'

'Where close to the beach?'

'Not on no cliffs that's for sure, one em low-laid villages that push right into the sea.' Ia turned on to her back and closed her eyes to continue her story. 'We'll have a boat for fishin cus you love the sea and I'll have a garden for fruit trees; I'll only grow what we like won't be one vegetable in our yard.'

Evie closed the photo album and joined Ia in lying facing the clouds. 'Strawberries and blackberries and raspberries,' she said. 'What else?'

'Oranges,' said Ia.

'Don't be daft, can't grow oranges in Cornwall.'

'How we know if we int tried?'

'*The Book of Cornwall's Countryside* don't say you can grow oranges.'

'Stuff the book, not everythin's in the book.'

'Mum says it is.'

'Then she's wrong.'

IA OPENED HER EYES and smiled. She returned to the caravan and lugged the sack to the kitchen tipped its contents on to the floor and put the fruit on to every surface into each corner like lamps they lit up the van gilded the walls happy.

She bent to pick up the one remaining orange and put it to her nose her cheek her lips like a living thing she told it she was sorry for the bite, the slaughter. The slow undressing as she split open the fruit, the sour juice dripping through her fingers as she put it to her mouth; the smell the taste the swallow, revelation.

When she had finished eating she wiped her hands in the tea towel; the tears on her face she left to dry they came from a good place she would wear them today, tomorrow, wear them until his return.

She sat amongst the oranges and held on to their memory like old hands; all through the morning she remained beside the things in her care, they were gems to be guarded, gifts from the deep. She told herself to cherish the moment make a memory she could return to but it wasn't long before old thinking ways resumed position: nothing was ever enough she was never satisfied, most days he told her this. She wished for more was all. More than nothing at all it wasn't such a reach, for all the shells and smooth belly stones she wished for better brighter beautiful moments to fill the muted space more than this mist.

Something good was coming something better it was long overdue. Ia knew it was only a matter of time. She left the van, heading toward the scrubland behind the ruin in the hope of finding blackberries one thing sweet; she found the bushes veiled in mould, the drupelets dried gone over before their time, it wasn't a surprise.

The cove was a beautiful tragic place, its parts made up of every kind of perfect pretty, but it didn't fool Ia; she knew its worst, had the scars and scratches to prove it.

The scrub was the highest point above the van, it caught an ill wind, the seasons that came in too fast went too slow, the salt air that went nowhere. Recently those fields sprouted more gorse than good crop; Ia knew what once had grown there would grow again have tough stems and weak roots; nothing much got tended on that part of the coast except plot-land the bit of earth each man woman could see, protect, fight for. The northerly hills were punctured with mineshafts; together with the reef of rocks to the south they captured Ia in their gape, a baited trap. There was no escaping the cove she would be absorbed by that sharp silt soil it didn't matter it was the sea that had her most days.

Out on the water she could see a rowing boat; it looked to be heading toward her. She watched it hang at the reef edge one minute, realize its mistake and about turn and Ia ran from the scrub, past the ruin and down on to the beach in time to see it; she wanted to shout about the oranges, share her beautiful bounty. She stood in the surf and waved, best face. The sight of a boat meant there were other people besides camp folk, she knew other places existed beyond the cove she wasn't alone just lonely was all, but they never came closer than looking; the rocks meant there was no way into Cold Acre Creek there was no way out either. Occasionally she got lucky, a lone lobsterman feeling sorry might tip his hat throw her a wave, but those times were rare mostly they got busy looked down at their hands, the families were the worst, Ia didn't blame them, the place was doomed you didn't have to know it could see it the campsite was to blame.

The campsite gang didn't trouble that part of the creek; there was no route through the rocks to take a boat nothing on the land but the ruin that housed the caravan and Ia rattling inside, the lonely woman who talked to herself a little downbeat drumming within. If anybody chanced getting close they would hear it she was a time bomb ticking Bran said without her medication she was set to explode; he told her she was lucky not to have been locked away aged twelve he said if it wasn't for him she would be there now said it was called the funny farm it sounded perfect.

Ia's only pleasure was the tide; whatever drifted out there beneath the ocean current she deserved, the things that were fated for that rootled cove were meant for her they helped her to forget in time she hoped to remember.

She continued to walk beside the curve of freshly laid seaweed; clods of bladderwrack and kelp tied together with dead man's lace. She kicked the slop with the heel of her boot and bent to swat the flies found limpet shells and mussels, those clear of tar she pocketed and moved on toward the rocks.

She stepped amongst the pools of water and into each new dint she sunk her hands an unlucky dip she returned to the sand and took a stick to mark and prod the wet shingle remembered the oranges and imagined an exotic ship. All those oranges, it had to be Spain perhaps someplace where the sun still shone, a place Ia Pendilly would never visit but here it was visiting her, a better visitor than any. She wished she had the imagination to take her there.

At the left flank of the bay she headed toward the rock that was her favourite and climbed the five-foot crag to sit. Occasionally from this vantage objects appeared suddenly from beneath the shifting silt, the retracting tide or a keen wind blown revealing the pinnacle of something red, rusted.

High tide spring tide neap tide certain times of the year the waves did their own thing came with the moon's pull and dug so far into the cove they bagged up the sand and in their alarmed retreat took up the beach left nothing in return but the hulks of metal the winches and the wheels of forgotten industry. Ia didn't like those tides; she called them bullies they robbed the bay of beauty.

Last winter she had found a bomb the size of a hawthorn bush. All through those worse wet months she spent her days straddling it like it were a good horse; she imagined herself gone in a blaze of glory wished it so until the sand returned rebuilt and reburied.

Nothing but the sea got to leave the creek she knew this, nothing but the wind the waves the seasons' change and the dead baby-buds; sometimes she thought her senses were about to take leave, one empty shell remaining a little space for her to rattle away the days. She pushed away the bad thoughts and jumped from the rock to resume the forage, found nothing but debris, broken bits, plastic beads rinsed pastel the shade of former glory. Ia couldn't place them, but she knew they had been around the world so many times no doubt they would go round again.

She left the beach and headed toward the smokehouse to fetch her fishing line, found a crust of dried fish on the floor and together with a purse of hooks carried them across the rocks to the basin of water where sometimes she got lucky. One mackerel perhaps a rainbow trout if she was blessed one fresh fish for frying instead of smoked to carry home before the last flash of afternoon light cut out. Food because she did not have much what remained she made last, she was never far from a frugal day but the oranges had changed that her lucky number come up.

She threaded the hook to the line the fish to the hook cast off with her feet wide her knees bent she told herself she would not move until night and tide made it so.

An hour passed maybe two, Ia wished she wasn't so quick to make promises to herself she was about to accept defeat when she saw something a little white thing caught up in her line she reeled it in.

'Carrier.' She swung the bag on to the rocks and cut the knot with her pocketknife; it was heavy it held her interest.

She sat beside it and pushed her hand into its contents a few items of children's clothes a tin mug and a leather case she flipped the cover and lifted it into the sky to watch it move it refused, a cracked compass stopped at south and that was her coast the place she was born and raised and come from. South-coast Cornwall her true home where the bearing pulled her most days, her heart in the softer south her head skull-hitting at the north-coast rocks the ruin the winched-in caravan. She put the bag under her arm the rod over her shoulder no fish for frying it didn't matter; Ia had her own curiosity hooked she headed home, tomorrow on her mind.

One more day of freedom, one more day to play at this other life before the rope retied the box kicked and Ia left swinging. Her time without him was precious it was freedom a minute.

'And I won't say a word bout what I found what I bin doin,' she told herself, 'and nothin bout the baby.'

THAT NIGHT SHE ATE little; instead she drank the orange juice whilst sitting and thinking on the life that had held the things she found in a knot: the rag of blue plaid neither dress nor shirt, the compass and silver fishing-floats and the dented tin mug like the one Branner used, twisted up in the bag and washed ashore together; they were going somewhere. She took another sip of the bitter juice and coughed and looked out of the curtain to see clouds come in and become sea; Ia knew the cold wet winter would not be far behind. She stood and pushed the chair to the table took her hoodie from its back tied it to her own and went to the food store without light or looking, found the carton of cigarettes hidden not meant for her and she fingered out a pack and took it to the porch. Anything even cheap smoke was better than the saline gob in her mouth.

From her vantage at the side of the ruin, Ia could see the lights of trawlers dip and climb in the ether and she wondered which one was his which one coming or going or stationary nets down. Each boat in a world of its own the sea and its sanctuary in another, some nights they seemed to come so close she thought she might touch them imagined lifting their hulls from the water holding on to them like resting fireflies in the palm of her hand.

She lit a cigarette and smoked it thinking on those boats and her thoughts wandered about the detritus of an unidentified life strewn across the table. She wondered what her life would wash up nothing much it wasn't a maudlin thought just truth was all. Existence was an empty vessel Ia dragged about, mostly it rocked in her arms barely weight at all, but at times it got into her head it whistled her wild a storm blasting. The first year of her arrival to the creek, perhaps with the year gone full circle, that was when she'd first felt the shift. The want for family love, a man to look after and be looked after by and a baby to bub make the chain complete. At that time this was all she wanted: a family because she didn't have a family. Funny how stupidity preyed on the young she thought she could replace one life with another it would have been a job well done.

Perhaps if she had waited long enough she could have been picked or chosen by anyone, lodged herself and her one bag of sentiment anywhere, it wouldn't have mattered. Age twelve she was not a child, bereavement had made its mark all innocence had been taken from her, snatched without ask she would not get it back. It had been a long time ago but still the confining north-coast ditch was not her home. What was it then? With her heart not in it what was it? She turned her back on the sea and returned to the caravan, pegged the canvas door shut and pulled the cord that raised the flag put her in business and she locked up and went to bed.

There was nothing much to do in the van between visits besides sleep or try to sleep. No TV no radio since the battery rusted and bust and not replaced nor friends or family for gossip bar those in her head these days her sister Evie her twin.

Two rooms was all: one for living-eating, the other for sleeping plus a bathroom no bigger than a pin prick and the porch filled with junk the things that were either on their way out or on their way in never making it further than the floor on to which they fell. Everything in that place held together with string and ply and tape, everything tipped, sea-heading.

Ia entered the bedroom and lit her usual company candle in the ironstone holder brought from home, set it on the chair by the bed and pulled off her hoodie and jeans kept her favourite rocker T-shirt on for warmth. She swallowed one of her pills and lay on her back to study the ceiling for new shadows a new story to make up like the ones she used to tell Evie as kids to help them sleep. The things she thought about most were in those tall tales, the things that didn't make sense in daylight she put sense to them then. She told herself to think happy heart, make the most of Bran's absence, but with the baby gone she could only think of the silence, empty space.

Ia turned toward the candle and brought her knees to her chest. She watched the stub taper run to spit and spill go out, she closed her eyes to the pitch and let herself be taken down toward sleep, close enough but barely ever all the way. Some place not dream but aspects of fantasy and memory combined, a place of rescue and recovery and come morning resignation but night was a long time some nights they went on for days. She thought about the babies, the oranges, smiled, went sad.

Beyond the ply wall of the van she could hear footsteps entering the ruin the rush of ivy somebody pushing past.

'Who's that?' Ia saw light and shadow block her window and she waited to see the face it belonged to a stranger. She sat up.

'What you got me?' she shouted.

The man held up his lamp and then a chicken; it was unplucked but dead at least.

'What else?' She watched him think a minute he was drunk the best kind would give her anything in that moment. He shrugged.

'Any drink?'

He shook his head.

'That a leather coat?' she asked.

The man looked down at himself he nodded said she could have it. 'Int mine anyway.'

'Come round the front.'

Ia climbed from the bed and cosied the blankets to keep

in the warm she knew this wouldn't take long. She put on her jeans, Mum's lipstick and heels and negotiated the dark van, lit the oil lamp in the kitchen and went into the porch to let him in.

'Follow me,' she said, 'and take off that coat.' She led the way into the van and told him he could do what he wanted but no hitting and the kitchen was the only room he was allowed and she pulled down her jeans and bent across the table the objects and oranges staring her in the face she looked away.

'This what you want?' she asked. The man grunted she guessed it was one of the campsite men they weren't good at talking spoke more with their fists their teeth she told him not to bite. Five minutes later ten all in Ia had a chicken on the side and a new coat hidden in the porch it smelt of pig fat but Ia was used to that it was the scent of all of them.

She stood at the sink and halved two oranges forked the juice into a glass near enough routine now and she sipped and spat and went about the last chink of night like it was day; filling the kettle from the porch hose that ran from the top field spring and lighting the stove she picked up the chicken and baby-bounced it to measure the weight swung its head to face forward and folded it into the corner shelf where the toaster used to be. She leant against the thin fibreglass wall of the van and watched the steam rise made a cup of tea with the summer mint she'd found growing amongst the outback weeds used the flotsam mug it pleased her to do so. The smallest things they were the ones that got her, mattered most, moments of stop and stare and smile once in a while.

She went to the table and put down the lamp pushed back the odds and ends and wiped it with the cloth, brought the compass into the light the arrow had found its spark was making up for lost time it held a secret she wished it would spill.

'Int no good if you don't stop turnin.' She put the cord around her neck took up her tea and returned to bed and listened to the crash of waves she knew the surf crawled close. 'You bring me somethin you hear?' she told it. 'Tomorrow you bring me somethin proper somethin that don't need fixin somethin for fixin me.'

She pushed her pillow up against the wall and stretched to get her thinking back on track wished there was some quick-hit way to shorten the gap between past and present but there wasn't. Her previous life was strewn in any case when she searched for one thing positive she could only pull up root-and-bole memories, unwanted thoughts that went so deep they made no sense at all. Ia's past was torn, she sat in the hollow the place of most damage, so far burrowed into that valley she went unnoticed some days she did not recognize herself. She lay down and pulled the covers up closed her eyes so she might sleep or dream or remember right; the story starting with her and Evie out on the rocks collecting winkles early days must have been. Before Dad hurt his back and couldn't fish and Mum broke into so many pieces she couldn't be fixed. That was when they put a pipe to it; those days when petrol was still a thing you could buy. Burrowed in sleep Ia still wondered what had got into them, what was it that had them think to leave their girls behind. Something so hard so complicated they couldn't just put them in the back seat strapped and buckled and told them they were going on a journey, that they would never return; every day Ia knew that would have been a better option to this.

Two girls same coin but different sides always so good at behaving making use out of the detritus that surrounded their childhood chalet at the edge of the world. They never asked for more than what they knew their parents could provide in any case. Ia and Evie never asked to come home see it dark and cold never wanted to hear the car ticking in the lock-up and yet no way in, the engine coughing out the last of its fumes. It had taken three neighbours to kick through the metal door; Ia tried to remember who they were but in sleep each man had the same face, the same expression, gobsmacked. Hers and Evie's eyes reflecting in theirs, just kids they kept saying and Mum and Dad sitting there, driving somewhere, already gone.

She tried to get her dream back on track, return them to their favourite pool in the rocks but it was too late the pleasure had been taken. She turned on to her back and listened to the waves, to gauge their depth the current and all the exchanges beneath the surface and she held her breath with her ear pressed to it so she might catch more meaning, what was meant but not said out there down there somewhere. Any movement not hers was what she wished for, anything other than her soul and the sea sidestepping going around.

I A WOKE TO THE sound of the waves crashing close; a high tide had come in overnight. She wanted to see if it would take the sand it had been so long since she'd seen it happen.

She pulled on her boots and hooked her coat to her shoulders ran to the cliff path to stand and watch the tide turn the red of sunrise, muddying the water. Part-way down the steps she stopped to greet the rollers goaded herself to go further felt the slick water beneath her feet the spatter against her face. She closed her eyes to the salt-spit splashes on her lips in her mouth as she laughed a sound she had not heard in so long she'd forgotten how beautiful. It was the song of purity of childish pleasure; green fields blue sky sunshine swimming. It was the sound that Ia believed freedom made, a door unlocking opening finally splitting the dark into light.

When the sea began its civil retreat Ia followed it; with each step forward she imagined herself going away wished the sea would part and let her.

It was a fast-drawn tide; already the flat rock plateau could be seen stretching away from the cliffs toward the ocean ridge. When water exposed the first spit of beach Ia jumped the last of the steps and stood at the foot of the cliff where sand used to be. She bent to the wall of rock and stuck her fingers into the bare sediment, saw flint pebbles and clay, she fingered a little into her hand plucked the splinters of slate from its fibrous hide and rolled it into a ball.

'Pottery.' She smiled.

How many times did she and Evie try to make something from nothing? Sitting outside on a summer's day, the washing-up bowl between them, getting wet making a mess, building objects and memories despite the fractures, widening.

Ia pushed her thumb into the putty met it with her finger made a ring and put it on. She looked for the morning sun and saw the bleed of red rising it came toward her a warning perhaps but she was not ready to let go of freedom no matter how fleeting the moment how brief the flight.

One step at a time one more inch of rock instead of sand Ia shadowed the sea as it continued to dig at the cove, she gave it the circle of clay took out the compass to check for change but nothing it kept on running rings. She held it out in front of her lifted it above the water saw the cove reflected its misery compounded in its face it was enough to wipe her smile land her back down to earth.

Something in that creep-dog moment made Ia turn abruptly;

she saw the gulls return to the bay their white gone to black becoming crows she looped her eyes along the cliff edge to settle on the ruin saw movement in its shadow shifting light it was then she saw it: a figure standing idling in front of the ruin, just looking.

'Branner.' She tucked the compass into her coat fixed her face to start the pleased-to-see pretence despite the shock of his sudden arrival.

'You're early.' She started to walk. 'You int meant till tomorrow.'

'What's with all the mess?' he asked. When she was close enough he said it again.

'What mess?'

'The oranges and the shit everyplace I look.'

Ia climbed the last few steps her heart bottle-stopped in her mouth she tried to think of a way around explaining the oranges and the beauty they had brought to the bay.

'What?' she asked, stupidly.

'The oranges.' He stepped forward. 'The fuckin oranges.'

Ia kicked at the stubble-stone earth she noticed the first frost had yet to melt she would make a note of that in her journal. 'I int bin stealin,' she said.

'Did I say that?'

She looked up at him and saw the rose gold of her locket flash in the dark and dirt of his chest it pushed like a razorblade beneath his throat. She saw him swallow, his Adam's apple threatening the skin.

'You pretendin to be crazy?' he asked.

Ia put her head down digging the ground, she wanted to know why he was early why the morning he never arrived home until late afternoon. She counted out the days counted them back, more confused than before.

'Or is it true what they say, like mother like daughter, all said there was somethin wrong, put a spell on my dumb-fuck cousin, some days he said it himself.'

Ia had heard the stories a thousand times it didn't bother her the campsite gang said this about everyone that wasn't them. Her mother said her own blood was ancient it ran with well-water came from bedrock it was strong and Ia tried to remember this draw from its strength it ran deep.

'From the south coast is all,' she said; she wanted to say more, how Dad had been cut from their north-coast family's flesh like rot just because he'd fallen for a stranger.

'Is all,' he repeated.

'I done nothin wrong.'

When Branner raised his hands as if to catch her explanation she flinched and told him they had been washed ashore.

'And what bout all this shit on the table?'

Ia didn't speak. She looked at him tried to catch his eye with a smile but his gaze had returned to the sea. What it must have been like to have so many images to choose from, his life twice hers in years his memory good his days filled with fishing and hauling and a life of boats and cargo ships what did he have to be angry about? He had seen things big and glorious, Ia only got to see the small, the discarded and the broken, nugatory half-objects.

'I was goin to bake some bread,' she lied.

'Saw the chicken on the side, spose that washed up the same.' He put up one finger before she could explain stabbed it toward home. 'You got anythin to drink?' he asked.

Ia shook her head said sorry she was always sorry. She followed him into the caravan and waited for him to settle at the table, watched his boots go wide with the kick.

'You want a cup of tea?' she asked.

He ignored her and pulled his bag into his lap got out his radio headphones and put them on stretched his feet across the table the hopeful things falling becoming useless on the floor.

'Don't disturb me,' he shouted. 'I need to listen to the mornin news; em put army on the streets to stop the lootin.'

Ia went into the bedroom and sat on the bed and wished for more rooms. A hundred would not have been enough his wrath so huge he pushed it into every corner kicked it into the splinter-wood of every floor punched it into every wall. When he closed his eyes to concentrate Ia moved to the edge of the bed so she could see him; like a childhood dare she forced herself to look fully at what he was. An old man with a girl's chain choked at his neck he was a ridiculous man. Ia remembered when she and Evie had been given those necklaces; it was a birthday a good one, Dad still working Mum not yet off the pills, and the lockets the photos two wings a butterfly clasped to each girl's chest. They had worn them like medals, shields of protection, never had Ia been so mistaken.

She leant back and looked at the mould on the ceiling; a subtle change in weather had drawn new veins of pink and blue they stretched out toward the light fitting and stuck to the flex, streams going somewhere then nowhere Ia knew how they felt.

In the kitchen she heard Bran swing his feet to the floor felt the van rock and he shouted something at the radio called Ia to come here.

'What you say?' She went to him.

'Said I'm crossin to the campsite.' He shrugged his coat to his shoulders and stamped his boots, what now? What was this new hurry?

'You're just back.' She followed him into the porch and out into sudden daylight saw the sea at the corner of her eye its hurried retreat eager to get away.

'Need to speak to the lads,' Bran replied. 'There's some mackerel in the porch needs guttin.'

'You eaten?' Ia asked. 'I can make you somethin for breakfast if you int eaten.' She looked at the face of the man she had hoped one day to love, his pale skin grey hair fallen his black eyes searching but not for her.

'I'll eat at the pool,' he said. 'Em fixed up a grill; I'll eat there.' He looked at the van. 'Get that shit cleared up.'

IA COLLECTED THE ORANGES into the sack and carried them to the furthest headland precipice. She set them free into the last of the leaving tide and like a flock of dying birds they flapped toward the surf their plumage dull toll-taken from their brief visit to the cold grey cove. She watched them take turns giving over to the sea and with their parting the want that had consumed her was want no more, nothing remained her spirit black where for a moment there had been colour.

She returned to the caravan and cleared the things from the floor and boiled water for wiping the sides the windows the walls, got to her knees to mop the linoleum. A few good hours lost with usual chores they helped her to forget while she told herself not to be hard on Bran there were things on his mind anger was just his way. She remembered the first time they had felt true happiness, the first baby and his joy the promises that he made they didn't stop. Everything Ia wanted she could have nothing was too much her imagination ran wild; she still had the pages in her journal the ideas the designs the what would go where. Grey pencil-sketch plans. When that first baby slipped suddenly he never promised her anything again never offered any other shade.

All the while the compass swung between her breasts her secret find, unlike her locket he would never know about it never see it to take it from her. One beating thing to hold on to, another's heart.

In the porch she found the roped fish hanging from a nail

stabbed to the side of the van and she unhooked them and went outside to where the gutting knife and board were kept drying against the ruin wall and carried everything to the cliff edge so she could throw the entrails to the seagulls. Ia watched them snatch the guts in flight and swallow, be gone. They knew nothing of Ia's life or the country's crash, nothing except the seasons, knew nothing of the things Bran said were getting worse on the outside. Beyond the cove Ia supposed changes for the worse mattered, but where she lived nothing was worth bothering everything was whittled and worn just the same. She knew she should be grateful, nothing to lose nothing worth stealing she was safe in her shanty life safe in her ignorance. But still she envied the gulls.

She sat down and wiped her hands in her jeans thought about yesterday's yesterday baby and last year's and the ones going back close to a decade. How many were there how many had fallen in between? Ia imagined their memory of the place lodged in the gaps in the furthest rocks their fate like bullets dodged and stuck, debris for another day. It was for the best was what Bran said each time another one slipped from her, perhaps he thought it was the right thing to say considering, have her know what harm could come fucksake she knew what already.

'Just somethin mine,' she said, 'somethin to take my mind off, take it away.'

From inside her coat she produced the compass and she opened it and watched the needle slow toward the sea it paused a moment and returned to the spin she told it to pack it in or it would find itself returned to the sink, she meant it.

When they were kids she and Evie had found one at the bottom of a cereal box; it took them so many miles from home they declared it useless when it didn't return them. A full day and night they spent squatting in a field of maize, the farmer brought them home they hadn't been missed.

Early childhood they had got away with lots of things, everything. Ia thought her parents were the best in the world, they didn't make them go to school never forced them to do anything they didn't want to just as long as they were happy stayed out of the way.

They had *The Book of Cornwall's Countryside* by way of education; Mum said everything they needed to know was in that book. Ia and Evie learnt the alphabet by reading its glossary of insects learnt to count by flicking the numbered pages both girls could count to 455 before school age that's what Dad said. They made up stories from their imagination could draw every animal from memory nothing got past them.

Ia watched the seagulls return to the sea the white translucency of their tails catching a little sky colour; they left nothing behind but clouds dropped them off like something inevitable.

'Fuckin fish,' said Ia. Every week there was something for gutting something for going into the smokehouse something coming out; all afternoon would be taken up with this one chore, she'd been at this job since twelve, she knew there was no way round the stick on her fingertips the stench in her hair it got everywhere.

Bran said it was tender, without it they would be poorer than ever but Ia knew from thirteen years observing most mackerel caught and cured went bartering toward the campsite store. What returned in way of exchange was drink and smokes, rarely did the right thing come back around; Ia had made do with the payment she received from her own secret slog.

She took up the knife and hit the heel of her hand against the steel spine it wasn't long before she had all heads chopped and bellies slit she pulled the guts and stripped the fish to bone. Occasionally the gulls came back and swooped close and Ia watched them cling mid-air and strain their necks to watch her handle the flesh, patiently waiting for her to pitch something more their way; she ignored them and thinned the meat into delicate slices piled them on the board for carrying.

The smokehouse was five sheets of corrugated iron one sheet with a hole for the roof and chimney made from the same; it held together with bent and buckled nails they caught the rusted metal like fish-hooks. Bran had built it on a jut of land halfway to the beach, it was where he found the washed-up ready metal, had said it was as good a place as any but Ia wasn't so sure. In certain weather the wind went under the eaves it was a constant battle to pin it down with rope and rocks she swore the thing had a mind to take to the skies and be gone; twelve thirteen years it had been threatening this.

She wrenched the bolt out of hiding opened the door and pulled the metal bath into daylight still brim full of salt water, her shoulders strong her thighs used to pitching low, she tipped the fish slices into the brine and secured the plastic lid with rocks; she knew the gulls were watching they watched everything. Tomorrow she would loop the strips of fish on to the suspension rack and light the wood and leave it until the fire burnt out.

She returned to the caravan and filled the basin with suds water to wash her hands and she scrubbed with the nail brush until the dry cracks split wide and bled and she wrapped them in a tea towel and looked for other things to do it wouldn't hurt for him to see her busy. At the front of the ruin there were crooks and corners where somebody in the past had declared garden, Ia wondered about its former glory. The patch of briar out front had a path running through it and sometimes she took up the hatchet, clearing beneath the bullying green, she often found the yellow buds of daffodils she loved them let them see light. Flowers that had been bulbs dug into holes they gave her hope somebody had loved this place, perhaps somebody would love it again.

Out at sea Ia noticed dusk was not far from falling; she realized she'd spent the day preparing fish and he not even around to see her toil. She stood and watched the pending cloud close the space between land and water a pinch between her thumb and fingers and in the last of the light she found some late-blooming crocosmia spiking from the bramble; she picked the flowers high at the stem and brought them into the porch, found a jam-jar a little water.

They would do for one day of colour; she set them on the table and sighed when she remembered the oranges.

'I should bake bread,' she said and she sat and waited and watched the dark claim the flowers watched them be captured and disappear from view.

NIGHT FELL AND BLINDED the windows with all the colours of dark and Ia remained at the table with the compass gripped at her chest; she lit the lamp and turned the object over. Outside she could hear the turn of bicycle wheels heard footsteps on the grit-ground and she bent to the stamp-hole in the kitchen floor and pushed the compass where she should have hid the locket all those years ago, before he had a chance to call it payment and claim it his.

'Got you somethin,' he shouted through the kitchen window.

Ia patted herself tidy and went outside and she stood beneath the mantle of the ruin where the door was supposed and she smelt smoke, some distant fire come in on the breeze.

'I said I got you somethin.' He wheeled his bike to the side of the building and untied the package from the rear rack.

'What is it?' she asked.

'Loaf.' He passed the bread to her and she thanked him and

watched as he pulled three bottles of Plymouth gin from out the bag told her it was bootleg not the real thing.

'Thought you might like the bottle.' He held one up so Ia could see the label.

'Is that a galleon?' she asked.

'Some sort of sail boat; when em drunk you could I don't know put a candle in em.'

Ia nodded. 'If I had a candle,' she said.

'Never grateful is you?'

Ia looked at him and his eyes drifted past, always two ships they were oceans apart. If one was lost the other was gone from the earth completely.

'Come in, I'll open a bottle.'

He followed her into the caravan and Ia thanked him again for the loaf. She set one bottle on to the table and put the two tin mugs the same and she wondered if he would notice which one was flotsam found.

'How's the campsite?' she asked.

'Same.'

'No more fightin than what's been?'

'All em other gangs too worn I reckon. Int bin botherin you have they?'

'Who?' Ia rubbed her hand over the table, remembering.

'Lads,' he said. 'Lads in general.'

'Why would they bother me?' They both looked at the chicken and she said she had found it wandering out on the headland thought it too old for eggs had snapped its neck where it stood.

'You know there's some fucker folk about don't you?'

Ia shrugged.

'You think it's funny?'

'Don't think anythin.'

'We know that.'

Ia kept her mouth shut it was best.

'What would I do if I came home to you slit all which way, what then?'

She wanted to say he would probably find another girl over at the campsite, raise her up into something that resembled a wife better than what she managed herself.

'Sorry,' she said, she didn't mean it. She unscrewed the bottle, poured his mug first and then her own. 'How's the fishin?' she asked.

'Same.' Bran took off his coat and pulled out a chair and the stench of fish returned to the van. 'Feet are killin.' He took off his boots and a little nit-sand danced on the floor.

Ia sat across from him and turned the bottle over in her hands.

'Should quit it,' he continued.

'What's that?' She helped herself to the pills her nerves were pins she needed to blunt them out.

'The fishin, int you listenin?'

She nodded. 'Course.'

'There's other ways to make money I know it.'

'Fishin's honest that's what you say.'

'That's what I say what the fuck do I know? You got to wonder why bother with honesty workin for shit when all round int, and them that int live in built digs and all the food and drink em want.'

Ia shrugged and she kept her eyes from looking out the window at the ruin. She didn't know what was good for him or what he was talking about and she remained silent filled her mouth with drink. She sensed him looking at her wanting answers to questions neither of them knew how to ask.

'And then you got all em feet set beneath the table think em owed somethin.'

'Who?' asked Ia; he was confusing her he always did when he was in this mood.

'The blow-ins, the foreigners and em coloureds blown in backalong, em think they got the same rights. Then you got the politicians, them that's in hidin em the worse, beats me why they set em free in the first place.' He waited for Ia to agree; when she didn't he slammed his hand on to the table.

'You got a job?' he asked.

Ia thought about the smokehouse.

'No you int, do I?'

'You got the fishin—'

'Fuck the fishin; you know why we int got jobs?'

'Foreigners?'

'Course, and people wonder why we got gangs gettin bigger; course em gettin bigger, we gotta fight for what's ours.' He looked at her with a question mark etched into his brow.

'Our country?'

Bran nodded. 'Our fathers dint fight in em wars for this.'

Ia wanted to say his father was a violent drunk, hers an addict, they had not fought for anything but the right to do what the fuck they liked.

She glanced at him when she thought he had finished talking and caught him shaking his head. 'What?' she said at last.

'Oranges.'

'I found em, thought they'd taste decent, juice or whatever.'

'Did they?'

She shook her head.

'Spend enough time trawlin up crap in the net, don't need it cloggin the van the same.' He stamped his feet and Ia thought about the twitching compass, a beating heart buried beneath them. They split the bottle of gin in two, occasionally raising their heads to look out the scratched perspex window beside them, he then she, then both together.

Ia wanted to say yes the ruin was still there: a relic a monument a champion to the cause a plight toward happiness. If she'd had nerve to say this she might also have had the courage to add that he could still do it if he wanted it so bad. In the beginning when Ia was first brought to Cold Acre Creek to cook and clean whatever, he had boasted how he could fix up the old fisherman's cottage in six months. That was his claim his dream the reason for his existence. Six months to source supplies winch the caravan back out of the quarters and make good what they had got. Get a gang of site boys to help, but that was before he pulled her into his bed and they became something other, before he claimed ownership of her and then the fear of losing and the hatred that came after.

'I gotta do somethin,' he said suddenly and Ia knew his thinking was the same as hers but they never knew how to say it.

'We int talked.' She didn't know what about but the connection between them was loose, two elements dangling they never sparked.

'Somethin's come up, I got business to attend.'

'What business?'

'Site stuff; I'll be a while so . . .' He pushed the chair and stood and hooked his coat over his arm and Ia watched him tie his good shoes into knots in a rush to get away; she knew tonight he was after his own prison break tonight he would have the site drunk dry.

'Bran.' She waited for him to stop one moment and look at her, wanted to ask why he hated her why didn't he let her go why did he return at all? He couldn't bear to be around her, when he came home his eyes set to leave.

'Thank you for the bread,' she said and he nodded and made a mess of kissing her cheek; he took up a fresh bottle got on his bike and toward the coastal track and gone. A man come again and then been and gone and Ia wondered which was worse, waiting for him to come home or waiting for him to leave. If sudden tragedy hit him if he returned home later than the usual week would she notice? Would he notice himself sunk at sea? Wasn't he already drowning, close to drowned? How much more loneliness and fear could she endure more than that which had already been forced upon her? Every day she told herself to be grateful and every day she failed. She reached into her coat pocket and took out the journal and flicked through the pages of photos and memory stubs to look at their childish postings, Evie's delicate drawings and observations, her own hand rough-sawn, digging, niggling the page.

She looked out of the window for inspiration and through the thin lamplight the ruin returned her flinty glare. Her own reflection her sister looking in.

She went to the drawer and found the pot of ink and the stubby artist's paintbrush she'd found in the seaweed one time and she sat. If she could paint what was in her she could understand better but when the ink spilt it only made things worse. The dye flooded the page it would take all day to dry it, a good page wasted, a blank black page, void. She sat at the table and closed her eyes leant her head against the van. If sleep came it was without substance another shaft in which to fall.

When she hit the bottom she woke with a start stood and looked out the window and tried for good things happy thoughts and she remembered the oranges squeezed them for a moment of pleasure but it didn't last. What had broken inside she could not say it rattled her shook her down to nuts and bolts nothing felt secure. With Bran home and without the baby to hold on to she had fallen hedge-way, there were no signs to point her right all thoughts tangled in briar. Each time Bran came home she searched for new beginnings, how they might find one right track on which to walk but the space between stretched wide it was gully deep, rocky.

The days of contentment were the ones when she saw him away and she was gifted with silence, peace upon her. Some days a week to be alone create a world worthy, this was what she lived for if she lived for anything at all. The grief was easier to contain; thirteen years her parents had been dead but it wasn't what they took away it was what they left behind; isolation was a noisy place it was chaotic made a mess of the mind.

Ia took the pot of pills from out her pocket and rattled them. 'Still some.' She took one straight and looked over the van; it was neither house nor home a holding crate was all with punch holes in the walls and doors for looking; she went to get the compass and looped the cord around her neck took up the remaining bottle of gin and hid it out in the porch.

She put on her coat her sister's scarf and left the van went about the ruin and imagined it like a fully formed house, the home she desired. The moon, full bulbed and great company as always, it joined her as she stepped through each room and together they passed beneath the granite lintels and stopped to dress the windows, every view framing something of the sea but with curtains and cut flowers she could keep from watching wondering about the world. If this was her home at some point she must learn to like it love it even, after all it was meant for her perhaps the things that were lost would one day be found. It was called hope it was a lonely word it remained untrusted.

She stepped on to the bank of earth that sloped up the rear wall and climbed to reach the space where the roof should have been. Sitting where the last trusses crossed the divide Ia looked toward the campsite and the fields that fell between and still not one soul about and along the cliff path he not one step closer to coming home. She watched the moon drag forward the west rim of the bay in sight, its belly full but fading and mouth hung dry, the sight of Ia rooftop dangling had it aghast, it was a worrier moon. That she might reach for it jump the sky somehow but Ia knew her limitations, knew she would end up skidding against the mouldy lid of the caravan her head in the skylight looking down on her life.

In her coat pocket she felt for the pack of cigarettes and the lighter and she lit one whilst waiting for the sun to rise, her eyes sticking pins in the east. Any colour any tint not sharp silver the sand the sea the setting moon. With the cigarette smoked she lit another with the dying butt and watched the trawlers come into view each rig-light following the next; the fight was on, the battle not always for fish but passing cargo whatever could be made use.

'So he int comin home.' She took one final pull of the cigarette and flicked it toward the path. 'One loaf of bread and he int comin back tonight.'

Ia wished she had kept the oranges, just that. Find the feeling make an effort to hold on to what it was they made her feel what was it? Strawberry picking in the southern flank fields of home in summer the smell of sunshine the taste of laughter dripping. Some years she and Evie ate so many berries their stomachs ached with the sickly sweet and they had to shit in the scrub where they stood.

Strawberries came first, then wild gooseberries and in early autumn the raspberries that prettied your lips and bloodied your hands to butcher blocks. Some jobs paid but most jobs didn't it wasn't a bother Ia and Evie were all about the gorge, mostly. What they didn't eat they brought home; Dad was always hankering after jam and Mum was forever saying tomorrow. Tomorrow came and went Mum always said there were plenty tomorrows but the fruit knew no better in that house other than green then black and blue. Fruit was special it was summer it was sister Evie. After the raspberries came potatoes; they tasted of soap, potatoes were no fun at all. And then the oranges, heaven tasting, then taken.

Ia was the custodian of the ocean that was all, an observer perhaps protector of all the things that went mostly unnoticed. She could tell by the change of colour in a new tide, the depth of opaque fog in the surf just how the weather would turn.

All seasons from new beginnings toward abrupt end she saw everything in that water, something in its movement too, it was there now, oil on water it curdled and placed itself wrong in the distance. Autumn she knew would end prematurely, perhaps it had ended. The bright startling breath of fresh and the bonus morning light were moments gone, Ia would have to get used to the rain.

Every day every night she watched the weather watched the tide come in stop about turn. There was something about the cove that made the ocean do that, pause for thought and then think better of it, retreat. Maybe it was Ia, like all else something about her made the north coast current recoil and push on into the next inlet, she didn't mind, it was expected.

Some days most days she knew she liked the beach and all the water more than it cared for her, it saw better places had more variety to choose from. She thought about Branner in that world away, all the streets the places he could choose, why did he want to come back to her? They were once in some kind of love she supposed. Ia Pendilly had been searching for the looking-after and then the happy-ever and Bran wanted a woman just and maybe a baby a family but that was never going to be, Ia was bumping barren she had fucked around the houses and still nothing more than the occasional foetus drupe for her to set on a raft push into the surf burn out to sea.

In the moonlight she waited for the last of the rock pinnacles to reveal themselves above the surface of the falling tide and what remained of water she watched settle and become mirrors reflecting. She slid from the top wall and into the room that most days she fancied as the kitchen and left the house with no door to close no way to shut that dream behind her.

THE WALK TO THE campsite wasn't so far, buried in dull dawn morning it wasn't far at all. There was nothing to stop Ia, have her hide; she was free to stand and watch the fools dance and drink themselves down to piss puddles, so far gone they wouldn't have noticed an army stamped there.

On certain nights when she couldn't sleep and Bran all at sea she did this went looking when seclusion cracked and a little world wonder seeped in. Curiosity was all. To see how others did it, how did they do it so at ease unaware of themselves?

She sat on the backless iron bench that was meant for sealooking and faced the camp, the vans like hers but grown over with ply and corrugated box-bits, it was a jungle an alien place. Where windows had been put out the plastic fertilizer bags and coal sacks amassed from backalong caught in the wind they rattled and snapped continually this was the soundtrack to the camp it never stopped never faded it had driven them all mad.

Through the haze of coming light she could see the last of

the revellers sit around the bowel bends of the swimming pool the fire pit still burning rubber in the centre of blue, their eyes on it their lips on the bottle.

'Where you at?' She lit a cigarette and drew her knees to her chest; she wished she hadn't bothered it was better thinking he was there than knowing he wasn't. She wondered what van he might be in getting laid or wasted in any case she was glad to see most teenage girls were hanging in the play park God knew he liked them young. They sat on swings and the spring-thing animals some good spirit still about them their lives determined this way always, some had been stuck twice, their Lycra guts grown fat with new life this circle they'd been caught both relentless and vicious. There was no beginning no end it spun continuous three girls on the roundabout high as fever it would not stop.

Ia smoked the cigarette down to her knuckles and she wished herself over there a gang-member but it was too late she had her ways and campers had theirs despite shared blood and anyway she was a woman of twenty-five she should know better act her age.

If she had the house to fancy up and learnt to cook maybe the older women would visit on invited days when loneliness threatened. Not friends but familiar faces they could talk things around to their way of thinking the way some women did. Apart from Evie, Ia had no friends and sisters didn't count; anyway she and Bran weren't the type for friends he told her this in the early days and she knew what he meant. Mum and Dad hadn't been the type either, they were each other's life and soul of their own party they had their gear what more did they need? Love and peace and crack and fighting until love again. That last night Ia had told Evie it was the best way to go considering, maybe their folks knew it someplace deep within the clatter and chaos, knew something of saving grace. Ia wondered what they would make of this place this life she had been put to, was it what they imagined? They loved each other they would see no love here.

SHE FLICKED THE BUTT from the side of the cliff and pulled the bottle of pills from her pocket rattled them and helped herself to what fell out, she would have to ask Bran to score more, he said depression drugs were easily bartered in the lane outside the old doctors' surgery in town it might have been a lie she'd never been. They came in all shapes and sizes these ones blue, Ia didn't know if they worked in the way they were supposed she didn't think she had depression but the risk of living without was too great they were the kind Mum took, the ones she stopped taking. She popped another.

'So,' she said, 'he int comin home tonight this mornin either.' She got up to head off but when she heard voices beyond the campsite perimeter and saw the swing of lamplight, instinct was to duck.

Men more men than usual appeared at the brow of the hill they were high in spirit Ia could tell by their boom there was too much bravado bursting from them she could hear it in their voices see it in the way they jumped in and out of the light.

Ia returned to the bench. What was this now? she wondered, she hoped Bran was not involved it would do no good to have him heated he was all brawn had no head to him at all.

How many men? She counted them fifteen twenty coming over the hill like a marching band the piped lead and winch-chains turning tuning up in their hands. She tried to see their faces it was hard to tell one from the other their trackies muck-heavy and hoods pulled to shadows in the cast Ia could see their brows were set on something.

'Idiots,' she said, whatever wrongdoing they had been up to they were idiots and she returned Bran to one of those vans, it was easier than thinking him otherwise. It was in her interest to help him hammer out the hard she knew if they rediscovered the soft silence he would be a better man. Early years he had been a quiet man. Content to sit in silence let Ia do the talking she never stopped. Sometimes he smiled, her stories her questions her words, but mostly he just listened to the sound of her voice back then it was music to his ears. Now it was just noise, she made a racket even with her mouth shut the sight of her was enough to have him take off. He thought loping about with younger lads was where the glory was thought himself something more he was a fool everything he did was foolish.

He used to be somebody he told her this, top dog in a pack of dogs, he'd gone to them now, a hound at the bottom of the barrow. Ia could see it hurt but he wouldn't talk about it tried to keep the dream beating by running with the boys but it only proved the point that he was older, slower, weaker. It was he who made the noise.

She stood and saw smoke rise from the high ridge fields to the south in the wake of the men, it looked to have unfinished business of its own. She could see fire too; the towering flames reached toward the bay, lit the way their faces masked with rage, victory, destruction for the sake of small-world glory.

Ia crouched behind the bench and waited for her breathing to slow her heart to restart so she could slip away. The men were close; she could smell their sweat the ash could taste their brine on her tongue. All around them tiny flames fell from the sky like stars they landed in the bracken became flowers, beauty finding Ia when she needed it most.

The men stopped in wonder.

WHEN SHE WAS SURE she had not been seen Ia pulled up her scarf and hood and ran. She told herself she would make a hot-jar bed, the morning was too long in coming now it was here it was too strange too cold too miserable to contemplate. She could still hear the men shouting singing some business complete got done and won they were in fine form. She could imagine them joining the others returned to the drink she thought about the bottle hidden at home wished the men would bring more but it was the bottle emptying that brought them sniffing around her in the first place. Perhaps it was the thought of comfort or lost sleep but Ia's mind was addled taken-up she didn't hear the footsteps see the shadow of a stranger cross her track the hand at her mouth the arm against her throat.

'Don't scream, don't even speak, I int goin to hurt you.' The stranger's breath was heavy he struggled to catch it.

He asked Ia if she understood of course she did she nodded yes and wished he'd hurry up and get on with whatever let her get home get warm. He took his hand from her kept a fist to her chest, when she did nothing he apologized and let go of her coat.

Ia pushed her hands further into her pockets. 'I int scared,' she said. She waited for an explanation and when it didn't come she told him the campsite was that way.

The man nodded and looked toward the ruin the whites of his eyes dyed red from smoke.

'Not that way,' she continued. 'Keep goin.'

'Who lives down there?' he asked.

'I do, me and my big fucker man lives down there.' She went to go on and he stood in front of her.

'He home?'

'On his way, he int far, he's at the site, as I said, just over the rut there.'

The man nodded and stepped to let her pass and in the dawn

light Ia could see he was tired he had been running. She looked into his eyes two burnished stones set in dried tilled sod-skin his hair the colour of burnt umber autumn leaves these were her favourite colours.

'You int from the campsite is you? Int headin there neither.' She stood back to get a good look at the stranger, saw the army greens beneath his military coat the banger-boots they had seen better days. In that split-second moment Ia knew she had the better of him, it would have been so easy to shout out get calling but kind eyes were a mystery to her.

'You on the run?' she asked and she waited for him to answer why was he taking so long? 'I int goin to shout; you can say.'

The stranger looked past her toward the campsite and she laughed told him the men were finished with the hunt.

'You know that?' he asked.

'All in all pissed, they won't be headin out now; besides, daylight's here, site folk don't do much besides fuck and sleep in daylight hours.'

'You one of em?'

'No way I int.'

'Your old man one of em?'

'Some days.'

'Today one of em days?'

'I'd say he's over there.'

The stranger nodded his head heavy fear was not far from him.

'You from round here?' Ia asked.

'Not far.'

'So go home why don't you?'

'Can't right now.'

'Cus of em?' Ia pointed to the camp and he nodded.

Something about the way he concealed himself, his darting eyes and his red hair wet with scrubland dew, had Ia think of a running fox, rip scared.

'I int afraid of you.' She said this to herself it surprised her. 'My old man int likely home if you want a hot drink; either way I'm goin onward, puttin water to the stove, it's freezin out here.' She continued down the hill shouted if he had alcohol on him she had things she could barter.

'I int got nothin but what I stand up in,' he said.

They went toward the ruin in silence Ia up front fevered with provocation the stranger behind his skin loose and worn from all the in-out jumping.

'This is our ruin, the van's inside, we're goin to do it up.' She told him to step up if he was coming; she couldn't account for men blowing in on the wind they had a habit of catching and stopping on the step like driven leaves.

When they reached the van she held open the door to let him pass, like a badly beaten cub he went slow and sorry, he was a different type of man shy or simple maybe both he smelt of fire recent smoke. This man was not used to disorder he was not used to low-expectation getting by.

'I'll lock the door,' she said. 'One drink and then you go.'
She told him to sit down and he did.

Ia filled the kettle in the porch and brought it to the gas and
she asked if he was hungry if he was injured, he said no just
worn was all.

'I int good at small talk,' she said and he nodded. She saw
him pick up the journal the ink stain dried into different shades
the light grey birds taking flight and the fractal trees reflecting,
where the ink pooled darkest that was the river it went nowhere.
She took it from him and tucked it into her coat pocket.

'Some things private.' She caught his eye and smiled, felt
stupid. Nerves but not nervous, heat but not hot.

She cleared her throat. 'Spose it's true what's bin goin on.'
She took off her coat and hooked it to a chair.

'What you heard?' he asked.

'Gangs gettin bigger, goin at each other and the army drafted
in and now everythin churned up, everythin worse.' These were
Bran's words but still it felt like she knew stuff had something
to say.

'Things is hard all round,' he said.

'I int arguin with you there.' She looked at him to see if he
had a story to tell, she knew he had but he kept it well hidden.
His eyes were for her, deflecting.

'You round these parts?' she asked again.

'Close enough.'

'I don't know you, spose I don't know many of anyone.' She

looked him over; in good light she could see he was restless, what nerve remained stood upright, bristled.

'Em camp lads after you?'

He shook his head.

'Course not.' Ia noticed the cuffs of his coat were burnt. 'Everybody lyin, everybody fightin, why tell the truth?'

'Some things are best left.'

'So army is you?'

'Long story.'

'In a gang? Don't say you int, cus all folks is, even army's a gang of sorts.'

'I int gang minded but you've made your mind up anyhow.'

Ia shrugged. 'You int sayin otherwise.'

'I int in no gang.' He looked at her straight, he meant it.

'What then?'

She could see something imagined tethered to his back, something that didn't belong to him but he had to carry it in any case. When he didn't speak she turned to the stove and put her hands out to catch the warmth; it felt strange, funny to be talking to a man both clothed and sober.

'Mint tea is all I got,' she said when the kettle was close to boiling. 'It's better un nothin.' She put the two tin mugs on to the side and counted out the leaves got pouring and all the while she felt the stranger's eyes on her this sudden kindness of hers surprising them both.

'Mint tea,' she said again. She set the mugs on the table

opened the blinds a little told him if anyone was coming she would see their shadow pass through the ruin the light was different there.

'Thank you.'

Ia nodded and sat down, his reticence caught her interest, she wanted to take out her knife and peel back the layers move closer take a look inside.

'So you're on the run.' She took up her mug and sipped and waited for him to speak, she wasn't used to pushing. 'Them campsite lads will go after anyone who int them.'

The man nodded picked up his mug put it down again. 'You talkin bout the colour of my skin?'

'I was talkin bout them army greens you wearin under that coat more un anythin else; that's somethin gonna get you unwanted attention, your colour comes second to that. How your paths cross?'

'I live up the hill there, used to till the army, my mother still does and them site lads bin comin in and callin her all sorts to get her out.'

'Maybe she should just go.'

'You int met my mum, she's stubborn and proud, she int likely to be run out no matter them stolen everythin.'

'Her land em after?'

The man nodded and she told him again these people were worse than what he thought, but he'd been running he knew this already.

'I saw the smoke,' she said.

'That int our land, was a barn close by; I tried to help, tried to put it out but then em come after me. I had to run.'

'Least it weren't your digs.' Ia nodded told herself not to get involved.

'You say you know em?' he asked.

'Kind of.'

'Maybe you could talk to em, if you know em.'

Ia ignored him. 'You look like shit; you eaten?'

'I don't want to take nothin from you. I'll drink this, catch my breath and go.'

'I've got some smoked mackerel; I cure it myself.'

'I know money's tight.'

'Int tight if you never had.'

She got up and went to the cupboard where she stored the fish; there wasn't much she gave him what she could.

'Just take it, bring it to your mother; you'll have somethin, int that right?' She tore a square of the paper wrap and folded it around the shrunken corpse. 'Here.'

When the soldier looked up and thanked her Ia blushed, most folk she knew just took what they wanted it was the way things worked.

'Looks like you could do with fatnin up is all.'

'Could do with a lot of things; I int slept in days.'

'Well I can't help you with that.'

'I int askin.'

Ia went into the porch and dug out a blanket; she bundled it tied it with twine and put it at his feet. 'If you get to sleepin somewhere tonight that int home.' She told him not to thank her. 'I int used.'

They sipped the tea in silence and Ia sat to watch him drink, his hands cradling the mug his face circled in steam like a fog his eyes fixed on the coming storm.

'Thank you,' he said when he was finished; he put down the mug pushed back his chair and stood.

'Right then,' said Ia.

He lifted the fish from the table, unfolded and refolded the paper, put it into his pocket.

'I int done nothin wrong if you're thinkin it, I might be army but we just bin doin what we was told.'

'You shouldn't have got involved with your mum and all; they might have left things be, might've seen some nerve in her and left it.'

'I int no coward.'

'I don't reckon you is, you should heed is all.' Ia got up to unlock the door. She stood and watched him step from the van, followed him out of the ruin; he too was part derelict the bare bones suited him.

'Best you head inland,' she told him and she pointed at the path. 'Wherever you're goin from hereon that's the best way; take your mother away from here.' She handed him the blanket roll and turned her back before he could thank her it was nothing. When he was gone she headed down to the smokehouse; there was work that needed doing and work was good she knew what it meant.

Outside the hut she removed the plastic sheeting and scooped the fish from out the bath and carried them inside to drape on the rack, so used to the job in hand she worked with her shoulder to the gloom.

When it was time to light the fire Ia took a moment to enjoy the ritual and she knelt to the woodpile with the tinder lit ready and slowly came the fire. She crouched close to the flames and watched them grow great, unbuttoned her coat to let the heat infiltrate. In the distance she could hear the camp revellers had settled a little, their rage falling with the rising sun. She thought about the soldier and told herself she should know better, she wasn't meant for common talk her thoughts were out of her mind they went on without her she wished she could get them back. A soldier of all people, that was worse than stranger, worse than sleeping with Bran's pig-cousins, so what he slept with his own.

She stood when the flames reached too high and pulled the wood back blocked the draughts with soil-sand, once the little hut burst with smoke she backed out and bolted the door. She looked at the sky for rough time and etched a number into the fish board with her knife and returned to the van.

On approach Ia could see the shadow of her man. He stood in the doorway of the ruin leant against what bricks remained he had a bottle in his hand held it loose against his thigh.

'Where you bin?' he shouted.

'The fish,' she said.

'Just?'

Ia looked into his slit eyes, the way he watched her every move was all wolf. 'Set the fire,' she said.

'Just?' One word and he had it slurred.

Ia nodded and said yes, just.

'Woman, what you do with your time?'

Ia wanted to say everything, she even provided for herself. 'I do my best.'

'Int good enough.'

'Fish'll be done in a few days . . .'

'Few days? What I got to barter till then? I need it now.'

Ia thought for a minute, she wondered why he couldn't put the night to bed before the day arrived fully. 'Got that chicken,' she said. 'I could pluck it.'

'Fucksake, don't bother.'

'Cook it in the smokehouse, site folk would swap you a bottle for it.' She went to pass into the ruin but he wouldn't let her.

'What you know bout site folk?' he asked. 'What you know bout the in-outs of this life? You don't do nothin to know nothin.'

Ia looked at the bottle in his mouth his hands black with soot she remembered the fire.

'Maybe you should just come in.' She wanted to get inside whilst the warmth of the smokehouse was still in her.

'And what?' he asked.

'Get changed, get cleaned up, get to bed.'

Bran threw the bottle into the ruin it hit the wall where Ia's dream couch was supposed it slumped to the ground. He looked down at his hands and then at Ia. 'Some fire,' he said.

Ia nodded and said she could still smell the smoke it smelt like just about everything had been burnt.

'Most of everythin did.'

'You was there?'

'Maybe.'

She thought him softening saw his shoulders go down she asked him why he bothered.

'With what?' He was about to turn in, he turned back.

'The lads at the site, all that runnin round, you've had your time.' Her words came out wrong she knew they did saw the letters fall and try to dig for forgiveness in the earth. Too late. She fell backwards her journal slipping from her pocket her coat blown and pinned to the ground she lay still and waited for his next move. From the corner of her good eye she could see him thinking things over, he wanted to go but the compulsion that overpowered him on certain days grew too great, he caught her looking.

'I used to be somebody,' he said.

Ia sat up; she could feel the blood rush to the punch point on her cheek.

'You are somebody,' she said. She watched him like a hawk his eyes all over the ruin it shamed him.

'Don't speak.' He went into the caravan and returned with the chicken dangling from its craw; Ia hoped nobody at the camp would notice it gone come back.

'I'll be seein you,' he said.

'OK.'

'What's that?'

'OK.' Ia could see the dog was still in him, could see the snarl his hackles hitched up. 'Just OK.'

She couldn't remember if she said more; she saw the chicken swing toward, its claws like razorblades they scratched at her flesh ripped out her hair swapped blood for blood.

She lay with her knees to her chest her bleeding hands patching against her head she heard him shout blame as always. She could feel the blood on her face tiny rivers running. Silence. The wind dampened the sound of constant water gone no tide to pull her. She got up. Dawn sat out on the far horizon an orb of light looking out for her beneath the graphite cloud it held all the colours all answers were inked in its detail she went to it.

IA RAN TOWARD THE cliff edge, to keep moving meant a part of her was going away. She stood at the top trip of steps and looked down into the bay her eyes searching for some way to stem the splintering it dug deep.

At the shoreline she stumbled out on to the rocks to find water, a rock pool big enough for cupping and she crouched, careful to hold the wet to her face let the salt sting lick her wounds. Cleansed, Ia pulled at her sleeve rubbed the crud-blood from its creases, the feathers she picked away. The blood knots in her hair she hacked with her pocketknife, once she started she couldn't stop the blonde gone rooster red she left it where it fell a sunk stray in the surf.

When she was clean she bent to a fresh dimple of water and bathed again; salt water, rain water, river water. Ia kept her eyes closed and turned her face to the wind let it dry the salinity help heal, she wished it could mend the slow bend the snap inside she was a woman of two halves. Thirteen years of cruelty and still it was easier to think up excuses; she used them like plasters, sticky tape, anything to cover up the festering truth. Mum said it wasn't Dad's fault when the punches took flight, Bran was the same, all that kin were; wild animals Mum called them, a pack of wolves the crack born into their fists.

Ia left the rocks and ran to the cliffs, a ledge of rock to hide beneath a place to sit and gape at the gotten world. Familiar things, this is what she wished for what she craved; familiar sea familiar faces familiar spaces in which to be set free, somewhere less lonely, less alone. She lay down in the sand and watched the clouds shape-shift in the sky, a little light winking, her sister's eyes. Ia pulled her hood down over her face, she needed to rest her head it hurt inside and out.

'Shut the door,' she told herself. 'Lock it behind.' She closed her eyes and waited for Evie to come comfort her.

'DAD HIT YOU?' HER sister asked.

Ia shook her head. 'Dint mean to.'

'What then?'

Ia bunched up let her sister sit beside her on the bed they shared. 'He went for Mum, I was in the way.'

'Mum's fault then, the wind-up and all that.' Evie put her arm around Ia's shoulder, told her it was nobody's fault.

'OK.'

'Just got in the way is all.'

Ia nodded.

'Always in the way int you?' She wiped the blood from Ia's face, linked arms around her, gathering safe.

'Don't go yet,' said Ia. 'I need you.'

She remembered Mum calling them, shouting food on the table, the loaf and the meat and the make your own. Saw Dad asleep in his chair; fucker waster shush, these Mum's words.

IA WOKE UP WITH a start and she sat and saw that time had moved on, beyond the clouds the stum sun had crept a few hours west. She pulled the compass from out her coat held it in front of her asked, 'Which way now?'

A little movement a tiny tremble, it told her to get up keep walking, it took her toward the westerly cliffs. Ia never had reason to climb out on to those distant rocks. The bay beyond was steep slate crag not even campsite kids bothered to venture there, it was half fallen and buried only a small beach remained, it was to that cove that Ia went.

Occasionally the needle changed course and she followed obediently the burden of rope loosening a little childhood innocence returned. She imagined Evie walking up ahead, her long blonde hair swinging from side to side as she talked she was always talking, asking. Ia ten steps behind, forever daydreamer she never caught full meaning, shouting at her sister to stop-still start again.

When they were kids and things slipped got out of hand they headed toward the beach and to the cave that they had claimed as theirs where the waves slammed and shut the world from view. Their secret hideaway decked with shared ocean finds, shells and sweet-sucked plastic, driftwood netted and hung from the splinters of slate rock above their heads. Everything found, everything found a use for. Ia wondered if their childhood cave had remained the same, the falling jewels and the nook where they hid secret messages to each other in a screw-top pickling jar. Evie always said if they got split up torn apart she would return to that south-coast hideaway and leave a message for Ia and she was to do the same, put her whereabouts and a plan to bring them back together. If she closed her eyes she could still see the cave's hollow eye peeking from out the rock face and her sister going on that last time way up front, her favourite white dress flapping catching in the late-autumn breeze; Ia could still hear her cry, an animal caught in a snare it was a sound she could not name.

'Evie,' she said suddenly.

Ia stopped walking to let her thoughts catch up to her senses and she called out to her sister saw her clearly against the dim dusk light and she watched the last wave pull away, the distant figure fall small, flatten, curl into the rocks.

She stood a moment more and waited for her daydream to swallow, the thing to move; she rubbed her eyes and checked the compass its bearing pointed toward the body in the surf.

Ia called out she screamed and shouted for help. She jammed her rubber soles against the coarse barnacle rocks and ran toward the body her knees giving way her hands bloody from the fall, when she sat and put out her arms it was a child she pulled into her lap.

'Wake up,' she shouted. 'Wake up, you can't die here.'

Ia shook the child and she dragged it from the water bundled it on to level rock and looked toward the ruin, she wished Bran was there this one time he would know what to do. She moved closer and looked into the face of the child the white of it the grey temple veins like pencil marks rubbed out.

'Who are you?' she asked. 'Where you come from?' Ia rested her palm against the child's cheek the skin clammy with salt water and freezing cold she snapped it back. She looked at the ocean the cliffs and the ruin barely showing in the distance, nothing familiar everything ill wishing. 'OK,' she said, 'all right.' She would carry the child home dead or alive if this was all she could do then she would do it.

Ia leant toward the body and she pushed her hands beneath the doughy backbone and lifted it to her the weight no more than washing picked from off the line. A bundle of rags part human part damp fetid thing she carried it across the rocks in the direction of the caravan.

Not once did she look down at the body in her arms not once did she stop to check for breath, her eyes on the beach her heart in her ears, her head, her mouth. When she reached their bay she carried the child to the base of the cliff-path steps and placed it on the sand.

She sat beside it and took the compass from out her coat. 'I reckon this is yours,' she said; it was a stupid thing to say to think but when she opened it and saw the needle pointing to the child she pulled the cord from her neck and put it into its hand.

'There.' Ia watched the surf turn white and draw a line around the perimeter of the furthest rocks, it wouldn't be long in returning she would have to carry the body up the cliff she wondered why the bother.

She thought about burial or cremation if this child was dead what was she supposed to do this was somebody else's child? She heard ticking coming from the tiny hand, she bent to it saw something move what was it?

Ia jumped to her feet. 'What the fuck?' She backed away and stood at the edge of the rocks where the sand dug and dipped made a moat between, held her fists in hard prayer, gripped to this, waited.

The first things to move the very first things were the hands, a strong grab around the compass and to the chest and then the head twitching as if waking from a dream and Ia held her breath wondered when the eyes. She stepped closer.

'I should give you my coat.' She undid the top button but stopped when the child started to cough. 'Shit.' She knelt and rolled it on its side watched the seawater dribble from the mouth and disappear in a foam in the sand.

Silence and the curious child turned its ear toward her.

'Open your eyes.' Ia crouched closer despite the fear kicking up stones in her chest, rattling her; if she could see the eyes she could see this thing human. 'Please,' she whispered. She saw the lids flicker, the blue buds blooming into pink; somebody was in there, struggling to get from the sea get home.

Human nature returned to Ia in that moment and she wiped the blood that still trickled down her own face and stood up straight. She took off her coat and cocooned the child carried it up the steps and across the clearing, an eel that kept slipping it took all her strength not to drop it. Through the ruin and into the caravan she kicked open the doors went to the bedroom and laid it on the bed, an object, one found thing.

'You'll do well to warm up.' She pulled the coat from under and covered the kid complete.

'Now what?' She went to the window and opened the curtain; her nerves were itching she took a pill and leant against the door jamb, it creaked and made her jump. She closed her eyes, wished the child gone wished her back again.

'What am I supposed to do?' She looked at her own reflection it told her this wasn't a game she knew that already. She turned toward the child, wanted to hit her, hug her.

'Where the hell you from?' Ia stood at the foot of the bed looked at the pale limbs twisted wrong from beneath her coat the soft head wet against the pillow. 'You int campsite, I seen em all, no blonde kid lives there.' Ia moved closer told herself not to be afraid.

'You want a story?' she asked. 'Spose a story's good for calmin, it always worked on Evie, need it for my own peace.' She looked to see if the child was about to move show some kind of interest but it didn't, just lay there.

'You ever heard the story bout the Mermaid of Zennor?' Ia cleared her throat, serious. 'When we was growin up we was told it; you washin up got me rememberin.' She coughed, dabbed her forehead with her sleeve and looked toward the window at the tiny rivers of water that roved there.

'Once there was this maid who used to sing in the pub; she had a beautiful voice, enchantin they called her, and she was beautiful and never seemed to get old, anyway . . .' Ia thought for a minute and closed her eyes to remember the story, it was for her own benefit. 'Anyway, this maid had a habit of disappearin and it went noticed cus all everyone had a fancy on her, especially some lad, Matty; he followed her after a night's drinkin, up on to the cliffs, and was never seen again. The story goes that he was lured into the sea by the mermaid.' She looked at the child. 'Anyway, she was a mermaid, like you, only she went missin and you bin found. Maybe that's it, maybe you're her returned.'

The child didn't speak didn't move and Ia closed the door and left it with its eyes still fidgeting and hands frost-tight around the compass. She went to stand at the window in the kitchen always her thinking place her place of safe retreat, waited for her reflection to tell her what next her other self looked away. She took down another carton of cigarettes and smoked one not bothering with the outside pretence and all the while she thought about the child not hers in the bed.

She went into the porch to find the bottle of gin took it to the door and stood unscrewed the cap and put it to her mouth. She sucked the bittersweet liquid and ignored the bloody claw-catch in her lip it tasted of rose hip and iron-licked lips she swallowed and waited for the sun to go on now and leave her be, she had thinking to do.

She carried the bottle and a blanket to the cliff edge and laid it on the ground sat and swung her legs above the beach imagined them walking step by step she went over the day. In the down dusk light she could barely make out the rocks where the child had been found, perhaps the sea had absorbed them she couldn't tell. Half in half out the tide lay tethered, the discovery of the child had it stopped complete. Its work done the ultimate gift delivered, been born.

It was as if time had stopped at that mortality moment and turned back, life in reverse; the child turning to baby and then into her womb where she could love it as her own. If only. She looked down at the bottle in her arms and pulled it closer.

IA WOKE TO THE sound of hounding waves the tide returned she heard a voice it was calling to her. She sat up and dropped the empty bottle searched for the moon but clouds now, looked toward the ruin saw the blue-moon girl stand naked at the threshold her found eyes huge with wonder.

'You'll catch your death,' she shouted. 'If you int already, you'll catch your death.'

Ia stood up and she took the blanket to the child and knelt to drape it around her shoulders. The smell of the ocean was everywhere on her not just skin but the blood and bone of her so gone through was she with seawater and Ia touched her head her fingers sticking briefly to the damp, fleshy skull. The sea had the girl faded, it was only a matter of time until the mist thinned her down to an aspic puddle and the chance of something the opportunity would pass.

At that moment the night might have drifted by and into day and night come again and still the woman and the child standing staying stopped-dead, neither of them speaking neither of them knowing how. It was as if memory had been replaced by new memory. Everything Ia knew she had forgotten except the child watching her every slight every move its head tilted in curiosity her blue-green eyes on Ia the way a child looked at kin it was too much. She pushed her away, pulled her back, asked her all the questions that were in her, when the girl didn't speak Ia answered them herself. She returned her to the caravan lit the lamp and shoved her into the bedroom, mum rough.

'Get into bed,' she told her. 'One thing to have you here, it's another to have you goin bout usual.' She pulled back the covers watched the child climb in, her knuckle-bone spine bulging like a fist gone through the belly.

'That's better.' Ia tucked the bedding around the girl tried to ignore the questioning eyes following her every move.

'I'll sleep over here,' she said, 'keep watch.' She cleared the bedside chair and sat put the salt-water blanket across her lap kicked off her boots and stuck her feet into the side of the mattress.

'No more wanderin,' she told her. 'No more nothin tonight.' Ia blew out the lamp and listened to the girl curl and settle to shell, her tiny body bumped beneath the duvet barely anything against the dark. 'Good girl.' She closed her eyes and rested her head waited to be carried somewhere new; a long walk, slowly taken.

Dust path, pollen fields. A meadow filled with all the greens the blues ever to exist. Milkwort and dog violet, speedwell, rampion, Ia could name them all. Ferns, flowers and grasses and forget-me-not so perfect that when she bent to touch them she promised she would never not recall this. She lay down and let the heady scent of bluebells and wild garlic catch in the breeze come close surround her and she studied the sky for imperfection, a cyan lake reflecting she found absolutely none.

She closed her eyes, sleep within sleep and then the sky scratched the meadow gone the flowers replaced by rock stone earth.

IA WOKE IN THE tomb of bounded night and she called out, 'Girl.'

How long had she been asleep? How long the child gone missing from the room?

She stood up and felt for the lamp turned it on and headed for the kitchen.

'Where you bin?' the girl asked.

Ia looked at the naked child sitting at her table and she did not answer, this was wrong it was everyday talk.

'I was waitin,' she continued.

Ia rubbed her eyes it helped with the unseeing of things.

'You hear me?' said the girl.

Ia noticed the girl's feet they were black, thick with mud.

'You bin outside.' She went to the stove and turned on the

gas, she lit a match to fire it and told the child if she was cold then better come forward if not she should do the same because that meant something wrong, she knew this better than anyone.

'I int cold.'

Ia ignored her and she filled the kettle with water the big stew pot to the brim and she waited until close enough to boiling; she carried both to the bath and filled it hot and cold.

'Come here,' she said. When the child ignored her she went and pulled her from the table and pushed her into the water.

'Stop there,' she said.

'I int cold.'

'Like fuck you int, standin round in the middle of the night.'

Ia watched it stand and stare the eyes stretched wide, greedy, waiting for something that wasn't there; she told her to sit so she could scoop the jug run the water over the tiny thing the fair hair thinning and sticking like candyfloss the eyes swimming used to water. With warming done Ia passed the towel and told the girl to dry off and to stop with the maudlin, her mother's words borrowed made to fit her own mouth.

In the cupboard in the bedroom she found her white child-hood dress and together with thermal vest and johns she brought them into the kitchen. When the girl returned she told her to get dressed and sit.

'Food is what we need.' Ia put more water on the stove and sliced the loaf and warmed it in a little oil; when the tea was made she sat.

She watched the child eat and she ate herself and neither of them spoke or looked or moved; when the girl was done she picked up the compass.

'This is mine,' she said.

'You reckon?'

She glanced up at Ia and nodded.

'You remember it do you?'

The girl unfastened the lid and looked at the workings, the barring pointing toward her.

'What else you remember?' Ia sat forward. 'You remember what got you here?' She put her elbows on to the table. 'Was you on a boat? Or the cliff? Fall did you?' She knocked on the table to make the child look up. 'What?' she continued. 'You from the campsite?'

The girl closed the compass and looped the cord around her neck and crossed her arms. They finished their tea in silence and Ia kept her eye on the kid, waited for a sign of something that might lead her toward understanding. She was a peculiar girl, not just because of the spoon-hollowed eyes and parchment skin but the righteousness it got to Ia.

'Just so you know, this is my van,' she told her. 'You abide and we won't have no trouble.'

She got up and told the girl to do the same and she ushered her into the bedroom and said this time sleep; she told her when the sun hit the bay they would sit in it get colour and talk more about whatever this was.

'Goodnight.' She returned to the kitchen and ate the crust from the girl's plate and she stood at the window and searched the horizon for trawlers wondered which one if any was his.

Dishes washed and all things wiped Ia took up the lamp and returned to the night and she stood out on the headland to watch the boats come in, the distance between lug and land closing, pinched in. Now what? She had no way of telling if Bran was on his way home no communication, Ia was used to counting the days from departure but she didn't know if he had returned to sea at all. Sometimes when he was drunk he volunteered for mate on other boats it kept him from coming home kept him from the shame. Much had happened in few hours, so constructed so perfect it was like something lifted from a daydream; first the oranges, the flotsam, then the soldier and finally the rescue the innocent child the chance for Ia to prove herself. The shame came with what felt right not being right; the child that lay in her bed was an unbelieving thing, Ia had not made it or traded it, there was a word for that if she was not given back soon, the word was stolen.

SHE WENT TO THE rear of the ruin and to the outhouse used backalong for shitting and she set the lamp in the damp shingle-grass so she might rummage there. The small tongue-and-groove door still hung to hinges just about and Ia was careful to lift and peg it open.

The things in the hovel-hole were rubbish she knew: unfix-able knots of net and plastic fertilizer bags filled with builders' sand why bother and the lobster pots from the year he decided to put a punt on lobsters. The stinking nets were the first to go, an easy haul out into the muck and she pulled them into hiding toward the gully behind the side wall. This was the place where the first foundations were to be made, Ia remembered it clear as day that sweet-sixteen summer, the two of them hammering going mad with the spades. From memory she could see them smiling, laughing even, imagine that.

Ia took her time to carry out the pots and she banked them in front of the ruin where she hoped they would dry and the sand-bags she dragged to the wall put a plank across and that would do for a shelf. If the child was going to stay awhile she would have to sleep in a room out of harm's way. She put the lamp on the shelf and paced out the square and there was enough room for four lobster pots together they would make a rough bed.

She returned to the porch and went to the storage box of nice things soft things the box that Branner called hers and she counted out the blankets old coats and remnants kept for maybe curtains and she told herself it would have to do hoped it was better than what the girl was used to.

In the kitchen Ia checked the time and listened out for noise for voice but nothing thank God. She put the lamp on to the windowsill and sat down. So this was what it was like to have to look after a child? It felt strange, more of a curiosity to look at dip her toes into the deep to test the water. She knew this moment would not last of course it would not, the kid had family good folk perhaps, but what else was she supposed to do? She had no map for looking nobody for telling until the girl started to remember her life before the sea Ia would have to make do with this, instinct. She settled into the seat by the back window and hitched the blanket across her shoulders rested her head against the wall of the van. If Bran arrived home she would hear him, make a fuss to keep him from the bedroom get the kid outside somehow and into the cubby.

Ia closed her eyes she couldn't help but smile. She had been gifted with a child after all. She had not asked for this but here it was an offering, precious find. She pulled the blanket to her smelt the salt water and felt the waves rock her toward sleep maybe a few hours before dawn perhaps the meadow returned.

AT FIRST THE TAP at the kitchen window was a branch of ivy come away from the ruin wall Ia dismissed it as an ongoing battle the ruin was more weed than mortar. In the morning she would cut it back, she told it this by way of warning.

The second tap came at the side of the van Ia jumped got the kindling hatchet from the porch and swore that she would chop the lot perhaps the walls would go with it let in the light. Outside the night had stopped rascalling, the wind blown out the clouds paused for breath.

'That don't make no sense.' Ia stood in her bare feet pulled up her hood the blanket tight to her back she felt about for the rogue vine attempted to chop but it was too thick for bothering.

'Somethin int right,' she said, she had been here before.

'I got a weapon,' she shouted; she put her back against the van wall held the small axe with both hands.

'You seen the flag up? Cus I dint put the flag up.' She waited and in response to silence she told them to come out. Through the opening at the side of the building Ia could see the figure of a man, he stood wondering she could tell.

'Too late now I seen you,' she said.

'Sorry.'

Ia knew by the way he skulked head down the one word of polite that it was the stranger the fox; she pulled down her hood and tidied her hair told him he was lucky that she was half alone.

'Come out,' she said, 'I know who you are.'

The shadow pulled from the window eclipsed the space where the door should have been like a curtain falling black. He stumbled and Ia stepped back; she asked if he was drunk.

'I int drunk.'

'Cus men can change when em on the bottle.'

'I int bin drinkin; bin runnin.' He put a hand out to catch himself hung on to the ivy vines for support his eyes digging at the earth wishing it would spade up bury him there.

'Thought I told you to get gone?' she said.

'I thought to go, but it's our land, why should we?'

'The beat is why.'

'It int right, just cus there int no laws a moment.' He tried to catch his breath.

'You can't stay here; this van is snare land.'

'I int askin, just . . .'

'Make it quick, I int got no boots on.'

'I bin hurt.'

'You need fixin up?'

He didn't speak she supposed he nodded she said he could come indoors a minute, she led on.

'We're on borrowed time here.' She imagined Bran coming home to this mess of folk not family; he would ask what the fuck twice over would say it with his fists until passed out.

'I'll get a smack if my old man finds you here; he int a man for sharin, specially with brown army lads.' She pushed on through the ruin lit the porch lamp and carried it into the van, her mind on the child her precious find.

In the candlelight she could see the full stagger of the man he was beat she pulled out a chair but he remained standing no smile this time.

'Where you bin got?' she asked.

'Shoulder, maybe my arm.'

Ia stood behind him and pulled the coat from his shoulders; she could see the red pressing on making its mark and she told him to unbutton his shirt.

'I int no nurse,' she said. 'Not even close; my old man says I int got one considerate bone. I'll do my best.'

'Thank you.' He turned toward her too close; she stepped back.

'Int done nothin yet.' She went to the kettle and set it to boil, told him to sit and he did.

'Stabbin, looks like.'

'Was.'

'You get a blade in?'

The man shook his head, said he was too busy running.

'Sometimes runnin's best.' Ia knew he was looking at her face some scars you couldn't hide.

'What happened?' he asked.

'This? Tis nothin.' She turned her better cheek.

'Don't look like nothin.'

'Was in a fight, another bird could say.'

When the kettle was close enough to boiling, Ia swilled some into the basin poured it clean and added a little salt, she went to the cabinet in the bathroom for a fresh washcloth, she wished she had more for helping but this was all she had.

'I'll clean it up,' she said when she returned to the kitchen. 'Clean it up, put a stitch in it; that's all I can do.'

Ia crouched beside him with the basin between her legs and she soaked the cloth and rinsed it pressed it to the wound on his shoulder, when he flinched she put her other hand on him it felt right.

'Int nothin major bin got,' she told him. 'If it had, you'd be bleedin all over.'

The man watched her his eyes following her every move, when she spoke he listened made her feel like somebody.

'Maybe it don't need stitchin,' he said.

Ia shook her head. 'Does.'

'But if it int bleedin.'

'Infection.' She kept at the wound wiping off the blood the crud of scab and cloth, one ear turned warrior toward the front door the other a wary mother pointed at the back.

'Hold that.'

He took the cloth from her and pressed it to his arm and Ia went to the drawer where she kept something of everything sought the cotton reel and the tin of pins found the curved needle meant for fixing chairs and cushions and brought it to him.

'Already threaded,' she said.

He nodded looked heartbroken for the beat the beast that was all of this, he was a man used to other things.

'Won't take long,' she told him.

'OK.'

Ia couldn't help but feel sorry for him she asked for his name.

'Jenna.'

She started to smile.

'What?' he asked.

'Nothin.'

'Why you smirkin? It's a good Cornish name init?'

'For a girl.'

'How you know?'

'Was my mother's name.' She touched his skin one moment, remembering. 'I'm Ia.'

He tried to smile but it didn't work, Ia wasn't swayed in any case she pierced the skin and passed the needle across the wound to the other side she didn't stop until the fourth.

'You bin runnin since last I seen you?' she asked when she had double-knotted and bitten the cord.

He nodded. 'Then I came back, my mother wanted back so.'

'Bet you wish you dint bother.'

'Some things are worth fightin.'

'Love and land,' said Ia and she rinsed the cloth and held it to his wound; one final moment to catch the last rivulet of blood one moment more to touch, to stop.

Jenna closed his eyes and let it pass between them.

'Thank you,' he said.

'Just doin what's meant.' She pushed her chair and stood, she was shaking.

'I don't know many good people; I'm grateful for what you done.'

'All little things,' she said. 'As it is you don't know me, if you did you'd know the stock I come from int great.'

'No.' He got up and took her hand and Ia felt like she might fall without it. 'You're a good woman; don't know what other folk say but I'm sayin it and I know the difference.'

She pulled her hand away and said goodbye; this man was a distraction she only had head and nerves for one. Even still, something in her had paused and changed direction with the sea-thing child and her old life seeping from her own wounded world she felt daring, the dare was everywhere.

'You stoppin nearby still?' she asked.

'Close enough.'

'You see a flag go up on the ruin and you're hungry, you come over.'

Jenna nodded.

'If you're hungry I int got much but seems you might need your strength for whatever you got planned.'

'Thank you for not askin.'

Ia didn't watch him leave. She pointed to the door and locked it behind him sat to gather herself closed her eyes to keep this in. Some things she would never understand but still it did not stop her from picking, a memory slowly unravelling.

NIGHT FINALLY LEFT THE bay. It removed itself from the north coast completely and still the sun did not bother to split the fog did not look through the window to wake Ia so deep in sleep was she, a child again. In the dream things were different from how things were, Ia could tell by the way she spoke the way her breasts felt beneath her shirt how her hair fell petal-soft Evie's was the same.

'They int dead,' she said.

Evie grinned. 'Mum's in the garden.'

'You sure?' Ia knew this dream it came from the place that should have been.

'Blackberries,' shouted Dad; he sat smoking against the door jamb like always. 'Mum's goin to make jam.'

Ia smiled found herself brushing her hair it was longer than what she was used to lighter in colour.

'My hair smells of jasmine,' she said. 'I int smelt jasmine since home, I'd forgotten how it smelt, imagine forgettin a smell like that.' She said this out loud, her real voice rough, ruined, not the voice of a teenager, clean and clever, chaste. A what-if world created from spit and stitch and good wishing.

The good dream didn't last they never did, the image of her dead parents washed up on Ia their waxen gape reminding her of the ocean child. She woke up and let go of the tangled matted mess of hair in her hand.

'Shit,' she said. She had waited so long for morning to arrive she had fallen into wrong sleep, wrong time.

She pushed the blanket and stood to look at the clock and she tapped it and wound the key and listened for the tick and she told herself the child was more important than wishful fancy, she was real she was here right now.

She went to the bedroom and knocked and called the girl it was time to get up. 'You hear me?' She split the door expecting to see her gone; the sight of her made Ia flinch, step back.

'Hungry?' she called.

Through the gap in the door she could see the girl shrug.

'It's breakfast, for real this time.' She pushed into the room and stood at the foot of the bed and crossed her arms.

'Right little mermaid int you? Way I found you floatin without a hope in hell, what you reckon? Mermaid you is: Mermaid of Zennor.' Ia grabbed one toe sticking from the blanket and the girl laughed.

'Thought you'd have a big old fish tail stickin out.' She pulled off the blanket and told her to get dressed come on.

Ia returned to the kitchen and put two pieces of bread into a pan of oil to heat and the water on to boil and she looked to the window for signs of sun-life the autumn weather she had gotten used to. She made the tea and at the back of the cupboard found the last jar of blackberry jam her own and she spread it on the toast one each and sat down.

'You remember your name yet?' she asked.

The girl put down her toast and shook her head. 'No,' she said.

'Where you from even?' Ia sat back and folded her arms. 'Just so you know, I int alone, so don't start thinkin you'll get your feet under permanent, if you're workin some kind of scam; I int got money but I got a man and he's due home; he int as accommodatin as me.' She looked across at the girl. 'I'm goin to stick you in the shitter till I work out what to say. Don't worry, the shitter int no shitter no more.'

'What's a shitter?' the girl asked.

'You'll see.'

They finished eating and Ia gave the girl Bran's boyhood boots and she went outside and told her to follow and to hurry up, Bran wasn't a morning man but he might just appear dark cloud coming over the brow of the hill.

ALL MORNING AND INTO the afternoon Ia had the child lug the pots and sweep the floor and carry the soft things to the new bed. A good worker she told her, her man would like that, a good worker and what was she seven, eight years old? Ia did not know children to be able to tell, perhaps she was older.

When the cubby was arranged to near enough room Ia put the oil-lamp on to the shelf and she gave the girl the spare box of kitchen matches so she might find light if she needed it in the dark. She told her it was the last of the oil and if she didn't use it at all that would be perfect, the camp store had been cleared of any kind of fuel months back.

'You can put the compass on the shelf if you want,' she told her. 'Maybe later find some shells to pretty things up?' She thought of their beach hideout hers and Evie's, the last time the worse time seven days they had lasted, seven days a full week and all the nights, surviving on winkles and cliff-falling rivulet water. Ia looked at the kid alone in its world she knew just how she felt.

'You'll be right,' she promised her. 'When I int around I gotta lock you in, but you'll be fine, and this here lock inside is from backalong uses, you slide it the same. Two locks is better un one.'

The girl nodded and Ia told her she was a good little mermaid.

'Reckon you is an all, turnin up near-dead in water and then comin back alive.'

Ia took one last glance around the tiny room and told the

girl she'd seen worse. 'Spose I should show you round the land just in case, just so you know where not to go.'

She took her hand and it felt odd to be holding on to something so malleable, it was a seashell that had yet to exist, this girl was a spirit child.

They walked across the wasteland toward the cliff path and stood a moment to catch the weather the waves the way things were in Ia's world.

'This is me,' she told her. 'This is all me, my life, nothin changes here.'

The girl looked up at her and something written on her face read disbelief.

'To the right there you used to be able to go a good bit round to the next bay but few years back the storms took a bite out of the land and every year since it's taken a nibble bit more. Nobody goes that way, nobody comes.' She looked at the girl to see if she was listening.

'Most important is what we got here on the left.'

The girl nodded but her eyes were dug in water horizon heading.

'On our left we got problems all over.' She started to walk toward the headland the first pinnacle of land where the campsite hitched into view.

'In daylight I don't go no further un this point here and you int to come here at all; em slides and swings and frames is littered with needles, it int for kids. All em will skewer you and put you over hot coals.' When the kid looked up she told her they'd snack on her bones for days use her ribs as toothpicks this made the child laugh.

'Truth is I int one of em much myself, my dad was and Bran's his cousin so he is, but em dint like Mum for reasons absolutely nobody knows, so don't ask. Them there int nice is all you need to remember and if you're thinkin of makin friends with the kids, don't; all em inbreeds more un most, you listenin?'

The girl nodded.

'Say it.'

'Yes.'

From their vantage Ia could see a group of boys sticking a dog it was grovelling on its forelegs she turned the girl homeward.

'All this land int ours, just bin taken bit by bit, can do what you want without laws. Spose you know somethin of it wherever you from.' She looked at the girl to see if she understood. 'The crash, the collapse or whatever they call it.' She returned her gaze to the campsite. 'No tourists, no comins, no goins; all roads is fucked anyhow.'

They walked slowly toward the cubby and Ia finished off her tour by waving a hand over everything to the north. 'One track in, same track out; nobody bothers cus of all the barb and briar and mines; most know Bran lives here and he's a fuck and those who don't soon find out.' Ia thought about the men that came to trade with her. 'There are exceptions to the rule, but you don't need to know bout things you int likely to understand.' She told the girl to nod and she did.

'Right then, you like drawin?' She took out the journal from her coat pocket and tore a page and sharpened the pencil with her pocketknife.

'Sometimes,' said the girl.

'Well let's hope this is one of em times. Here.' She gave her the paper. 'I'll come check on you later when evenin's passed and I'm sure he int comin back tonight, OK?'

'OK.'

Ia left the child hooked and staring like the part-fish she was and she pushed her into the tiny stone room heard her call out like a calf taken from the tit and she ignored her had to she was not her mother.

When she returned to the van he was waiting for her on the ruin step, the soldier the good man Jenna.

'I saw the flag was up.'

Ia smiled, she had forgotten to take it down maybe she'd put it up by mistake, since the kid she had forgotten certain duties.

'How's your arm?' she asked.

He lifted it put it down and shrugged. 'I'll survive.'

She told him she was going for a walk on the beach. If he heard the captive kid he'd think her hard she was she knew this.

'Walk with me if you want, nobody bothers me, don't bother with this cove either, it's rocky, there int no way in.' Or out, she thought.

Jenna nodded and got to his feet said he missed walking he'd been hiding out in a rope shed.

'The ropery? I thought that had collapsed. I know it.'

'You do?'

'Course, up the track and right, that's where I get my blackberries cept this year em rotten.'

'Full of brambles.'

'That's em, best fruit in Cornwall I reckon, usually anyhow.'

Beneath the final fall of evening light they headed toward the path and down the steps the tide was out the sand groomed and stretched, it had done this for them.

'Could be any point in time in any year,' said Jenna. 'No wars, no fightin, nothin.'

'Is that what it is?' asked Ia. 'A war?'

'I reckon it is.'

She saw a tiger cowrie in the sand hadn't seen one in a long time years even she bent to pick it up. 'Wars end,' she said.

'Not this one, it int got enough shape, nobody knows how to handle it, how to take it apart.'

'Course it will.'

'It int a war in the common sense, it's a loose battle, all em fightin just cus; bin over a year now.'

Ia rubbed her fingers over the smooth skin of the shell kissed it and put it in her pocket. 'Never known anyone to fight for anythin worthy, not the folk I know.'

They walked toward the rocks where Ia had found the child

it got her wondering what if she was an orphan? Her heart quickened.

'This fightin battlin whatever, towns as well as country is it?' she asked.

'Town's where there's unrest, but em gangs are everywhere burnin houses, stealin land; its chaos all over.'

'And em that can't fight, on the move I spose.'

'Them that got somewhere to go have gone already, but I heard whole country's the same.'

'Init just Cornwall?'

Jenna looked at her and smiled. 'Cross the river's just as bad, maybe worse.'

'And how they go, them that's gone? By road or boat?' Ia put the shell to her ear for the comfort of customary waves.

'Both, cept roads are wrecked and them that have gone went before the real shit hit.'

'What bout all that's left?'

'Cornered, sittin on their hands hopin somethin's goin to change or somebody goin to step in.' He looked at her and told her the army had been the last resort.

'And that's how you got involved?'

'Flash points they call em, sent us in to keep the peace.'

'Did you?'

Jenna looked at her. 'No.'

'I can see some of it got to you, can see it in your eyes.' She meant this. The hurt and horror were pooled in the black of his pupils they were flooded stretched wide too many images gone in, got seen.

'Truth is I dint know which side was which, who we was supposed to fight, who to protect.' When he stopped walking Ia did the same.

'Protect your own, int that right?' she asked.

Jenna shook his head. 'I was meant to protect the people, em that couldn't protect emselves. I failed.'

Ia linked her arm into his it felt right. 'Let's keep walkin.'

She took them to the far end of the beach to sit in the part with most shelter, a place they could talk without the wind, see each other without being seen. Ia looked out to sea and thought about what Jenna had told her. The girl was an orphan she had to be, her folks long gone dead, another part of the puzzle that created a picture of her new life. The child and this man, objects washed up for her to discover if Ia could find the right way to piece them together.

'You got a woman?' she asked; she needed to know for the picture perfect kept her eyes on the shell.

'My mum just.' He looked at her and his hair caught a shard of sunlight and brought it to her.

'You got her hidin out somewhere safe?'

'She's safe.'

Ia smiled and she asked if he had a dad worth bothering with.

Jenna started to laugh. 'No, he int worth botherin.'

'Int around then?'

'Nope, was army is all I know; Mum still has a photo of him in his uniform, can't tell you why.'

'Maybe he weren't so bad.'

'Reckon he was.'

Ia sighed. 'Good people are hard to come by, em worse when things get rough; what they callin this that's goin on?'

'If I had the words to describe what I seen I'd tell you.'

'Spose I should be afraid.' She wasn't, her own private world was enough. She looked out to sea and noticed that the serene waves that had invited them down on to the beach had been replaced by bullying breakers, they entered the bay at an unusual angle looked to be spoiling for a fight. She turned the shell over in her hands and her fingers traced its freckled back the white-toothed smile.

'Why int I seen you? I'd recognize you if I had. Both your parents black?'

'My mum just; Dad was white with red hair.' Jenna pointed to his own.

'Campsite folk int keen on dark but they hate the Polish most of all.'

'Why's that?'

'Em first in.'

'That don't make sense.'

'Hard workers; Bran said em show all else up.'

'Your people . . .' He didn't know what to say shook his head instead.

'Int my people, em died years back.' Ia watched the horizon for turns in the weather she saw the sky and sea merge exchange rainwater for seawater the clouds were black with it.

'Hope that storm stays off.' She looked at him and smiled, a way to show that she had surrendered to fate a long time ago.

'I brought you somethin,' he said suddenly; he undid the top button of his coat and pulled out a bottle sat it in his lap. 'To say thank you for helpin.'

'Give it to me then.'

He passed it over and Ia noticed he was shaking his nerves still in parts if he had found them at all.

'You thanked me a hundred times already but I like a drink.'

'More un for helpin, thank you for bein good; all else int.'

Ia didn't know what to say she twisted the lid from the bottle and drank. Truth was he didn't know anything about her nobody did. She thought about Evie and her heart split in two like a mouth it called out.

'I int so good,' she said and she returned the bottle.

She watched him drink, his brown eyes closed his auburn curls falling covering he was a man suited to hiding. Perhaps he had become used to it, the same way as Ia had, every crack every fissure in her held the potential for falling hiding hoping.

He caught her looking and smiled, despite everything he held on to hope. Ia had never known this in another; Bran had let go, the ruin was proof of that. She took back the bottle asked where he had found it she knew he wouldn't tell her.

'Int good to go down to the campsite,' she said, she recognized the taste.

'I int sayin nothin.'

'And I'm just sayin.'

'I found it.'

'That int likely.'

'Was left behind.'

'Where? In the blackberry bush?'

'Not far.'

They both laughed and looked out to sea, saw a buzzard short cut across the water, it hit the cliffs like a thrown blade.

'How's your shoulder?' she asked.

Jenna pulled off his coat his shirt and turned his arm toward her.

Ia moved forward. 'Int infected.' She traced the serrated ridge where the thread still held ran her thumb against the bruised skin.

'Does it hurt?'

'Not now.'

She bent to the wound and kissed it let her mouth linger there his smell his taste like newly discovered things she wanted to savour this. Slow to kiss slow to love slow to open up to trust herself. The salt of this man the sea air the waves calling cheering shouting. No fists. No fire except the uncontrollable burn. Ia looked into his eyes as he bent to kiss her mouth, her eyes reflected, falling stars falling for him. Jenna was warmth, a beautiful flame; all night he shone for Ia gave light where she thought there was none. Her moon.

Hours passed and night straddled the two lovers but still they did not move didn't dare if they did old worlds would come crashing reality returned.

'Wish we could stay like this.' Ia pushed her face into his neck when he started to sing she felt the vibrations his music everywhere.

'Leavin home,' she said. 'Leavin home never to return, it's a sad song.'

She listened to his story the chorus tying around in complicated knots, the slow unravelling of thread; when he reached the ending she felt his pulse lessen go flicker flame slow, hushed heartbeat, muted and Ia knew he was crying.

NIGHT COME NIGHT GONE it took him with it Ia woke with light come round again she found herself alone, he was not a man for standing in full light there was enough in him in any case it was his gift to the world.

Ia kept herself buried in his coat and listened to the waves crash far out against the sandbar it was the sound of comfort it always was. She pulled the wool fabric to her face and smelt smoke the bitter bite caught at the back of her throat it was not his smell or the cove's but in recent weeks that was all she smelt.

She sat up and looked toward where the sun should have been, paused in anticipation but the clouds were stubborn they spanned the wide mouth of sea made fog of both headlands.

Down by the rocks she could see Jenna stand his back turned to the wind she could see his head was heavy with new day thinking, she called out to him.

'I found somethin.' He walked toward her his hands in his pockets. 'Close your eyes.'

Ia did what she was told she put out her hands felt something soft curl against her palms she opened her eyes.

'Buzzard feather,' they said in unison.

'My spirit animal,' said Ia. 'I'll keep it always.'

'Saw you collected things, shells and bones and whatever else.'

'Where you see that?' she asked.

'In that porch of yours.'

Ia smiled he was the first man to notice her nature table. 'Found a fox skull last spring, no frame to it, just the head.'

'I dint see that.'

'I keep it wrapped, Bran says it's witchcraft; it's just a skull.' She moved to let him sit down but he remained standing.

'You goin?' When he didn't speak Ia stood and passed him his coat. 'Don't get into no more trouble.' She helped him put it on.

'I'll try.'

She told him to try harder asked if she would see him tonight, when he didn't answer she let him go he had given enough of himself.

She watched him walk slowly across the sand his hands behind his back his head down like a crow going over a newly reaped crop. She put the feather to her mouth and felt the tiny wing fibres tickle her lips she put it to her cheek felt its strength become her strength.

'Rebirth,' she said. 'The bird that eats death converts it, life from the blood and bone and bite of death flesh.' Ia had read this in her nature book it was true of every carrion thing and the buzzard told her this shouted it to her every day. Life continued: this would be her mantra from now on. She threaded the quill through a buttonhole and went toward the ruin she wanted to show the child her gift.

'It's mornin,' she shouted when she reached the stone hut. 'You awake?' She slid back the lock and pulled the door and waited for the girl to appear from the gloom.

'Look what he found me.' Ia put the feather into the child's hand and told her to wait whilst she checked the van for the all clear.

'He int likely,' she told herself; she would have heard him shout out her name felt the stomp of his feet splitting the earth, even still the fear was in her like a disease it had her riddled.

Ia went into the caravan and called out his name the porch the kitchen the bedroom nothing touched, no man nowhere she lay on the bed and sighed the heat still in her. Above her head she checked the ceiling for new damp marks it felt like forever since she had lain in her own bed, recently she'd found everywhere better, it wasn't hard. Each day added turning year the van grew tired its walls heavy with sweat and wet seeping through the floor more soft in corners than last time she looked and the roots of plants put down and come up to reclaim. Ia jumped from the bed she could no longer stand the place. She went outside and leant beside the ruin she needed the child to pull her straight she called for her told her to hurry up and together they went into the kitchen the kettle filled the pan to heat a bit of bread and fish divided.

'It's a buzzard feather.' Ia looked to see if she was interested, she wasn't she dropped it on the table and brought the compass from out her dress.

'You're a good kid,' said Ia. 'Never known a kid so quiet, I don't know none up close but you int like site kids, that's definite. You see em you keep away, you hear me?'

The girl nodded.

'Say it.'

'Yes.'

'I got a name.'

'Yes Ia.'

'Backalong em used to come up to the peak of the cliff path every day till Bran put a stop to it.' Ia remembered how they used to call her names throw rocks and dog shit toward the van they fell short by a mile that pile of rubble and stink became a natural border in those early years.

'Em bad kids,' she said. 'Bad men now.'

After breakfast the child helped Ia with the dishes and it made her laugh this little person so malleable like cliff clay in her hands. There was nothing she wouldn't agree to do not yet anyway and nothing done without Ia's say-so. She was hers, not her daughter but for now she was hers to govern and there was belonging in that. Not since Evie had she belonged in this same way it was as if this were somebody else's life she was living. Her thoughts had become found objects, treasures, she spread them out in front of her put them everywhere for looking they were better than any mollusc bone skinned thing.

Morning chores completed Ia and the child climbed down to the cove and they sat out on the rocks so she might remember something significant from her short life.

'Do you remember your name?' Ia asked again.

The girl shook her head. 'No.'

'Can't keep callin you kid.' Ia looked about the beach for inspiration something to give by way of identity. 'Mermaid.' She clipped her chin to see if the child cared either way, she didn't. 'Bout the shipwreck,' she continued and the girl made the face she did when the subject didn't interest her.

'Bout then.'

The girl twitched and looked to the horizon, picked up a rock-pool stone and threw it.

'What you remember bout the boat? Capsized I reckon, I think we'll take that as fact.'

She watched for signs of anything other than indifference and wished Evie were there to help. 'Just to get a name out of it,' she said to herself. 'Anythin more un nothin.'

Together they watched the waves split and break beyond the cuff of rocks, the swell climbing the same way it did each day and the dull scratching clouds come down to meet the ocean it had drawn the last colour from it.

'Rain's gettin closer,' said Ia. 'I can smell it even more today, it smells like sewage, it's close.' She looked at the girl and asked if she wanted to look for shells and she did and they returned to the sand and walked the bay, corner to corner, filling their pockets with the hole-through limpets so they could string and garland them later. What would she think of the cove in springtime? When warmth returned full palette and painted all the colours back in?

'You might never leave,' she said and despite her restless heart she knew she was smiling.

A little light melody music ascended from childhood, whistling her happy. Ia was grateful that Bran was missing, wherever he was he was not here the space was open she was free to move beyond dreams maybe he would not return. She sat down lay back on to the crook of one arm and thought about what Jenna had said, she imagined the fighting could only think of brief standalone moments of violence: her parents without their gear, camp lads on the can, the men who came sniffing in the early days, badgers ripping flesh-shreds beneath the summer gorse. What were the streets like before? What would they be like after? She looked at the child building towers out of the damp sand and she sat up to help.

All the things Ia liked to do the child liked the same. All day long they moved at the same speed stepped into each other's footprints it was a dance learnt and forgotten and remembered again. There was comfort in that, comfort in the silence that surrounded them it had four walls and a firm foundation the sky no matter what shade was their roof. The inside of their world was full of colour and texture, the more time they spent there the more Ia could not imagine being anywhere else. The happiest day the happiest night there had been nothing to compare to this if she had a palette she would paint it all the colours of the rainbow.

When the sky started to lose light and hunger came crawling Ia walked the girl up the cliff toward the smokehouse.

'This'll be your job one day,' she told her, 'give me a rest; don't worry, I'll teach you.'

'Fish,' said the girl when Ia slid the lock and opened the door.

'What you reckon?' Ia stood back, proud.

The girl nodded she went in hands everywhere, Ia pulled her back.

'These int shells for maulin, em food.' She lifted a couple from the rack. 'For eatin.'

'I know,' said the child.

They left the cliff and returned to the caravan Ia deciding that the child had experienced enough of the cove for one day.

She tied back the canvas door to the porch and dragged the kitchen chairs into the entrance so they could sit and watch the first rainfall.

'You like rain,' said Ia to the girl, it came as no surprise. 'Keep your feet in, won't be much left of em otherwise.'

'I like rain,' the girl repeated.

They drank mint tea that Ia had left to cool in a jug and she poured it into tall glasses and they ate the first batch of smoked mackerel from a slate propped between them.

'You want vinegar?' Ia asked.

The girl shook her head she didn't or didn't know what was on offer.

'Girl,' said Ia. 'Can't keep callin you girl, wish you'd come with some kind of tag or tattoo in way of identification.' She kept her eye on the kid but she ignored her, happy to be toe-tapping in the mud.

'I got a tattoo, want to see it?' Ia pulled the sleeve of her hoodie up toward her shoulder.

'It's a human skull,' she told her. 'Mostly it's a skull and a load of other shit that means somethin to the gang; don't mean nothin to me. Bran said we all got to have one in case; had mine fifteen, sixteen, early on anyway; Dad had the same but better, mine was done by a blind man or drunk, maybe both, just as well of been.' She looked at the girl to see if she was up for laughing she wasn't and Ia told her to pull her chair back from the puddle at her feet that she would not tell her again.

'So that's my lot anyway, you got a gang where you from?' When the girl didn't speak Ia squeezed her chin and turned her head toward her. 'No?'

'Don't know,' said the child. 'Can't remember.'

Ia pulled down her sleeve and took the bottle of pills from

out her coat, when the child looked over at her Ia returned them to her pocket. 'Don't need em,' she said. 'You got me calm as pool water.' Together they finished off the fish and watched the puddles that had formed in the ruin tessellate become tiles to form a floor.

When the storm sky leaked into porch corners and the child curled to sleep Ia put her coat around them both and carried her to the cubby put her to bed with the one song Mum and Dad used to sing the only song she knew.

She returned to the porch and sat with a cigarette to watch the pitching rain the damp misery that was ocean fog, Ia waited at her post by the door she knew it wouldn't be long before he came to her.

'You bin waitin for me,' he said; he stood at the entrance of the ruin his manners were Ia's delight.

'I was hopin.' She smiled.

'You put a seat out.'

Ia looked at the chair beside her and nodded she hid the child's glass by kicking it toward the canvas wall.

'So sit on it.' She watched him come into the light his eyes lambent with flame not the good kind.

'What?' he asked.

'You don't look right, somethin happen?'

'Em cousins of yours have gone quiet, you int heard anythin since this mornin have you?'

'I int seen nobody to know nothin, int seen me old man

since whenever.' She looked at Jenna, could see he was thinking something.

'Bran int a part of this, he's out to sea,' she said.

'Know that do you?'

'If he was he'd be rattlin round, keepin watch; he int a quiet man.' She watched him fidget in the seat beside her, his hands scratching, tapping, tied.

'You want anythin to drink?' she asked. 'Tea just.'

Jenna shook his head. 'Don't need no bloody tea, need to talk to someone, find things out.'

Ia sat back. 'You can't go strollin into the campsite askin questions, you just can't.'

Jenna took her hand in both of his and pulled her toward him. 'My mother's gone missin, since last night, she's disappeared.'

Ia didn't speak, she turned her hand in his to hold it pull them back to last night.

'I seen that tattoo on your arm,' he said, 'seen it on em others; you're one of em.'

'Never said I weren't.' She pulled her hand away.

'You could talk to em, find out where she is, she's all I got.'

'One tramp stamp and a name don't mean nothin; me askin where I int meant gonna make em worse.'

'Worse un what? Int nothin worse un this.' He went to stand and Ia jumped back in her chair they both watched it fall.

'You think I'm goin to hit you?' he asked.

'You're windin up to somethin.'

'You reckon, after last night?'

'You blame me for last night, if you weren't with me your mum would still be round.' She went to stand at the caravan door. 'You should leave.'

Jenna put his hands in his coat pockets. 'So that's it, you int even goin to try talkin to em?'

'What would I say that won't make em wonder on things? Bran can't know bout you and me.'

Jenna bent to pick up the chair.

'I int used to this,' she said; she wanted to explain her futility.

'What int you used to?'

'Talkin, thinkin, I don't know.' She took the pill bottle from her pocket cracked the lid with his eyes still on her she swallowed two.

'What em for?' he asked.

'Nerves.'

'You int got nothin to be nervous about Ia, maybe that's your problem.' He neatened the chair and turned to go, left a space an opportunity for Ia to step into she stepped back and closed the door.

IA STOOD AT THE kitchen window and watched the sea for signs of life she wondered where Bran was wished him fully away.

She sat at the table and closed her eyes her head against the window she listened to the lilting wind. Tomorrow the trees that hedged the track and fields would shed the last of their leaves have them pitched into the breeze.

Since the girl's arrival Ia had been spending more time sleeping at the kitchen table. At that end of the caravan the windows were both sides she could rest her head with an ear turned for listening the child her lover the men her man. No matter what time of day or night Branner returned she would be ready for him but with each passing day each night she dared herself to dream that he would never appear her heart beat crazy thinking it.

She stretched her feet to the crossways chair and hooked the blanket over her head to make a tent so cold was this new night come in it had taken all good things the happy the heat Jenna's warmth gone tepid she was not who he thought she was.

'Too much thinkin,' she said to herself. 'Too much gone in, can't get it out.' She pulled down the blanket and lit the lamp put her hands to the glass to catch the flame. A moment warm she returned to the beach her fire fox he had given her everything wished for, more.

'I can't talk to em,' she whispered. 'Don't know em, cept . . .' She got up and lowered the flag.

Beyond the ruined walls something not wind was howling shouting calling for her.

'Shush now,' she said. 'You gotta shush, don't make this an unhappy thing; you all I got.'

She folded the blanket and went into the porch to smoke the last of the cigarettes, the call of the child had her nerves torn and tied. She felt the knot constrict in her gut its rope stretch toward the girl, Ia knew it was she who tugged a little more each day. The girl shared Ia's speared, spit-heart ache the loneliness, if she was not her mother how come she felt this way? The guilt was the worst of it, bricking up the child leaving her in the damp the cold, no matter how well nested it was far from right the girl was feral but not animal.

Still Ia would not go to her, not until she knew Bran was gone for good and the fighting over she would not let herself get too close. She thought about Jenna, his eyes his voice her golden boy. 'Fuck.'

Ia finished the cigarette took one of her pills and stamped the boots put on her coat and walked a little way out on to the headland no light but memory enough to gauge the edge. In half an hour maybe less the girl would know she was not going to come she would settle down set her default to mute until morning. In that time Ia would search the campsite see it clear of the people she knew this was all she could do.

Outside the ruin walls she searched the sea for light but not even the lighthouse beam could be bothered she heard the foghorn blast its warning, so dense was the night the sensor had been triggered. Black on black the sea the heavens the sod beneath her feet, everything tarred, all things Ia knew to be her life her home threatening to come down heavy. She could hear it reeling on the wind, smell the thing that was close to fear it crawled the cliff path like a winch-chain it begged for mercy in a coil at her feet. Something was happening further down the track something odd more odd than what was usual, she went to it.

Ia kicked a little of the cliff to hear the scuff of falling scree, world falling. She bent to feel the damp earth the tufts of heather in hiding and she hunkered down amongst the cliff-tight gorse to watch the campsite men and women go on toward their bay. It wasn't much more of a beach than Ia's they used it as a dump for the very last of things the dead-end waste the broken shit-bits they barrowed over the cliff to let the sea come pick at the bones. Sometimes the current fancied an armchair plucked to spring and hair or a melted plastic toy but mostly it made dunes masked everything with sand some things were just not worth the bother.

Despite the fog the dusk Ia could not chance being seen she sat with her legs out straight and bowed her head so she could spy through the scrub there was an atmosphere about the folk that was close to revelry the moment before mayhem. She counted them out and there were many too many to know their names their faces they bred like wildfire spreading.

Down on the grit-sand Ia could see the shadows of children shouldering driftwood they carried it toward the centre of the beach a fire was coming good the soot smoke fused with the dank wind it grew great and came at her like a manifestation of all that was bad about that place.

'Someone,' Ia said, remembering Jenna's words, 'someone to talk to, someone to ask about his mother.' She saw one of her regulars standing at the pool, he was stumbling drunk, had too much whooping to him to be of any use. She moved closer, her hands in the grit her knees scuffing rocks she saw the chicken man hunched to a run of tyres, he didn't look too far gone there was still time, if she could sell herself for information she would.

Ia stood up brushed her knees pulled a slate splinter from the pad of her hand. She cleared her throat and spat, felt her thighs her cunt tighten. When had this happened? When had she become not that kind of girl? Fucking was fucking for fucksake.

'Since fifteen,' she said, told herself it was for Jenna that she would do this but the thought only made her worse. She rubbed her head her ears the noise of camp was getting louder.

She wondered what day it was that might warrant celebration; they were forever celebrating something aligned to the seasons the weather, old ways Bran called them. Every tradition rooted and earthed in farming but not one single soul right for work or worrying beyond seeing the night through to morning. Campsite people were built for going after their own needs their hands soft their bellies softer; nothing physical in their lives no hard work except the fight, their ferality made them fearless. Ia knew fear was what made the difference, with everything it made the difference.

When the smoke consumed the hills the horizon and all that was in between she moved closer saw a dozen strangers get pushed toward the pyre. She pulled her scarf over her face to keep from breathing in the smoke squinted her eyes to concentrate. Each face same colour flushed red with heat, the flames so high their flesh looked to be on fire. Ia turned her head away from the smoke, told herself it was just a threat this was what site folk did intimidation was a favourite pursuit. She rubbed the smoke from her eyes and turned to go when she heard screams she turned back. A woman tied to a door, lifted, settled into the blaze like wet wood. When the flames found her dress her hair the crowd cheered. No kerosene to spare it would be a slow death.

Ia ran. She would not be a part of this she wished herself planets away.

She headed back to the security of their own scrubland and set her thinking straight, she looked skyward and realized if there was a place for thanks it was in that moment.

She and Jenna and the girl they were alive Jenna's mother too she was sure of it she would tell him this. No black woman down on the beach she was sure, just strangers was all.

Ia closed her eyes wiped the savagery from them. She thought about the buzzard feather it reminded her that life came from death, always she would remind herself this. Good from bad, the child had come to her at her lowest point one seed fallen from a felled tree.

As she walked she could still hear her calling out and something else too it was the gate at the end of the track it opened and smacked shut, three times shit shit shit. Ia ran toward the kid and she shouted for her to shut up if not this would be it the end of their perfect dream hadn't she said he was a violent man?

In the distance she saw the bike light turn flash stony and she began to run. Past the ruin walls toward the outbuildings and the illuminated girl, a standing anemone. Ia took the lamp from out her hand.

'I gotta lock you in,' she said, 'and you gotta shut the fuck he's comin right now he's here.' She pushed her into the cubby took the lamp and secured the door, what concrete blocks lay scattered she lifted and jammed against.

'I'll be back in the mornin,' she whispered. 'When it's all clear I'll come see you, promise.'

She blew out the lamp and stood with her back against the ruin waited for Bran to come fully into view.

'Show yourself.' She focused her eyes on the puddle of light its beam spread thin, flattened in the fog. Two figures moving, stepping into the light, first one and then the other they stood together, defiant, broke apart.

Ia cupped her ear when the wind changed direction it caught Bran's voice and threw it her way. Then another voice, Jenna's. She closed her eyes told him to save himself go running. Suddenly the bike moved and the light fanned out a dust cloud settling she saw Jenna walking away.

Ia was quick to make her way around the wrong side of the ruin she climbed the stone sill of a window and into the van the table and sitting.

She relit the lamp found the feather and put it in her pocket she tried to remember why she was up why was she?

'I couldn't sleep,' she told herself. 'I can never sleep.'

She scooped her hands to the back window to see if he was coming around and stood to look through the front watched the light go in and out of the ruin saw his silhouette he was slow to move.

She went through the porch the ruin and stood opposite him in the yard.

'You're home,' she said.

She heard him grunt he turned his head to keep from looking at her face. His damage done.

'I was worried.'

'Doubt it.'

'You int bin home.'

'Know that don't I?' He put out a hand and she took it thinking good things but he did not want her except to lean upon. 'Get me inside,' he said.

Ia took his weight and helped him toward the caravan she watched his feet go slow and noticed he wore military boots his good shoes gone. So many things she wanted to ask, so many questions where the hell had he been? She stood behind him and watched him ascend the scatter-brick steps into the van and she kept her hands ready the lamp still swinging if he fell she would try to catch him.

He went so slow that the time in Ia's life was pressed to pause. Everything about him measured, his fingertips gripped against the aluminium doorframe his head down full-stop. If Ia's life had moved on at a pace Branner's had taken a turn for the worse he had become an aged man old before his time. She felt sorry for him, the guilt it knifed her cut her in two.

She watched him go toward the bedroom and he told her not to bother with the petting the looking-after, he'd hurt his leg and that was all, he asked her please woman leave it there.

That was the moment Ia's two worlds collided. For the first

time she could see fully the cracks they had always been there, the split and splinter of so many things destroyed and only one thing left dear, one damned thing it didn't even belong to her he could have all the rest.

She followed him into the bedroom and scanned the space for traces of the kid, saw a few strewn items of childhood clothes he would not think anything of them. She watched him stand and stare at the bed something was catching up to him a realization that this was his life.

'Dint I say no pettin?' he said.

'Just seein you right.' She watched him flick the blankets get in fully clothed, in that moment she hated him more than she ever thought possible. That was her bed this was her home she'd earned the right had made it so.

'Can I get you anythin?' she asked, the familiar servitude bone-stuck in her throat.

'Not right now.' He pulled the covers up to his head. 'If I think of anythin I'll shout you.'

'OK then.' She remained at the door.

'What?' he asked.

'Bout your leg.'

'Not now Ia.'

'How you do it though?' When he didn't answer she asked about the campsite lads, it wasn't him it was Jenna who was on her mind.

'What bout em?'

'What they doin? I saw the fire.' She swallowed hard, remembering.

'Fucksake, you bin spyin?' He sat up found the candle holder and threw it into the hallway.

Ia stepped back and watched it hit the floor the pretty blue petals torn and flipped white.

'I int bin spyin,' she said. 'Was just askin.' She pushed the ceramic shards away from the door and closed it returned to the kitchen to sit.

HOW MANY WEEKS HOW many moments merged? Good days and bad nights it didn't end.

A string of lights joined together by dark spaces and Ia dangling motionless between the man and the child. There was no escaping the mess she had made she was living two lives; Bran in bed shouting his leg getting worse, the girl out playing in the backyard scrub. Two lives and neither one belonging to her she wished she could return to the place that made most sense.

If Branner could see what she saw, understand the map she carried in her head then maybe they would have a better shot with the one bullet that remained. She saw things from such incredible height some days she found it hard to explain the detail of such big pictures.

Time passed and the honeymoon light that was Jenna had dimmed he had lost interest in what little she had to offer. All good things faded the way Ia knew they would, he was a beautiful exploded star, blown. She supposed he had taken her advice and run for good, but still it was a shame, kind eyes good manners it was a great shame.

She stood at the kitchen window and asked the stubborn waves for answers they had nothing for her the white-tipped crests catching the wind she saw the entire ocean join forces with the cloud be rain and fall back down to earth. She wiped the sides and made a mess of cooking porridge with a few discovered oats, mindless. Her head fallen between unwanted and needed, neither man nor child cared for her their love was incomplete. Two halves but joined they would make a whole if only she could bring them together.

'She has no name,' Ia decided she would tell him. 'No family, nobody, nothin.' She would bring the child to him stand back and wait for him to see her the way Ia saw her, see their new life manifest itself into what they had wanted from the start, a normal kind of life a life they had once imagined something to grab hold of keep them upright. But deep down Ia knew she was clutching at straw her hands itched thinking it.

THE FOURTH MAYBE FIFTH week since Bran's return Ia stood worrying at the kitchen sink there were more things to niggle her than usual. Bran's leg had gone from bad to worse, he hadn't used a splint was healing wrong she'd seen it from afar looked like twisted ivy root. It put him in an unpredictable mood his blame pointed at Ia she didn't have time for him her concern was all for the girl.

Another morning spent at routine she had gone around with the tea the hot oats first the man then the child and she had noticed how much colder the dawn how the fog had gotten into the cubby it painted the walls with ice crystals the floor spread like a sheepskin rug.

Winter was close, she could smell its bated breath the underground water reserves slowing for the freeze the days were closing in both ends shortening losing light.

How much of her responsibility was this kid? Counting the given days when would she slot into place be one of them? Ia had been entrusted with her life, at some point she would have to stop with the lock-up. She wondered if she could make the smokehouse bigger put the kid in with the fire wondered if she could trust her in a way she couldn't with water. When Bran called out she took a minute to wipe the child from her mind she squeezed herself into an ill-fitting smile so he might loosen it was about time.

'Where's my drink?' he asked when she pushed open the bedroom door.

'You had mint tea,' she said. 'Mint from the garden.'

'We int got no garden, go get one em bottles of gin.'

'It's gone.' Ia leant against the door jamb and wiped her hands in the cloth she held.

'There was three bottles.'

'We had em away.'

'We did?'

Ia nodded it was easy to lie, his head so addled through fifty years of hard drinking since boyhood he had no memory no capacity for small detail.

'You got anythin for the pain?'

She thought for a minute. 'Got some mushrooms.'

Bran nodded and she went to the bathroom cabinet found the bag of dried mushrooms that somebody had bartered she didn't care for it he could have the lot.

'How's it?' she asked when he pushed a little into his mouth.

'Tastes off.'

'I mean the leg.'

'Fuckin hurts, what you reckon?'

'You want me to take a look?'

'Why would I want you to do that?'

'In case.'

'I twisted it is all.'

'Int cut is it? Don't want no infection gettin in.'

He looked at her and Ia knew what she was doing she was pushing but she couldn't help it. She knew what a bully he was knew whoever injured him had got worse, she narrowed her eyes tried to read him but he was a torn page she never got further than whichever mood. He looked tired, the days the weeks chasing after the site lads had taken its toll, he wore his skin like a loose veil his hair too long for his lupus skull.

'How you do it Bran?' she asked. 'How you hurt your leg?'

'Fell.'

'Drink, was it?'

He looked at her and said yes it was the drink but Ia knew he was lying.

'You best leave me alone,' he said. 'You standin there accusin, what the fuck you got to be accusin bout?'

'I bin leavin you alone for the past month, I'm worried bout you.' She meant it.

'Don't start Ia.'

'I int startin nothin, just wish you would settle some way toward your better self.'

'What the fuck I say? Had too much to drink is all.'

Ia stood in the jar the crack between open and closed. 'We was all right once weren't we?' She watched him think a moment saw the light come on perhaps this was the time for asking saying about the girl.

'Bran?'

'You was never right,' he said. 'You took everythin that was mine, made it your own, had me tied before I knew what was what.'

'I was a kid.'

'Fuckin baggage was what you was.'

'You had me workin fish before I was a teen.'

'Your keep was all.' He looked for something to throw, tipped the mushrooms to the bed and fisted the plastic bag into the air it went nowhere; he let his hand drop and together they watched the small carrier catch a mouthful of air and hang gaped in suspense they knew they hung the same.

'You int nothin without me,' he shouted. 'Wouldn't survive outside the creek one minute without me tellin you what and holdin your hand; you int got nobody but me, all em in your life left, don't you forget that.'

COME LATE AFTERNOON SOMETHING inside of Ia some kind of defiance had her bring the girl down on to the beach before the dark descended, she wanted to return to the place she and the child had created all those weeks ago the world where they were happiest.

'You be quiet though, you hear me?' she told her when she unlocked the cubby door. 'Don't go makin noises, don't go callin like you do in the night.' She held the girl's chin to make sure she understood and she told her that Bran thought a skulk of foxes had moved into the ruin someplace so let him continue to think that.

'Soon you'll be meetin him, you have to learn best behaviour, when he's better, when he's back to fishin and found somethin resemblin calm.' She held her tiny limpet hand and led her past the side wall of the ruin, when the girl saw Bran's bike she stretched out a hand so she could touch it and Ia liked that, she was connecting, they were all connecting.

'Be nice to play on the beach awhile won't it? Play some-where different than muck and mud.' She looked down at the girl and noticed in the new winter light that her eyes had changed colour, the sea blue gone the forest green darkened turned hazel and that was the colour of her own eyes.

'See if we can't find some more shells for the cubby, you'd like that wouldn't you?' Ia wanted to tell her it wouldn't be long until Bran left his storm behind, after the thunder they could start making plans.

'Cubby's still all right init?' she asked.

'The shitter?'

Ia nodded. 'Int too cold?'

'It's OK.'

They walked the sticky sand still wet from morning tide and picked their way through the seaweed and plastic to pocket their finds.

'You see any sea-glass, you pass it to me; I'm goin to make somethin for your room, got somethin planned, don't ask what.'

'What?'

Ia ignored her. 'Evie was the best at finding glass. One Christmas she made an ashtray for Dad.' She closed her eyes, remembering.

'Did he like it?' the girl asked.

'He loved it,' she told her. 'And really he did.'

Ia tried to think what it was her sister had made Mum that

final year, something similar but she couldn't recall exactly, only fragments, scattered.

When the girl looked up at her Ia smiled and she wondered what she remembered of her own life. The longer the further the days the more past life was forgotten maybe that was for the best.

They sat on the sand when the wind blew the grains dry and counted out their bounty it was a good haul.

'We'll have the porch plastered,' she said and she looked at the kid to see if she'd noticed the slip of tongue. She had decided to make a room for her there.

'You gettin some blush in your cheeks int you girl?' Ia pushed the girl's hair from her face and watched the last flash of sunlight set in her eyes. 'Bin out the sea how long now? Two months you reckon?'

'Maybe.' The girl reached for the shells and pulled them toward her.

'My little mermaid, you is.'

How different things could have been if Bran had hurt himself in a way that rendered him bed-bound for good, a little space was all she asked for a little room to escape. Every day on the beach sharing the sea its bounty its spoils without the runaround without the fear of losing the girl she was a peach.

'In time you will remember everythin bout your own life.' Ia said this as a matter of fact she said that she was OK with it.

'Some things shared and some things no, it won't matter cus

we got this int we?' She wondered if the child knew what she meant wondered if she knew herself. 'So if you remember stuff just say, I int goin to hold it gainst you.' Ia felt better saying these words it was something that had played on her mind it needed to be said. 'Come summer,' she continued. 'Come summer when we got heat and the unrest has died and Bran gets a hold on himself and goes back to work like what he's used.'

With routine resumed she would have more time to spend with the girl maybe Jenna would return they could visit him up in the north fields when Bran was at sea, she missed him missed his silence his touch, the tiny shards of flame he made and put inside her.

Ia looked at the girl, she was about to ask if she'd remembered her name if not she had a few ideas, good ones, but the child was distracted something had snagged at the corner of her eye.

'What is it?' Ia asked. She looked to where the girl gaped cliffward and saw Branner standing there she jumped to her feet.

'Who you talkin to?' he shouted put his hands to his mouth to go the distance.

'Just some kid.' Ia pushed the girl behind a rock told her to hide in one of the caves when she got the chance. She left the mountain of shells on the sand and ran the beach the cliff and up the steps toward him, hoping that he might understand this new chapter in their lives and have her explain things before he had chance to think them.

'What kid?' He capped his hand to his brow it was getting dark the night came stumbling close.

'A girl, I found her.' Ia gripped her hands to her knees to catch her breath.

'What the fuck, Ia? What's this now?'

'Don't shout, you'll scare her proper.'

'Where is she?'

Ia looked down at the cave thought she saw the girl crouch where the surf hit the rocks one moment gone then back again.

'I asked you a question. Where is she?'

'In the caves, you frightened her.' Ia noticed he had come out barefoot and without his coat. 'You'll catch your death,' she said. 'Why you out? You int meant for out.'

He looked down at his leg and said he was testing it.

'Won't heal walkin round, you gotta go back to bed.'

Ia went to help him part-way toward the van and she told him before he had chance to ask that she didn't know where or who the kid had come from.

'Belongs to someone,' he said. 'What's her name?'

'Won't say.'

'Don't want some fuckin waif wanderin round, not with everythin goin on.'

'She int no waif, no stray either.'

'I should bring her into the site.'

'Course, when your leg's better.'

'Call em. I wanna see em.'

'Stop shoutin, you'll scare her.' She noticed he was drunk asked him where he had found the bottle he ignored her.

'Kid,' he shouted. 'Get yourself up here if you know what's good for you.'

'Or what?' asked Ia.

Bran looked at her and she knew he was working his way up to something new.

'You should rest.' She reached out for his arm in the dusk and said she would help him in.

'I'm sick of restin, it's bin weeks, I got things to do, a way of makin money more un usual.'

Ia guided him to the entrance of the ruin. 'Is it straight?' she asked. 'Cus fishin is, you always sayin it's an honest job.'

'Since when you care bout what's straight?'

'I care right and wrong is all.' They reached the van and Ia helped him through the porch and into the kitchen.

'I'm sick of restin, sick of this life, sick of idlin workin no space between.' Ia watched him steady himself against the wall and fail, he fell toward her his instant reaction to put out a fist it clipped her cheek and they hit the ground.

Silence. This was the space Ia knew they would one day plunge, the earth divided, she had been avoiding stepping over she wondered why. Thirteen years Bran had been her universe she tiptoed around him in fear of the fall. He was nothing to her, thin air. Ia didn't need it she needed the child's water, Jenna's fire, survival things.

'Get off me,' she said. His weight was nothing but he had a way of pinning her always had.

'Or what?' he asked.

Ia looked him straight in the eye she did not blink did not cry for the usual pity didn't turn away despite the stench of his breath. 'We lose time.'

Bran rolled off her and Ia left him sitting on the kitchen floor, she returned to the night to look for the girl.

THE THINNING MOON NAILED itself to the space between transient cloud and Ia was appreciative of small light it got her to the cliff path and down on to the beach.

'Where are you?' she called. She stood in the curl of bay and threw her voice into the wind.

'Why you frightened? Don't be scared, we was just fightin, don't everyone?'

She went from cave to cave shouting for the girl to come back to her, out toward the rocks and into the next bay, that was when she saw her bundled against the brim that crowned closest to the sea.

'Don't move,' she said. 'Don't leave me, not yet.'

The water was drawing in, it filled the rock pools and circled the child.

'What you doin?' Ia asked, she saw her lips move and she crouched to listen.

'That's him,' said the girl.

'Who?' asked Ia.

'That man that made the light that crashed the boat.'

'That man?' Ia pointed toward the cliff and the child nodded. 'What you say kid?' She sat on the rock beside her.

'We was fishin and then the fog came and Dad saw the light, thought it was bringin us in, we int from these parts.'

'Light on the headland was it? The rocks?' Ia knew that trick it was the oldest.

The girl nodded. 'It was him,' she said, shaking.

Ia sat back and watched a little more of her boots disappear into the water. 'I gotta think what it is you're sayin here girl.' She thought back to when she had first found the child if Bran had been out fishing maybe he had.

'Spose you got a name now have you? Now you got your head back.'

'Gevelles.'

'That's a pretty name.'

The girl nodded. 'It's Cornish,' she said.

'I know, so's mine. Come on now, it int long goin to rain.' Ia stood and she reached out a hand to pull the girl to her feet.

'I'm gonna call you Geeva.' She looked at the child and told her it sounded familiar, like something lost, something found.

'And don't you worry bout Bran, he's addled, must've found my stash; he'll be flat out round about now.'

They returned to the shore and Ia saw the shells collected

from earlier she stuffed them into her hoodie pocket and into the girl's hands.

'You gotta stay in the cubby a little longer, you hear? Just till I work out what to do.' She wished she knew the way to new thought she had a habit of tilling old ground.

They climbed the path in silence and on toward the ruin and into the cubby the child on to the bed the shells on to the floor.

'Lock yourself in and I'll lock you the same.' She crouched and repeated her words and asked what was wrong the girl would not stop staring.

'Your face.'

'What about it?'

The girl came to her and pointed at the fresh cut on her cheek. 'He do that?' she asked.

Ia put her hand to the wound. 'His ring must've caught me.'

'He hurt you; he keeps hurtin you.'

Ia ignored her and pushed her through the door.

'He's a bad man,' the girl continued.

'I think I know that.'

'You gotta leave him.'

'I can't, he's my family, I int got no other.'

'There's another way.'

'Kid, what you talkin bout? First nothin, now everythin.'

'You gotta leave him now,' she said again.

'Cus the wreckin? The fightin?'

'Cus the baby.'

'What baby?'

'Yours.'

Ia looked toward the ruin, counted backwards.

'It int his,' said the girl.

IA SAT OUT ON the headland her legs dangling the world she knew so well a tumble of talus rock a fallen thing beneath her.

'A baby,' she said.

Did she believe the child? She didn't know. She was crying in any case. She wiped her face and put a hand against her stomach. Beyond the shoreline she could hear the waves smash against the rocks and go under.

'A new baby.'

If the girl was right and perhaps she was pregnant what now? The baby was not Branner's he would know this, the last baby she had got away with but not this one they hadn't touched in months.

'Jenna.' She had to find him the baby was his it had to be it came from a version of love that she could not ignore. She went from the cliff and slow past the ruin lifted the lamp and headed north through the gate and on to the path toward where she thought the ropery used to be she didn't think it far. She stood with her feet in the briar and looked for stamp-ground tracks, any trace of movement anything to give him away, whispered his name and hoped he hadn't left Cold Acre for good, perhaps he'd never returned to the ropery. She went on pushing, the lamp held high, her feet stretching booting the brambles into fists of weed.

'I know it's in here,' she told herself, she had seen it years back before the overgrowth when people still had a pride in things.

'Jenna,' she said. 'Where you at?' She looked to where she'd left the track and decided to loop full circle and that was when she saw it the hut the door gone the roof still holding, she went in.

Ia stood and waited for her eyes to adjust to the gloom and she said his name but knew he wasn't there. On the floor she could see the blanket she had given him on that first night neatly folded and placed like it was the only thing he owned in the world it nearly was. She crouched against the wall and lifted the blanket to her and inside a torn photo a mother and her son a man's arm at the tear nothing more she was quick to put it back.

'He int gone.' She knew this couldn't say why she turned off the lamp and settled herself to sitting waited for his return.

Some nights darkness suited Ia more than daylight, it was better at forgetting, it forgave the day. When she needed to think, it was a place to hide without looking. She pulled her knees up to her chest and dragged her coat across her lap and she tried to imagine Jenna in this tight spot she could not. Truth was Ia could not imagine him any place except hers the cove the beach her arm's reach, together they would have nothing to fear why would they? In her dreams he was never far even in nightmare he stood at the edge, a little soft guiding light. She wondered where he had been hiding these past weeks, he'd been gone a month, maybe two. There never seemed to be more detail than here and then away she couldn't help but worry. She knew he was lost, she could see it everywhere in him knew she had found him in stasis a holding place, it was where she found herself, a state of indolence. When she looked at him, talked to him, it was as if he were holding up a mirror, his float so familiar it confused her.

She pulled her coat closer and put her hands into the waistband of her jeans. 'All em years slaggin, spittin duds,' she said. 'A baby like this don't come from nothin but love, after all em cruel years, I can feel it special.' It had been eleven years the first five with Bran and near enough on her twentieth birthday opportunity came knocking with its pants down she took it. When the gifts got offered she took them told herself once the greatest gift came along she'd give it all up but never had one baby bigger than a thumb she'd never been loved.

'Not till now,' she said.

'Somebody in there?' he whispered.

Ia went to turn on the lamp and he knelt to stop her.

'I thought you was gone for good, thought I'd never see you again.'

'I int bin far,' he said.

'Why you int bin round?'

Jenna didn't answer and Ia knew what this was, it was the worst of things. She thought about the woman tied and taken toward the fire on the beach that day and she took his hand wanted to say sorry say something she said nothing.

He didn't speak. The something that was changed put him at a distance he was so far away he looked shrunken in size.

'The thing I'm thinkin,' Ia rubbed the back of his hand her fingertips pushing between the veins each gully a dead end, 'bout your mother.' She looked into his eyes saw a little light flash there a match struck and then blown gone out. She wanted to couple her hands around him whisper the flame into being until it became a fire, his fire.

'You're plannin, int you?' she asked. 'Plannin for good, the big full stop.'

Against the frame of dusk light she saw him nod said yes, it was time for revenge.

She squeezed his hand and put it into her lap, wished he could sense the baby the way she did it would have made things easier had them communicate with thoughts instead of words.

'I won't stop you,' she said; she heard him sigh for the things he had done the things he had to do.

'I int goin to ask, cept to say nobody has to do what they

don't want to do.' These words felt funny coming out of her mouth they didn't belong to her she was a fraud.

'There int no way round what I have to do.' He looked at her through the thin veil of light could see the crescent wound he shook his head. 'This land, these people, you shouldn't be here.' He pulled her to him, held her face in his hands.

'I int special, Jenna.'

'You int like them neither, don't reckon you ever was; this is a warning shot Ia, that smack, em killins, how long you goin to ignore all that int right?'

'I can't just up and go.' She thought about Geeva, the space she was going to decorate for her in the porch. 'I got responsibilities.'

'Excuse is all you got.' Jenna took her hand.

Ia closed her eyes she could feel herself slipping didn't want to touch the ground, if impact was imminent let it hit without warning. She could hear Jenna say how bad things had got since he'd last seen her.

'How I do it?' she said. 'I can't even decide what to eat most days, I'm adrift.'

'You make a plan and you stick to it.'

Ia nodded, she'd never made a plan in her life. Except one.

'And once you're gone don't dare come back, no matter how much you might think it's somethin lost, it int nothin like loss. Em people int your family, you got to leave the cove.'

Halfway down part-way through the fall Ia felt the air slow. Her hands discovered ropes and pulleys her feet found rungs a ladder going up. She took a deep breath.

'My old man who int, this place, everythin haunts me,' she said.

Jenna let go of her hand and reached for her face.

'I had a plan,' she said. 'Me and my sister, we had a plan.'

'So you'll go?'

Ia nodded. 'I'll do it.'

'When?' he asked.

'Soon.'

'Ia, sometimes we int got no choice for the things we got to do.' His hand went to her mouth and she kissed it. 'Where will you go?' he asked.

'Home, my real home, follow the River Tamar home proper.' She looked at him and told him not so far from where they sat was the source of the river, that she had always known this, it gave her comfort. Over the years she had thought about it often, a gut-string pulling connecting seas. In that moment a sense of belonging overwhelmed her and she felt its warmth its comfort it was a settling place.

'I'm goin to do it,' she said.

'You got a boat for all that river?'

'I'll walk, there's a notion in that int there?'

He nodded put his hands into his pockets he was thinking about his own plan.

'Tomorrow.' Ia stamped the word into existence it made a mark. 'What bout you?' she asked.

'Seven days.' He reached for the photo that was hidden in the blanket and folded it put it into his coat pocket.

'What's seven days?'

'Down the river there's a quay to your left, as you head you'll see a waterwheel; seven days and I'll meet you there.'

'Waterwheel?'

'You can't miss it.'

'What if I can't get there in time?'

'I'll wait for you; it's our plan, I'll wait.'

Ia nodded, she wanted to tell him about the baby, she looked to tell him and he mistook it for melancholy told her not to feel sorry for him, that these days had been destined.

'OK then.' She smiled and the dark caught it and put it somewhere safe. 'We've got a plan,' she said. 'We're together in all this.'

IA RETURNED TO THE cliff with the warmth of Jenna's embrace still in her his words in her ears each one was a kiss. She sat with the lamp in her lap about to go over her plan when something caught her eye she glanced back at the ruin and saw Bran standing there. The night clouds above his head the colour of sword and shield he'd always been protected so.

'It's goin to rain,' he shouted.

Ia looked toward the ocean told it she was going away.

'You'll get wet.'

Ia could see him hobbling at the corner of her eye.

'Don't come no nearer,' she said.

'What I done?'

'You know what.' Ia took her hand from her stomach this was not his baby he was a rotten man all those early years it was he who grew bad seed.

'What, the fight? Was just a fight.'

'You bin wreckin,' she shouted. 'Backalong, that's what you bin doin.'

'What the fuck? I told you, I was out fishin or else in town with the site lads, lookin for work.'

Ia turned to face him. 'Liar.'

'Why wreckin? What you bin thinkin up now?'

'The kid told me.' Ia saw him take out his pack of cigarettes and she asked him to light her one and he did.

'The kid? Some lyin scrag off the street?'

Ia took the cigarette from his outstretched hand, told him to stay put.

'Where is she?' he asked.

'You int seein her.'

'She's lyin, I got questions for her.'

'She's afraid of you Bran, like most folk is afraid of you.'

'She int got nothin to worry bout, int goin to hit no kid, just got questions is all.'

'Couple months back you lured her dad's boat on to the rocks and looted em and now that kid int got no father.'

'Fucksake.'

'Fact.'

'Some kid? You're takin the word of some kid?'

Ia nodded.

'I know what this is.' He started to laugh. 'You stopped takin em pills to calm you?'

'I am calm.'

'How many pills you take?'

Ia thought for a minute; since Geeva she had been taking less and less. 'This int nothin to do with calm or no.'

Branner started to nod and Ia knew he was mocking her.

'We gotta score you some more, up your intake, double it. Stop your imagination runnin riot.'

'Bran, I don't need no more pills.' She was shouting now she could hear her voice hit out it was a hammer looking for a nail.

'Ia.' He took a step toward her and Ia pushed closer to the cliff edge. 'I don't know what you're talkin bout,' he continued, 'or what some kid sayin, but if you int careful you're goin to go slippin or the storm breaks and you won't come in like last time and then you'll get sick worse than before.'

Ia started to smile and he caught her at it.

'Why you smilin?' he asked.

'Was thinkin em words more un you said to me in years.' She wasn't, she was thinking about the plan.

'Thirteen years is a long time to keep talkin.'

Ia smoked the cigarette down to her knuckles and she wondered if she could trust him this one time trust him ever. He had a way of talking her down with a little soft talk always had, she had wanted to love him for so many years. It was too late now but even still the usual bleed of bile and guilt rose up from her belly seeped into her mouth why was that? She was a conspirator had made a pact with a soldier to escape maybe this time she truly was losing her mind.

They had their chance to be a family a hundred times but this final moment had been lost in the wreckage. She was leaving him, a part of her had already gone.

They went slow toward the ruin a space apart, nothing on their lips but the mizzle-mist nothing in their heads except please keep this silence this clear space between them.

They walked through the house that Ia knew would never be a home and into the porch the caravan and she stood to fill the kettle.

'I'll make tea,' she said and she put the two tin mugs on to the table.

'You sure you int got anythin stronger, for the pain?' he asked.

'I'm sure.' She made the tea and sat crossways from him.

'What now?' she asked when he kept looking.

'That kid,' he said. 'You goin to make it sleep outside all night?'

'Bin all right so far.' She kept her recent concern about the cold to herself.

'You think it's right?'

Ia shrugged.

'What's that?'

'What?'

'Shruggin just.'

'Cus I int got no other option,' she said.

'Bring em in ere, that's an option.' He pushed the mug of tea away.

'She's scared of you.' Ia took up her mug of tea and supped despite the heat.

'I int done nothin to scare the girl, let me see her.'

Ia shook her head.

'Like a pet for you is she? Hidden in a cave like a wild animal.'

'She int in no cave.'

'Where then?'

'Int likely to tell you is I?'

'Bring her into this house.'

'House?' Ia sat back. 'This ruin, this winched-in van, you call this a house?'

They looked at each other and Ia waited for his mug to fly, violence was better than silence, she knew its edges, the shape, its texture made from familiar cloth.

'You goin to hit me now?' she asked for it, no longer afraid.

Bran got up and made toward the bedroom.

'Don't you walk away from me.' Ia stood in his way and she told him this was when he was supposed to hit her. 'In the face,' she shouted.

Bran clenched his fists, final warning.

'Don't make me.' He lifted his arm his proud right hook and Ia stepped forward to meet it. Face better than belly, fall final full stop.

He stood above her. 'Best thing you can do is leave.'

When he left the room Ia told him that she would.

SHE LAY ON HER side her hands protecting the unborn her legs bent wrong in the skid of spilt tea. She could feel her cheek rise with heat could feel his print his mark on her since childhood branded as his. She listened to the rain bit-flick the skylight a soft tap building turn heavy hammering she saw the first drops pool and fall into the kitchen for so many years a troubling occurrence it didn't bother her now.

She was slow to get up, first the knees drawn and then her hands out she felt different somehow curious on the inside. She stood and put on her coat and boots went into the rain the wet smarting her eyes stinging the cuts the thumps and claw marks bleeding again as she ran to the cubby.

'Tell me what to do,' she shouted through the door. 'You come to me out of the blue, tell me I got a baby comin, so now what?' Ia heard the child climb from the bed and she unlocked the door put an ear to the wood and waited.

'Go home,' said the child, appearing from the dark.

'I know, but I'm scared to leave, scared of out there, the road, everythin.'

'This int your home.'

'Since twelve it is.'

'Home where you was happy.'

'Evie,' said Ia. 'Evie was where I was happy.' She started to cry. 'I gotta head home to Evie.' She felt the girl reach for her hand put something into it.

'What's this?'

'The compass.'

Ia passed it from hand to hand. 'Keep from the roads, follow the river.' She looked up at the sky and noticed that dawn was breaking. 'It's a sign,' she said. 'Go put on all the clothes I give you, we got to go, got to go now.' She told the girl to stay inside the cubby until she returned.

Ia ran to the smokehouse and she cleared the remaining rack of fish undid her coat and dropped them into the pocket of her hoodie and returned to the caravan.

Inside the kitchen things had changed. It was a photograph for Ia to look at step into one final time. The smell of foul fish and misery, the peel of punches in the paper walls as she put out her hands to move through the grey dawn light, the boot-stamps in the floor when she stepped toward the bedroom. One final moment to check for the all clear, Bran passed out, drunk.

Ia was quick to grab the things from shelves and corners that she might need in days to come. Her knife and kindling hatchet, the last of the food, the tin mugs and lighter plus the half-bottle of kerosene and the blanket off the side; everything into a bin bag for dry the hessian sack for carrying she sniffed it smelt of sunshine oranges even still. The last to go in was her journal and the nature book and she tied the sack end to end with good rope and hung it crossways from her shoulder and she found woollen hats and gloves and the leather coat she'd hidden in the storage box she knew it would do for the kid.

She lit the lamp and left the caravan and the ruin for good her new life swopped and returned to the ancient.

'Put this coat on,' she told the girl and she helped button up the stiff leather pelt pulled the white bobble-hat over her ears and told her come on if she was coming.

River

THEY WENT TENTATIVELY TOWARD the cliff path and westward to the next looping cove and Ia was glad Bran was injured this head start was everything.

They passed the campsite under cover of darkness a little light riddling through gaps and cracks, Ia could see the spew of junk metal meant for mending, the soiled mattresses and sofa seats kept for summer sitting, she told herself that she would not miss this place; knowing her new baby existed was enough to take it to safety carry it from the creek before it had the chance to snatch it from her.

Occasionally the child disappeared from view and Ia thought her gone completely she'd shout her name Geeva tell her she needed her now more than ever and then the inquisitive eyes came through the rain and Ia would smile and say OK.

They continued in silence, in fear, keeping to the path the lamp swinging out a hundred metres above the rocks, the white froth surf lifted back-lit bright, a string of angel wings, waving.

'Don't look down,' she said to herself. 'Don't look down don't look back don't ever.' She saw the girl up ahead the coat hem dragging at her feet and she told her to be careful slow down please.

'Compass says we gotta go inland,' shouted the child.

'How you reckon?' asked Ia.

'It's pointin.'

'Let me see that.' Ia caught up to her and she took the compass and held it to the light. 'Spose we got to cut in at some point.' She looked at the girl and wondered why she trusted her, where had this belief blown in from? This seed that had landed, planted, now talking.

'Woolley Wood is where we're meant,' said Geeva.

'How you know that?' asked Ia. 'How you know, when you int from these parts?'

'You told me.'

'I did?'

'Backalong, when you said bout the river.'

'Don't remember that.' Ia supposed she didn't remember a lot of things, that was what Bran said she had a head full of fancy, daydream, she knew that much was true.

When the bracken blockade allowed they pushed through from the cliff path and into the first field and something about this new land had Ia wonder what it was she was doing. She never went further than the cove the path above, never went down the track except to look for Jenna when he stopped coming.

'You're goin to have a baby and it int his,' said the kid and she came alongside her and looked up and smiled.

Ia nodded. 'I'm goin to be a mother.' The words felt right in her mouth on her lips put out on to the wet night air; with the other babies she never said this never got further than a few weeks, one month, she never dared say it. Nothing mattered; Ia was going on moving forward a better life her baby inside, the child a gift beside and the man who would soon come to her.

This was it, this was what she had wanted had waited for so many years she'd known its meaning without thought without dare it was one word it had her stopped dead. Escape.

A NEW DAWN A new world Ia did not know if there was a place for her here but either way it was too late. She'd heard stories been told things that made her fear the unknown it made a noise merged with the rain a constant racket in her head. There were words she'd heard but didn't understand, they came in twos: civil unrest, social collapse, internal warfare. Away from the cove these things took on new meaning became giants she imagined them hawking their misery from one coast to the next.

It had been a long time since she'd seen anyone just Bran the young man Jenna a few strays with their dicks sticking trousers already down, the men from the campsite or strangers who thought themselves brave ignoring the trespass signs the razor wire they were lucky to get away. The cove had protected her from worse things and now she had left the place.

They continued hiking through foreign fields, burrowing through hedges pushing on no matter the sharp nail briar and hawthorn barb, the compass dictating, pointing. The rain at their backs heavier than ever a little sea-skimmed it bit at their necks their shoulder blades like teeth pulling tight lips it was the ocean telling them to come on home now don't be a fool.

'Never,' shouted Ia. 'We gone and did it.' She pulled off her hat and threw it into the wind told the weather to do its worse nothing could match past misery. The river was calling, good water, soothing. She looked toward the girl wandering up ahead and shouted that it would be a while before they found the source but the child ignored her and Ia shrugged her own indifference. She pulled up her hood and adjusted the sack across her shoulder and she told herself to trust in instinct the way animals were meant.

They came to a wide chained gate and climbed it crossed what was left of road, the tarmac lifted by drought summer wet winters no council money for fixing the last few seasons had taken their toll. This mess was another thing in her favour, Branner would be a long time coming if he came at all. Ia had time on her side plus the river once she found it, a through route, a burrowing worm way home.

They walked until their feet no longer felt pain the wet in them and everywhere about them numb to the nerves the marrow of every bone; their legs lifting going down for more sucking up the muck Ia could feel it permeate could taste the earth its nutrients she was a growing thing.

Despite the elements the fatigue nothing could dampen her spirit her strength she was making a move going on by her own accord she knew Geeva sensed it felt the same, they were lifted.

'You hungry?' Ia asked when the girl wandered close.

Geeva shook her head.

'Me neither, my gut's in knots.'

'You should eat somethin for the baby.'

'I got a heel of bread.' Ia rested the sack on the toes of her boots and she stretched it wide found the bread and split it in two.

'I told you I int hungry,' said the girl and Ia told her to put it in her pocket she did the same.

They continued toward the brow of the hill digging their toes into the sod, when they reached the vantage they took their time to take it all in.

The valley that stretched out below them reminded Ia of the landscape she sometimes dreamt about the scene she painted, sculpted, called happy place. A beautiful construction that perhaps did not exist, except it did she held it here in her hands.

Ia reached out a finger traced the lines of trees, deciduous on her left to the right a pine forest together they formed a V shape made an arrow had Ia pointing.

'So much.' She gestured toward the timbered landscape clinging to the valley and the child that was still in her smiled it was all too much.

'Look what we got,' she said. 'Look at all those trees, I int seen so many trees together.' She tried to think. 'Not ever.'

'Let's go down,' said Geeva. 'See what's what.'

They went toward the woods the walk taking longer than they anticipated, the land beneath their feet slippery the heavy rain speeding stabbing holes in the sod. The coloured canopy of trees still intact ahead of them and Ia wished for dry she would have liked to sit down and draw them listed what shade of paint she might use if she had paint one day.

'Them beech trees,' she told the kid. 'All em cept purple, them called copper beech.'

The girl gave her the look that could have meant anything and then she smiled and Ia liked that, she knew something it was free she was giving it away.

'You know lots bout nature,' said Geeva.

Ia shrugged and nodded yes.

'How?'

'Me and my sister Evie, we had a book told us everythin, if it weren't in that book it weren't worth knowin.'

'What was it called?'

'What?'

'The book.'

'*The Book of Cornwall's Countryside.*' She looked at her and said she had brought it with her.

'Don't you know everythin in it by now?'

'Spose.'

'Can I see it?'

'Maybe later.'

'I'd like that.'

Ia nodded and said she preferred reading to talking. She didn't speak unless there was something that needed saying, the kid was the same and that was good it meant she got to spend most of the time in her own head where she was used.

They entered the woods at the side flank and Ia said they wouldn't be long in passing. She yanked at her hood and hit the wet from its peak and she told the girl stop please one minute let us catch our breath, stretch, eat something.

With the canopy extended above their heads and cloud washed and draped in every corner of the sky, tall shadows stepped up to reinforce the circle of trees. Ia stood centre stage and she put her hands into her pockets and took a moment to absorb her surroundings. She saw the white of the child tangle amongst the branches and she smiled remembering the small woods near their chalet on the cliffs a different kind of wood a mixed bag she recalled.

'Don't go far,' she shouted.

'We're close, I know it.'

'You reckon?' She pulled off the sack and tightened the rope and returned it to her shoulder. 'Where's your coat?' she asked when the girl ran close.

'Int mine.'

'So? You'll catch your death.'

Ia found it bundled where it fell amongst the trees and she returned it to the child and did the buttons and collar tight.

'What you doin?' the girl asked.

'Lookin for fags.' Ia felt in the pockets until she found what she was looking for.

'This his coat?'

'No.'

'Em fags, this coat, these boots.' Geeva kicked her feet out from below the coat and tapped them together.

'Told you it int his coat.' Ia returned her hood and lit a cigarette allowed herself three drags rubbed the ember into the bark of a tree. She returned it to the pack for saving and together they went further into the woods, the trees changing shape and colour, their surroundings becoming forest.

'Pine cones,' said Ia. 'You see any, pick em up.'

'Why?' asked Geeva.

'To put on the fire.' Ia placed the open sack on the ground and started to pick up the cones.

'Em wood?' asked Geeva.

'What you reckon?' She watched the girl hold a cone to her nose to smell she took a bite said yes it was wood.

They continued filling the sack and Ia enjoyed rummaging through this new kind of flotsam when she found a fallen nest she squealed with delight.

'What is it?' shouted Geeva.

'Nest of baby birds.'

'Let me look.' The girl peered into the tiny twig basket she took it from Ia. 'Em dead.' She looked up at her for explanation.

'The nest gone fallen from the tree a while back; the parents weren't able to feed em down here.'

'Bones.' Geeva pushed her finger into each bird's skull she snapped them at the neck and laid them in a row on the palm of her hand.

'Shells,' said Ia and the girl nodded and together they returned the heads and set the nest into the low bough of a tree.

'Time to go,' said Ia and she tied the sack and shifted the new load on to her shoulder.

'Int rained for a bit,' said the girl. 'We're lucky now though.'

'How's that you reckon?'

'Water'll flood where it's meant.'

Ia looked across at her and shook her head. 'That int always right.'

'Tis, you'll see, where the river starts you'll see.'

'Know quite a bit for a kid with no rememberin to her.'

Geeva nodded without looking.

'Remember where you from yet?'

The girl stopped and spun around. 'When I do I'll tell you,' she said.

They continued on toward lower land and lost several hours that way, Ia quiet with wonder the girl fevered with talk since she'd started she hadn't stopped, so convinced was she that the valley was where they were destined. Wherever they walked all the collected water had potential for river making, it congregated in roadside cracks and ran from fields and into tributary lanes and Ia told the kid no more wandering let's just make our way south on what we know.

'Night's comin back in before we even got time to notice,' she said. 'Never knew to miss autumn till now. We should look out for some shack or outhouse, whatever, thick canopy would do; I'm tired, could do with stoppin.'

'But we int found the river,' said the girl.

'Things take time.'

'But look.' Geeva took the compass from her neck and held it up so Ia could see it.

'Stopped again,' said Ia.

'For a reason.'

'Maybe that reason is we should stop, maybe that's all.' Ia untied the sack and took off her coat and laid it out on the damp ground.

Since the definite baby and the maybe man and the plan that for now was on, Ia had stopped believing in childish fancy. The compass did its own thing it always did she knew in preparation for her new life she must stamp the stupid from her. She looked at the girl standing soldier between two trees the light in her eyes fading her spark pinched with finger-spit and Ia told her she was tired, she was sorry.

'Give me that thing.' She took the compass and studied it and said yes perhaps they were close.

'It's what we said.' The girl sat beside her and flicked the boots from her feet.

'I know.' Ia looked at her and said belief in things that you didn't understand was the best kind perhaps it was the only.

'I believe that,' said Geeva.

Ia nodded. 'Good,' she said, 'cus if you only believe in what you know, you're fucked widthways.'

The girl took the compass from her and said she knew the source of the river was close that it was fact was all.

There was nothing much more to say on the subject of hope and want and Ia said they should look for firewood to add to the pine cones if they were going to do this then they should do it properly.

They gathered what they could from the floor the fallen branches weren't so bad with the rot kicked out and beneath the leaves some sticks a little drier it would all do.

'You watch,' she told Geeva.

'I know how to light a fire.'

'It's all in the buildin.' She looked over at the girl out-stretched tapping at the compass and wondered when she had transformed from shy retiring into this. 'I used to be a cocky beggar, look where it got me.'

'On the run,' said the girl.

Ia cleared the earth of dank and she pushed the wet leaves into a barrier to keep the wind from nosing, she told Geeva all she knew of kindling, the girl wasn't listening but it was something to do. She sat with her legs either side of the fire the tiny flame playing her, goading, she was always the fool. Desperately she wanted to show her companion things, that there was more to her than what she reckoned but half an hour spent poking and she lit the lamp settled it into the wood-stack and said she was giving up everything was wet.

They sat with their backs against the trunk of the same tree the blanket across their laps and ate the bread from their pockets hunger had yet to catch up with them but it was something to do.

Above their heads the hands of trees clasped unclasped in the breeze and through the gaps the mizzle gathered took hold became rain and fell proper.

'Most folk would probably think it a stupid time to set out on a journey.'

'Why's that?'

'Rain and all and then the night comin in colder.'

'We int like normal folk Ia.'

Ia looked at the girl she'd found a stag beetle was guiding it with a stick.

'Spose not,' she said.

'And anyway, you got to do what you need to do when you got to do it.'

'That makes sense.'

'You know what you doin is right.'

Ia sighed.

'You do, you should trust yourself more, what's the word?'

'Instinct.'

'You should trust your instinct.'

Ia leant forward to run the beetle back to Geeva when it scurried her way. 'Don't trust nobody, int never had reason to.' She thought about those who had left her and wondered if she could truly trust anyone long enough to let faith take over she doubted it.

'That Jenna,' she continued. 'You reckon he's good for his word?'

'Never met em so.'

'But what you heard, what I said, whatever.'

'Don't hurt.'

'You think he'll turn up at that waterwheel?' She watched Geeva direct the beetle up a piece of kindling made it walk the plank.

'Probably not, but it don't matter; you're runnin from, that's all you got to remember.' When the insect fell Geeva threw it a lifeline a leaf on which to stick its feet. 'You got to keep runnin.'

'Keep runnin,' said Ia and she wondered when escape would

convert to freedom. 'OK, I'll take your advice, word from a kid but I int never had no other so just as well take it where I can get it.'

The girl ignored her she freed the beetle and lay down where she sat.

'That's a minotaur beetle,' said Ia.

'How you know?'

'Cus his horns, see?' Ia ran it toward the girl. 'Look closely.'

'It looks angry,' said Geeva.

'He's hungry is all.' Ia took out *The Book of Cornwall's Countryside* and looked up beetles.

'What's he eat?' Geeva sat up and came close to Ia so she could look at the book.

'Says here rabbit droppins and dung.'

'Don't be daft.'

'Don't knock it till you tried it.'

'Ia, you int never ate rabbit shit.'

Ia laughed. 'Made Evie eat it one summer up the back field.'

'No you dint.'

'Did, it was a dare and I won.'

'And she ate it?'

'Good handful, she always did what I said, even the bad things. She never wanted to disappoint me, spose anyway.'

'She sounds nice.'

'She is, can't wait for you to meet her.' Ia watched the girl stretch out beside her a little mizzle falling settling on to her hair like rain dust.

'Rainin,' she said. 'Least it int too cold.' She knew about the cold knew it better than most that last home winter the one that changed everything turned her from a girl into a woman one cold week, the last night saved for the worse.

'And now here I am again, night-settlin, sittin outside in the woods like somethin planned.'

She wondered if this was what she had imagined wondered if this was what she had thought if anything at all. A part of her asked what the fuck, and each time she undid the top button of her jeans put a hand on the flat she told herself this here was the fuck why. The unborn and becoming baby this was why she sat in the wet in the woods.

She saw the filtering fingers of the canopy soak up the dark and watched the girl curl into a mollusc stone beside her and she listened to the crows finish the last spat of the day she had seen their nests earlier the highest trees tangled tied to a hard life.

Beyond their silver circle all else was extinct. Even the night air contained no trace of humanity she was used to smoke it was the smell of others. For thirteen years Ia had known only two things other than the van: the sea and the campsite, the best and the worst of her own private world and now this place, what was it? Never had she felt so far away from any kind of home.

She lay down.

'Winter,' she said and she looked to see if the girl was awake but of course not she was an ocean child used to sleeping in the deep.

'Winter's here,' she said and she wished she could explain what that meant to her it was a loaded gun. It was a taker a robber of things, a snatcher in the dark it had taken more from her than parents her childhood what had been stolen she could not name but it was close to core. Each year it came around tripping Ia sensed that it held a secret, a silence, a haunting.

'Best thing bout winter is spring comes after,' said Geeva.

Ia smiled; even in sleep the girl had an eye on her she was a good kid.

THE NEW DAY CAME racing in and Ia woke prepared for it she surprised the child with a whoop come on.

'What?' Geeva sat up and she rubbed the sleep from her eyes and looked at Ia she had already started to pack.

'You hungry, there's a little dried fish in the sack.'

The girl nodded she liked fish it was the only thing she did like.

'Day two,' said Ia, remembering to make a note of it in the journal.

'Day two,' said Geeva, 'the best day, we're on the road proper.'

Ia agreed and she told her to get off her coat so she could put it on.

Packed set ready they left the woods with spirits up the rain had softened the sky finger-rub grey. All good things coming all great things on the horizon, Ia Pendilly was coming home.

'How long you reckon?' asked Geeva. 'Till home?'

Ia liked this kind of question, it was serious took some thinking whiled away time.

'Seven days till the waterwheel,' she said.

'Six now,' added Geeva.

'Six days till the waterwheel and then if Jenna comes in on a boat, well . . .' She thought for a minute pretended to know the river downstream from the Calstock viaduct she'd seen it on a postcard. 'Two days tops.' She looked down at the kid. 'Eight days in all.'

'Eight days,' Geeva repeated, she shouted it threw it to where she thought the river was snatched it back into her hands.

Together they decided it wasn't that long in the scheme of time eight days was not far at all. In Ia's case eight days subtracted from twenty-five years was nothing but a drop in the ocean and Geeva squealed with delight she declared it her favourite saying.

All morning they talked about the things they loved most Geeva with the water talk Ia with nature she hoped to teach the girl a thing or two whilst they were travelling companions.

There were things she remembered perfectly without the book the trees her favourite and the dormant saplings that gave her hope, she told the girl about the ash and the oak and April showers. She explained the art of water-divining and early that afternoon she found Geeva a wishbone stick it had the kid so wound Ia had to set her free a moment.

'Don't leave my sight,' she shouted, she was serious. She

watched the girl speed into a blur a hare out of the traps when she noticed she had left the field completely she called her back.

'I found somethin,' Geeva shouted through the gate.

'Come back.'

Ia stopped walking and waited for the girl to return she was making a point.

'I found somethin really this time.'

'You reckon?'

'I know it.'

'Spose you found the river.'

'Better.' She took Ia's hand and told her come on she pulled her across the field and out of the gate.

'What?'

Geeva stopped suddenly and pointed to a sign at the end of the lane they were about to cross.

'What's it say?' she asked.

Ia thought of all the signs Branner had stolen off the moor and put up around their land: danger, keep out, mine shafts.

'Don't want to go trespassin cept when we don't know.'

'It int red or yellow, it's blue, come on.'

The girl ran ahead and Ia followed reluctantly, she wasn't ready for people knew for sure people weren't ready for her.

'It's a picture of a boat,' shouted Geeva. 'Ia, read it.'

Ia pulled down her hood. '*Tamar Lakes*,' she said and she looked at the girl and said it again.

'Shit.' She grabbed the kid despite her usual pull-away and she told her she was a genius.

'We can go on, can't we?'

'One minute,' said Ia. 'Seems by lookin at that sign this was some play place and by that I mean it might have drawn a few folk in.'

'Nobody goin sailin,' said Geeva, and Ia told her to hold back and stay close in any case.

They climbed the iron gate and Ia pushed the girl from behind. Bran had told her about places like these. Centres he called them, this was where great swathes of people had taken over dug their heels in and claimed it as theirs, squatters but more than that, they were gangs come together not through kin but needful greed they weren't to be trusted.

'Nobody bin down here a while,' said the girl, she put out her hands to touch the overhanging laurel as way of proof.

'No cars just,' said Ia. 'Don't mean that there int folk like us scramblin.'

'If em like us, them all right int they?'

Ia didn't want to muddy the girl's naivety it reminded her of her younger self Evie too and it made her sad thinking of these things.

'Just go slow is all,' she said.

Through dark gummy leaves they pressed on, going toward the water like this were desert land. The woman the child the unborn life depending on this moment the lip the mouth of revelation. A thirst was in them, a thirst for the right track the river running south it would be so easy.

'Don't get carried away now,' said Ia, it was to herself that she was talking. Another sign up ahead. '*Welcome*,' she read. '*Welcome to Tamar Lakes*.' She grabbed the girl by the scruff it was instinct to hide take stock a moment and together they ducked against the bank of reeds at the side of the first lake.

'Int nobody around,' said Geeva.

'Shush.' Ia put an ear to the wind. 'I hear somethin,' she whispered, 'look.' She pointed to a swathe of purple material waving in the wind somebody's jacket they were moving coming toward them.

'Listen.' They held on to each other and heard the flap of cloth the pit-patter of rain.

'Them int movin,' said Geeva.

'Get down.'

'Them int doin much at all.'

'They seen us int they?' Ia's heart hit hard and her hand went to the pocketknife an instinct from birth.

'Fucksake, what you doin?' she asked Geeva when she started to laugh and Ia reached out her free hand to shut her up.

'That int nobody.' The girl pulled away and climbed out of the marsh. 'That there's a wind sail.'

Ia stood up and pulled down her hood and she looked at the purple and white synthetic rag and she too started to smile.

'Wind sail in tatters,' said Geeva. 'And look, there's a buildin over there.'

Ia climbed after her and looked to where she was pointing. 'Sign says *Café*.' She looked at the kid and told her to go slow stay behind.

They stepped carefully across what remained of the car park, the weeded cracks faded partition lines taken up and put back wrong the lake coming close and claiming. Ia knew others had been there, the tinder remains of benches circled black on the paving stones as they went toward the double doors, the glass put out and lost in the wet.

'You should stay outside,' she said and she pointed to an upturned boat blasted with pellet holes it made a good lookout. She told her to be brave, stay away.

'If you hear anythin at all, you get under that boat, you understand? Anythin at all.' Ia could tell the girl was thinking on ways to accompany her and she ignored her and pulled at the ivy so she could climb through the door.

Inside the vast hall the world that Ia knew fell away. Nature had not yet found a route to infiltrate it had its fingers wrapped around each window frame its face pressed to every open space but still unmistakably this had been someplace. The empty sales racks told her this so did the decaying posters promising best days out the aqua lake glistening, welcoming, nothing like the shit-flood outside.

'This is a big room.' Ia wondered how many caravans could

be lifted into this space it was heading toward ruin. She listened out for the girl, then went toward the back of the room the canteen so the sign said. What was it she was looking for? Food perhaps or shelter it was getting dark. She tried the side door found it locked and slid across the serving shelf went through the kitchen picking over the things already gone over by other pilfering hands. She thought about the cove the things she found most days were better than this.

'Nothin.' She pushed through the scatter of broken crockery like it was a stretch of sharp sand, reached into the drawers and cupboards quick to find things that they might need but it had only been this day and yesterday what was it she was after? Ia didn't like the place she imagined it a hospital a halfway house before death the creak of pipes filling with stagnant water she could smell it.

She returned to the main hall and her eyes swept over the chairs saw them occupied a hundred faces turned toward her she sat down. Bran said she would never be good in a crowd she knew this now to be true, even in her imagination she could see their eyes rubbing up against her their half-bitch mirth gripped and pitched toward, they wondered what she was doing here she wondered this herself she got up and when laughter blasted she ran.

'What you find?' asked Geeva when she returned.

'Nothin, waste of time.'

The child looked up at her and asked what was up.

'That place, I like out is all.'

'Same here.'

Ia nodded. 'We'll find a place to camp soon enough.'

They continued past the lake and then a second, their eyes splashing skimming stones looking for the river it had to be close.

'Be dark soon,' said Ia, she told the child to hurry up she wanted to get away.

'We're close, don't worry, I can smell it.'

'That's em lakes.'

'I can see it, look, through em trees.'

At the southerly reach of the second lake the water filtered forward, went somewhere. They pushed on through the bullying bushes gathering water from their heavy boughs the bind and leaves of ivy sticking to their legs their coats. All around them swampland the wet out to get them, sink them.

'There's such a thing as too much water,' said Ia. 'You can't argue with that.'

'The river's in there somewhere,' said Geeva, 'we just got to walk beside it a while.'

Eventually they made it through the undergrowth and in the fading light found a small clearing beside the riverbank, Ia declared it perfect. Covered and knotted with rhododendron she could have kissed those interwoven roots for the shelter they provided they even raised them off the ground.

'We int goin nowhere else today,' she said. 'Night int far

behind, we'll light a fire, make good from what we know of the day.'

She cleared the roots of wet leaves and in a foot-fork made a tepee of dry kindling from the sack and with close-hand wood she edged it and daubed a little of the kerosene. When the flames started to lick out and the scabs on her face began to smart in the heat she sat back.

'We won't want for nothin more tonight.' When the fire lifted she placed the pine cones and watched them open and release their seeds in the warmth and she told Geeva to take off the coat and lay it down in one of the tree hollows.

'You hungry?' she asked her.

'No, never much.'

Ia took out the parcel of fish and the water flask, told the girl to eat something drink at least and she helped herself to the food it tasted of charcoal, old fire.

She carried the spare canister to the water's edge and filled it and drank and filled the tin kettle for boiling.

'So quiet,' said Geeva, 'cept the river.'

'Int nothin more un big stream.' Ia thought about the sea she missed the boom and blast of waves. She thought about Bran one bitter brief moment and felt the back of her neck pinch he would know now have found her gone she could see him hitting out imagined the van punched to the ground. She tried to think of Jenna wished she had a photograph a recording of his voice she knew it wouldn't be long until she had him imagined wrong another misplaced fantasy to go with the rest.

They sat in silence and when the water started to spit Ia added a little home luxury the powdered milk and she poured it into the tin mugs.

'That one's yours,' she said to the girl. 'Got washed up round about the time with the compass.'

She looked to see if Geeva remembered but she just shook her head.

'Spose there's a good way still to come on all your thinkin.'

'I int remembered home yet if that's what you're after.'

Ia shrugged and took out her book and journal. 'Winter now then,' she said, and when the child looked puzzled she told her that was where she was in regards to the chapters.

'You write and draw somethin on each one?'

Ia nodded.

'What happens when you bin all the way round, got a year complete?'

'I start over.'

'Don't get bored?'

'Why would I?' She took out her pencil and knifed it sharp and looked around for something to draw. 'Rhododendrons are considered weeds to most.' She glanced across at Geeva to see if she was listening. 'Don't let nothin else grow them roots is so tight.' She started to sketch the vines but in dim firelight it was more from memory than actual account.

'My sister Evie was the artist more un me; got her sketches here, I'll show you.'

'I'd like that,' said the girl.

'You would?' Ia had never shown the journal to anyone it felt funny to be talking about it here. She rubbed her hand over the rough leather bind pinched its spine and passed it to the girl.

'Pictures,' said Geeva. 'Pictures and photos and words.'

'Can you read anythin?' asked Ia.

Geeva shook her head. 'I like the pictures, I like this one.' She held up the charcoal sketch that she and Evie had made of a fossil fish, it made Ia laugh.

'Found that on a rock in the sand.'

'Was it dead?'

'Course it was dead, millions of years dead.'

'That's a long time init, long time since alive.' Geeva flicked through the pages and shrugged, closed it and handed it back to Ia.

'You like it?'

'It's OK.'

'If you ever want to draw somethin let me know.'

'In the journal?'

'If you want.' Ia pulled her blanket from the sack and gave it to the girl.

'You plannin to draw all the trees?' Geeva asked as she settled down.

'Just the ones I can see.'

'That's too many.'

'Int such a thing.'

Ia flipped the pages of her journal returned to early days. She found the rose that Dad had given Mum one summer it was meant to say sorry for something it didn't work. It brought in aphids made a red dust mess of the table where he'd left it. The idea to rescue it from the bin was Evie's it took her all day to stick the stem the individual petals to the page. The mess she made into a miracle a new creation, better flower.

Ia ran her finger around the rose, kissed it closed the book and put it away. She lit the lamp and saw that Geeva had fallen into a deep sleep.

Darkness hit hammer hard there was nothing more to the world except the fire the child the sound of water and maybe that was enough. The immediacy of life bent and buckled together, minimalized.

She carried the lamp down to the river-stream a low bank rising water but no burst tonight the rain was lessening out there beyond the black. Upstream Ia could sense water falling she'd heard it when they had passed by earlier she wanted to go a little way to see where rocks divided and set the river on its new course. Reflected in the subtle lamplight she could see the fallen boulders their hunched backs slick with wet and weed their faces gone over grown old with moss hair. Every shade of green in and around those stones like living things themselves and something else above another rock but larger it moved with the current.

'Shit,' said Ia. She lifted the lamp and winched it out over the water to look at the thing when it returned her gaze she jumped and slipped against the bank.

'Fuckin horse.' She set the lamp down on the earth so she might climb toward it but it wasn't long before the stench of rotten flesh set upon her the sight of pocked and bloated belly was enough for her to retreat.

She returned to Geeva, the little fire had rubbed pink into the girl's cheeks and Ia added more wood and lay back from the heat. She closed her eyes and listened to the wind skate across the lakes, blown between the trees the sound like a key turning an engine over seen better days too much effort nothing returned. The leafless branches hitting hard, each slap a footstep coming going moving around and with the night capped tight Ia wondered if by some miracle she would sleep tonight.

The building by the lakes had her think people, crowds, all those chairs seated they were ghosts she could still see them poised toward, looking. Where was she what had she done?

Something strange went through her it didn't sit right beside the baby. Two seeds, one good one bad, the future a leaf drifting with uncertainty, the past made from apex root, she knew it, had been calling it home longer than her legal age. If Bran were to come after her now what would she do? Allow herself to be taken home a bad child needing the belt or would she keep on running?

Her head hurt thinking always on dilemma and now her gut ached she could feel the tightened knot unravel crawl out of her gullet and she stretched to be sick. Ia thought she heard the child ask if she was OK and she told her fine bad water was all and she lay with her head on the sack watched the fire go down and the tree vines creep like serpents coming close. Like lariats they circled her limbs and fingered her skin snakes that smelt of familiar home the creek the bind of barren land for a moment she felt as if she had fallen through the cracks to find herself returned.

I A LISTENED TO THE blackbirds sing announcing morning the first to rise and she heard sparrows somewhere getting louder amassing size their family as big and brash as her own extended kin.

'Got sick,' she told Geeva when she started to wake. 'Got proper sick.'

'You should eat somethin.'

Ia sat up when the giddy returned and she opened the nature book and looked to see if there was a remedy hidden within its pages.

'You ate somethin bad, the fish?' asked the girl.

'Weren't the fish; if you're thinkin of drinkin that river water, don't.'

'Why's that?'

'Dead horse up away.'

The girl shook her head, Ia's stupidity was something she

knew already. 'You should eat somethin,' she said again. 'Some-thin sweet.'

Ia sighed and she stretched the sack and found the pack of candied peel that she'd acquired at some point in time and she pulled a fist for sharing.

'Used to eat this all the time when I was little,' she said. 'Used to nick it out the jar and sneak to the cave, count em out equal.' She ate a few and passed some and returned the bag to the sack.

'We should get goin.' She packed and stood and waited for the girl to put on her coat and boots.

Through dawn hours the rain had leached and taken hold it crammed a little more swell into the river and Ia wished they were insects had a stick in which to sit set sail they would be downriver in no time.

They went in the direction of the water. The compass put away, their minds on other things besides. Between giddy and getting sick Ia thought about her true home and she wondered what might need doing fixing up and she thought about her sister had she returned?

In the end everything had to go back to the beginning, it had to. Someplace returned in spirit if not the physical location of childhood where things first took shape began to make sense. She watched Geeva stomp up front and wondered what was in the girl's head where did she think she was going? She had no home to which to return at least in memory she did not.

Perhaps it was Ia's fault for not pushing, she'd gotten used to not asking the child about her mother the siblings any kind of kin-blood that might have been out there somewhere bleeding for her return.

She thought about her own mother, spent her days never far from a bad day, bad months on end.

'She got sick or was she always sick?' asked Geeva and Ia realized she must have been thinking out loud like all the lonely folk that spent their lives alone.

'I'll have to think and get back to you on that one,' she said, and then, 'Yes, always sick.'

They continued with the river to their left, part friend part foe they never went too close. The earth beneath their feet gone of grit sieved through with a thousand tiny streams left nothing but slipping mud.

The winter was in. The rain the wind like last year and the year before come stripping tearing at the foundation of everything known and loved. The trees fallen jagged teeth showing in defence of weakness and the landscape changed a little each year, last year the cliff path gone Ia had to tramp through weeds took weeks of walking to make another.

'You think it's goin to stop rainin?' asked Geeva, behind her now.

'Int stopped yet.'

'The river goin on fast init?'

Ia agreed. 'All rolls off the hill when you're in the valley.'

She looked up at the slope to her right the rock ridges the water falling over running between. 'If this rain continues we'll have to move to higher ground.' She spied Geeva annoyed and jumping at the corner of her eye and told her she didn't want to either.

'We can't leave the river, Ia.'

'I know.'

'Now we found it.'

Ia put her hand to her mouth and nodded, she could feel the sick rising her stomach a clenched fist pushing what food upwards and she bent to a tree to get rid.

'Could've told you not to drink river water,' said the girl.

'I dint think.'

'You'll think twice next time.'

Ia wiped her mouth on her sleeve and stood. 'Be kind,' she said.

'You should rest up.'

'Can't.' She looked at the river the narrow bend from where it came all its shit getting faster when would it end? Like baggage it followed her if she went too close it would stick like arctium bur eventually all the small stickle-bits would weigh her down. She realized it wasn't the river she wanted, it was the sea the end of the rope the line she would not stop except for Jenna together they could endure anything.

They continued on through the sponge briar sidestepping the sapling trees the sycamore and the oak that in spring would leaf and inch toward light and Ia felt the nipple buds held on to them when she slipped and she saw the gone-ahead girl do the same.

'Slow down,' she told her.

'I int goin fast.'

'You're goin fast enough, don't forget I'm older un you.'

'Old maid is you?'

'Maybe not in years but my bones would tell you different.' She told the kid to wait up stop complete.

Dry retch now, nothing to purge just pain a little yellow bile dribble to cough on to the ground as she crouched, her ass sunk into the wet mud she didn't care.

'Seven days,' she said when the girl put an arm under hers and heaved her to her feet.

'And some days slow, some days fast,' said Geeva. 'Maybe this day slow is all.'

'I can't walk, let me sit a bit longer.'

'Over here, where it's drier.'

Ia sat under the tree where the girl had dropped her and she drank a little of the good water brought from the van and felt it cross her chest and poke her gut like a fine-tipped blade, making an example of her, a map with scar tissue. She pulled at her hood to contain the fever and wrapped her arms told herself the ache would pass at least she was warm something good to work on whilst she battled the bad.

'You there, girl?' she asked. 'Why you got to fuck off when

I need you most?' Maybe Geeva had gone to look for shelter Ia remembered her saying something hadn't she?

She pulled her knees to her chest and crushed them close a little rest was what she needed in this her own personal storm she would wait for calm.

'I'll wait here,' she heard herself say. 'I'll wait until it's safe, safe to go back to the chalet.'

She fell toward sleep and her old life waiting she went toward it sat down took a look around. The slate sand the same the sky and the sea between all the same; Evie had called it teal, those last remaining days it was teal all over.

Was this memory now or was it dream? Either way Ia had been here before it was the detail of all the small things that gave it away the silence amid bursts of noise the gaps and creases that fell between the two sisters as they sat in the cave.

'We can't go home,' said Ia.

'Can't stay out all night,' said Evie. 'People will worry.' Her words hit and dangled from the cave wall like thick gob-spit.

'Nobody will worry,' said Ia, she heard her sister say that she was cold, Ia linked arms and asked just tonight please. One night of dark to wipe away make the seen unseen. Their parents would be returned to them tomorrow, living, breathing life into a new day.

When the next day washed in a good high tide with it, all Ia could do was plead with Evie to stay another day one more night she could not bear to go home reality had set in.

Once that threshold was crossed there would be no way back no track ticket to return them to childhood. Two girls two empty shells hanging from the cave same as all the others occasionally catching being caught by the wind, sometimes apart sometimes colliding they made a whole Ia wished then as she did now that they could have remained as one.

Seven days they had lasted, she remembered this clearly a full week barely breathing eating surviving just about. This was all she remembered. The days that came after did not exist. No memory, no picturing, nothing. Those seven days they had remained in the cave, stopped; and then the fall.

'Seven days,' she said.

'Seven days, that's right,' said Geeva.

Ia opened her eyes to see the girl had returned.

'Where you bin?' she asked.

'Around.'

Ia nodded.

'How you feelin?' The girl crouched beside her.

'Like shit.'

'Better un?'

'Bit better.'

When the girl stretched out her hand Ia took it and got to her feet. She put her fingers to her head to feel the temperature gone and told the child that she would be OK.

'We should boil water for the bottle from now on,' said Geeva. 'And that int a dig, I'm just sayin.'

'We will, soon as we set up camp we will, just a little more walkin so the day int wasted.'

'A little more walkin,' Geeva repeated.

Ia could sense the girl was in playful mood it was her way of lifting them both but the fever the memory had Ia tipped wrong the bog-water at her feet heavier than usual.

'How long was I asleep?' she asked.

'Not long.'

'How long?'

'An hour? No longer un an hour.'

'Water's risin still,' said Ia and she looked up at the incline it hadn't shifted since they first set off. She closed her eyes let the water wash there. 'We should go up,' she said.

'Away from the river?' asked Geeva. 'You sure?'

Ia looked at the girl and said yes, that was where they were heading.

They left the woods and the riverbank to avoid the lower fields the corners drown-deep with run-off and she told the girl for now it would be enough to hear the river, God knows they knew it was there.

Another hour spent climbing out of the valley another back down the trudge took its toll, when they came across four posts a roof meant for God knows they stopped, it was good to sit down.

'I'm fucked,' said Ia and she found the half-smoked cigarette and lit it. 'And my feet are killin; how's yours?' she asked the girl.

'OK,' said Geeva and she kicked off her boots a habit she'd had from the start.

'Part fish,' said Ia and the girl agreed and she added that she hated the coat.

'Rather swim the river naked would you?' She sat down on the bench.

'Yep.' She asked for a toke on the cigarette and Ia ignored her. She unloaded the sack and took out the bag of dried fruit ate a handful and passed the bag to Geeva.

'Your feet don't look too good.' Ia told the child to stick them out into the rain to clean them Ia did the same.

'Blisters.' Ia took out her knife and pushed the tip of the blade into the bloated heel flesh.

'Ouch,' said Geeva. 'That looks sore.'

'It is.' Ia closed her eyes and told the kid to be quiet a little while. For all their hiking they had returned to the river it had pulled back would not let them go.

'I'm goin for a look about,' said Geeva.

Ia opened her eyes. 'Where to?'

'Down to the water just.'

'Not too close.'

The girl looked at her asked if she were stupid, when she disappeared Ia saw the boots and socks where she'd dropped them on the wet earth it was the kid who was daft. She watched her weave between the fence posts that flanked the river the wire long gone but still her white dress snagging occasionally on the nails that remained, she looked at the coat at the end of the bench and shook her head.

'She won't learn, int worth tellin her nothin.' Ia scooped a little more dried fruit from the bag and put the lot in her mouth she gauged her surroundings wished for one flat path a straight line one moment please. The river preferred gullies the deepest creases of land it sliced into the earth and made mountains out of riverbanks all surrounding fields went down at speed came up panting.

When she saw the child come running up the incline toward her Ia asked what she had hiding behind her back.

'What you reckon?' the girl asked.

'Just show me, I int never bin good with games.'

'Fish.' Geeva stretched out her hands.

'Let me look at that.' Ia rubbed her fingers across the firm lateral lines of the vertebrate she checked behind its gills its eyes for signs of disease stuck her finger down its throat this made the child laugh.

'We can eat it can't we?'

Ia took the nature book from out the sack and flipped through the chapter on creatures of the ocean and then to the section on rivers.

'What is it?' asked the girl.

'Trout,' said Ia and she studied the speckled markings made a guess at its size. 'Brown trout,' she said.

'Can we eat it?'

'Course we can eat it.' Ia made a hole through its gills with her pocketknife and she cut the cord from her hood and threaded it through the fish tied the ends and looped it across the girl's shoulder.

'Int too heavy is it?' she asked.

'I like how it feels, slimy wet.'

Ia pulled it behind Geeva's back, away from small hands; she told her to put on her socks her boots the coat there were a few good walking hours left before dusk.

'We're goin toward higher ground, proper this time; land levels out up there, I know it.'

The girl didn't look so sure.

'Wouldn't be so bad to find the closest road, see what sign-posts to point us south.'

'But we know we're goin south,' said Geeva. 'Followin the river int we?'

'I'm lookin for a short cut just.' Ia wanted to add that her stomach still ached and that she wasn't here for the journey just.

'Could do with the vantage,' she added, 'see what's what.' She looked at the girl and wondered why she had such a burning need to return to water. They were never far from it but still she stretched for the wet of it her eyes wide for the wonder the fill.

They went through an open-pegged gate and out on to an abandoned laneway, Ia could tell by the knee-high thistle and weed that split its length in two.

'Higher ground,' she said to herself, she looked at the sky and wiped her eyes added that the rain might not let up today but perhaps tonight tomorrow at some point it would stop.

The problem was how much rain in one drop to burst the banks lift the levels how many trees fallen bridges buildings collapsed to fill the gaps the spaces meant for course.

'How many storms come round each winter you reckon?' asked Geeva.

'Five or six on average, don't you remember nothin bout weather?'

The girl shrugged, she either didn't know or wasn't saying. 'I don't mind the rain,' she said.

'Course you don't.'

They crossed on to a main road and followed it but not for long, Ia thought she heard something strange she grabbed the girl pulled her into a hedge and hid.

'Int nothin,' said Geeva, 'just a cow.'

They watched the calf animal move blindly past, its head down ribs caged in hungered suffering, its haunch and hipbone hollow, kicked in.

'Why's it cryin?' asked Geeva.

'Callin out.'

'For its mother?'

Ia swallowed hard. 'Its mother.' They went into the next open field and climbed the sodden turf to its brow, when the levelling fog cleared it gave them by way of revelation far-reaching views of Bodmin Moor the Tor silhouettes Brown Willy the highest its peak unmistakable looked like the driest place on earth. In contrast everything below was gristle chewed fat land rinsed and spat.

The housing estates to their left filled with canal-run water the tiny mortared structures jousting like barges channelled wrong and landed, locked in. Ia wondered what town this was. She'd only lived as a recluse Branner had made her fear the world, these places could harm her those people were savages he painted them worse than site folk.

'Where's that you reckon?' asked Geeva.

Ia shrugged, she could see fires burning through the gloom the smoke chocked black with tar. She felt the girl's hand tug on her sleeve and she looked at her.

'We goin down there?' she asked. 'Could be good for shelter.'

'Maybe.'

'And the river goes through, look.' Geeva pointed to the band of mud water that ran past the buildings.

'Maybe it does,' said Ia and they went to it.

In the valley below she spotted a flock of starlings start their dance before dusk, a thousand small things and then one thing, a mark like an error drawn black against the grey.

'Like fish,' said Geeva and Ia agreed.

'Everywhere an ocean,' she said and she looked at the child and smiled. Everywhere was an ocean, the clouds contained more than they were letting on, came at them with such force it was as if some giant fissure had opened up had sucked the sea and blasted.

She looked at the town below. Not so big not so unlike a forest all trees the same. All those people what made her so different from them? She'd been hidden away her entire life but she had two arms two legs in recent days she had her head on straight and what wits she had she kept about her. She thought about Jenna and nodded.

'We're headin in any case.' Ia took out her medication bottle and looked down at Geeva, the dare was in her it was contagious, she took the one remaining pill. 'Come on,' she said.

Ia AND THE GIRL walked the day down to dark, wild animals crossing the town boundary entering from needs must a vixen and her young.

'Should find some shelter.' Ia wasn't sure what that meant just a roof would do a place to burrow and hide. They stood at the sign and read the name *Launceston*, wondered how to say it every way was strange.

Two lights tethered between bright and dim stood in the centre of the road their yellow hats cracked blue arrows directing wherever but pointless now. All cars abandoned no fuel trucks had crossed the border in a year.

Instinctively Ia put a hand to the girl's shoulder, she wondered if she was doing the right thing bringing her here. She was no mother but a mother in training there were things she could learn from this, things she had to learn.

'Stay close,' she said.

'I am.'

'Stay closer.'

'I seen towns like this before.' Geeva patted the broken light and nodded in recognition.

'Don't tell me you lived in a town.'

'Maybe.'

Ia didn't appreciate this flash of newly stiffened confidence, it made the child erratic, her eyes grown huge like splashed puddles she was taken up by the bright night.

'We should keep to the shadows.' She looked at Geeva. 'I know I'm no fun.' She sounded like other mothers not hers, had to admit it sounded good.

'You see anyone, put your head down, act like you don't see em and maybe they won't see you,' she told the girl.

'How?'

'Become invisible.'

'I can do that.'

Both sides of the road were flooded and the thick shit mud plastered the doors and windows of the terraced houses built sticks and branches into stairwells and entrances, colossal bird-nests they were something for Ia to marvel despite the devastation.

They kept to the centre of the road where the water lapped the toes of their boots and Ia was grateful for the night falling there was too much for her to look at too much water and none of it the river. Houses and then shops, she read the signs for bread, hardware, meat. She wished she'd had the chance to see the shopfronts laid out instead of boards and broken crock cemented on to the windowsills. It would have been something to see a little of the real world somehow she'd dreamt it better than this.

It had not been so long ago but now it was another time so much had changed for those society people who had lived their lives by the book had abided by rules and laws and for what? Everything dear to them had been taken, robbed off. For Ia it had been different, she'd been kept from it never had anything to lose, to Branner she supposed she should be grateful; nothing known nothing lost. When they first met he'd promised to protect her it was what she wanted never thought it was from him she needed protecting most. She dug for one good memory turned up broken bones. She wondered how he was where he stood in that old life. She wished she hadn't, imagined him behind her creeping close, the bind around her neck contracting, feet faltering, falling backwards. She could feel old weight on her shoulders, her chest tight, too tight, snap back.

'Ia, rain's gettin heavier,' shouted Geeva.

Ia jumped. 'You hear that?' She looked at the child suddenly. 'I hear somethin.'

'Like what?'

'Voices carryin on the wind.'

'Talkin?'

'More like shoutin, not shoutin, chantin.'

Geeva stopped walking and turned her ear until she caught something. 'I hear it,' she said.

'We should try some doors,' said Ia, 'get into one of these buildins quick, go up a floor.'

Where rising water and flotsam allowed, the girl pushed toward shop doors she tried the handles kicked out but when an alleyway appeared they took it for dry cover a moment to stop and think.

'This was a bad idea,' said Ia.

'We int done yet.'

'Should have never bothered, just followed the river where we knew for definite; I knew things was goin to get worse.'

Sudden shouts resonated out of nowhere and Ia wondered if they were calls for help or threat either way she could not risk getting involved she had the girl had her unborn baby to protect.

They continued down the alley pressing their palms their heels to doors and Ia could smell smoke the burn of desperation, anything to hand. She thought about those people huddled someplace close they weren't so strange just strangers what was it that Bran had told her? Hadn't they all been hit from both sides? The crash and now the floods they would not stop until early spring they never did. Each man each woman and child was a victim this disaster was a shared thing, all folk family now. She thought of Evie at home on the cliff hoped the tide wasn't so high that it had eaten into the foundations made a jut out of the front yard and pulled the chalet toward the sea. It had happened to three chalets some way down the bay when they were growing up and Dad said if a thing like that happened once it happened twice.

Ia supposed you could say that about anything nothing was for sure and she flinched and put a hand to her belly.

'Don't worry, it's still there,' said Geeva from up ahead.

They came to the end of the alley and the sound of voices dictated their movements another thing to have her panic, pray for the getaway.

'Follow me,' said Geeva. 'Trust me.'

Ia had no other choice but to run after the girl more alleys more passageways circling around.

'Where are you?' she shouted. She heard voices getting closer shouting maybe it was a gang coming for her she knew it she should have listened to Bran why hadn't she?

'In here.' The girl reached a hand from out the shadows and grabbed Ia's arm she pulled her into a low-lying window there was barely enough room to push.

Ia fell to her feet with a splash the water had followed them it crept over the window frame and fell like a curtain.

'We go upstairs,' said Geeva and she pulled her steady toward the metal stairs. 'This is a warehouse.'

Three sets of stairs three levels going upward it was a cliff they were climbing, the child in front holding the lamp and Ia following behind more child than any.

'We'll be safe up here,' said Geeva. 'Anyone comin, we'll hear them on the stairs.'

The mattress pushed against the wall the scat of charcoal bones, empty beer bottles and needles strewn these things told them others had been here before them.

'Don't touch them needles,' said Ia.

'I int plannin.'

'Them spread disease.'

'Know that don't I?'

Ia nodded. 'Good kid.' She kicked them away with her boot.

'Can I cook my fish now please?' the child asked.

'You still got it?'

Geeva unbuttoned Ia's coat to expose the fish dangling from its cord.

'How you get me to carry it without even knowin?'

The girl smiled.

'You got a way int you?'

'What you mean?'

'A way with you that's . . .' Ia stopped for a moment, wondered a word other than strange that was her own label that's what folk called her. 'A way with you that's different, special.'

The girl nodded she didn't care her head was all about the fish. She looped it from off Ia's shoulder and then the sack and she pulled the blanket and laid it flat across the mattress and sat down.

'We goin to light a fire int we?' she asked.

Ia sighed, she supposed a bit of heat for drying flame for cooking wouldn't hurt and besides if they heard footsteps coming up the stairs they could stamp it and hide there were plenty of places.

She took off her coat and jeans and hung them to dry on a nail that protruded from the wall she told Geeva to do the same and she set about finding wood for the fire it wasn't a bother. The room below them was filled with wooden pallets rescued from the sodden ground floor and then abandoned, people in towns and cities were always moving on dreaming of something better that's what Bran said.

Ia pulled a crate up the stairs and then another and she took up the hatchet she used for kindling and worked the wood into strip-bones splashed them with fuel it wasn't long before they had a fire.

She gutted the fish and placed it on the head of the axe close enough to the pyre to cook and sat back to wait, when the skin peeled into crisp flakes she turned it with her knife. They took off their boots and rolled up their sleeves to the heat stuck their feet toward the fire their socks steaming falling away. Pain.

Outside they could hear people passing by their voices thrown down kicked around. Everybody hurried a hundred things done a hundred more needed doing.

They ate the fish in silence. One fillet each a little water to wash it and then the girl lay down she'd done enough Ia let her sleep. She sat back against the wall and watched the embers soften where they fell and the smoke coiling away from them it had found a draught and chased it into other rooms.

'If we survive this night we'll survive anythin.' She looked down at the girl the compass laid open in front of her and she picked it up and watched the needle find water.

In the dull warm glow of flame Ia could see the rain had claimed something of the roof it tiled the ceiling in stains and fell from the light fitting a little firelight blinking in the wet where the bulb used to be. A new cave a different hole in which to hide.

She waited for the night-ship voices to pass by and took the pill bottle from her pocket to see the thing empty. What now? Thoughts were coming in to replace the silence, clarity so bright it scared her.

She closed her eyes. The extra skin of unbelonging that covered her peeled away, she could see she could breathe she could be.

Beyond the warehouse and the din of rain and wind she could hear a little music float through the alleyway seep into the building. A lone fiddle calling out for companionship and then there were two a beautiful conversation of love. Jenna.

Ia closed her eyes to listen to this version of heaven, if there were people making music despite then all things would come good because they had to. It lifted Ia and carried her a little way laid her down to sleep.

In her dream she was running. Nothing about her recognizable nobody bothering no voices except in her head, they doubted her everything. In childhood Ia had no way to understand this but in adulthood and in sleep it came to her; half-formed thoughts they told her she was useless did not deserve better than this life-sentence built on guilt and grief. There was no foundation worse than that; Ia knew there was no land good enough for her to stand and her running returned to the river.

THE NIGHT MIGHT HAVE become day returned to night and still Ia would have slept on so comforting was it to be somewhere soft and warm and almost dry. She lay with her face pushed into the blanket her feet to the fire even in dream she could feel the warmth she thought of home.

'Evie,' she said and the sound of her own voice made her jump. She pushed up on to her elbows and looked for the child and stood to put on her jeans.

'Where you at?' She bent to the fire and picked up her boot swung the heel to deaden the embers and put them on went to stand at the gape at the top of the staircase.

'Girl,' she shouted, 'where you at?' She didn't like it when the kid disappeared it always happened when Ia took down her guard.

'I'm here,' said Geeva and Ia turned round.

'Shit, kid, you had me worried; where was you?'

'In the other room just.' The girl pointed toward the door hanging from its hinges at the other end of the building.

'You think it's mornin?' asked Ia.

'Tis, I bin lookin from the window, stopped rainin too.'

'Let me see.' Ia followed the girl into the smaller room and she stood at the window and looked out toward the towering castle stub, a sore thumb pressing the clouds.

As far as the eye could see was water. That was just about all that was left of the streets and corners: water punctuated with a tree a post a steeple. They packed their belongings and put on their coats still bogged with yesterday's rain and together they went out into the new day.

It felt strange to be in open air, exposed and without rainfall to hide them Ia kept her hood up she walked with wide marching strides told Geeva to do the same stop pondering this place.

On the wind smoke and foul meat still bullied the air and the sweet-sour tang of sewage it was all around them.

'We came into this town cus we thought we was followin the river, we int got no purpose to stay.' She looked at Geeva. 'Just find and follow the river which way it's runnin is all.'

'Never said I wanted to stay.'

Ia nodded, some things were best left.

They passed through the centre of town the shit-water lapping the tops of their boots and not one place for stepping dry. In the windows above their heads children spat and pissed and asked them their names and Ia put a hand to Geeva's head and pushed her onward.

The first people they had seen in days they were different

from the stuffed-pig site kids, these were bone angled and vacant their bullet-blasted eyes peering from darkened rooms.

'Ignore them,' said Ia.

'I am, I'm tryin.'

'We int got time for nothin,' she kept telling her. 'Find the river, get out of here; them back there int your friends, don't want to be neither.'

More and more shotgun folk began to appear they climbed out of windows and dropped into the mire, their isolation alleviated come together out of hunger and fear. When they looked at Ia she looked down at the ground.

'He was right,' she said.

'Who?' asked the girl.

'Branner; said I weren't ready for the world, would find it too much and he was right; I don't belong here, don't belong anywhere.'

'You're doin fine.'

Ia wondered if she was doing the right thing she was used to this thought it came at her every day. When the child repeated her words Ia looked down at the back of her head pushing proud pushing on.

'Where you come from?' she asked. 'Really.'

'I told you I don't know.'

Ia told her to stop a moment. 'You know stuff bout everythin, why don't you know a small thing like belongin, what it is to belong?'

The girl stood with her back to her and shrugged.

'I int on the medication no more,' Ia said.

'That's OK,' said the girl. 'That's good.'

'Is it?'

'Course.'

'Cus em keep me calm.'

The girl turned she had been looking at something still held it at the corner of her eye.

'You're calm int you?' she said.

'For now.'

'Bout everythin you're calm.' She turned back and continued to walk toward where she thought the river was hiding.

'Geeva, come back.' Ia adjusted the sack and went after her.

A group of men heard her shout asked what the rush and Ia imagined their hands out for the grab an eye out for prey and she turned her hood hid her face her wounds her shame.

'Geeva,' she shouted, 'I can't do this without you. Come back.' She stood close to a run of flooded fields rinked full to hedges and she wanted to scream for the things she hadn't had time to love got suddenly lost in the storm.

'What now?' she shouted. 'What?' Ia felt in her pocket to hold on to the pill bottle never more had her anxieties been tested. She saw Geeva in the distance she stood on the downward edge of a hill and the girl waved.

'Look,' she shouted. 'Over there, look at that road.'

'What bout it?'

'It's headin toward the river.'

Ia made her way across the slope to get to the girl, she shouted for her to stay put.

'I told you I don't want to walk on no more roads.'

'Ia.' The girl was losing patience, despite everything it was funny to see. 'Over there,' she explained, 'is the river.'

Ia glanced back at the town thought she heard the scuff of collecting feet.

'Things are bad,' she said. 'Things are worse.'

'So come on.'

She went and stood by the girl looked at the sky filling with birds all kinds it seemed and she said all birds were bad omen.

'Who says?'

'Some folk.'

'Not you, Ia; you like birds. Come on.'

Together they went east from the town the road in bits it gave them something immediate to think about. The blistered tarmac pinched and plucked to stone and the grit beneath washed away at times Ia imagined the tide had been there these were the rocks of home.

They passed beneath the main artery road and stopped to look up at its underside. Nothing thundering, nowhere for anyone to go, they heard a horse its hooves hitting hard where landing allowed and they stopped in the shadow of the bridge road waited for quiet to return.

Everything Ia knew of trust she put into the girl, it wasn't much but they had lost the river somehow Geeva said she would get it back it was out there somewhere.

An hour's walk without diverting from the east and Ia kept her mouth shut her head on her aching back the agonizing pain of her feet.

'I can smell the water,' said the girl and she looked at Ia and said she could hear it, when she started to run Ia gave chase she was right the river had returned to them.

'And look,' shouted Geeva, 'over there, it's a rower; Ia, we found a boat.'

Ia stood to catch her breath felt the strange sensation of a smile settle in the creases of her face.

Together they climbed down from the bridge and through the hedge to where the small wooden boat had got itself lodged in reeds. Ia took off her coat told the girl to hold it don't move she would wade out.

'Has it got oars?' Geeva shouted.

'Wait, I int there yet.'

'If it int got oars we're fucked.'

Ia tentatively placed her feet on the uneven riverbed, good fertile soil had given way to swampland, every time she stopped she thought she might go under.

'Grab it,' shouted the girl. 'Please Ia, before it floats away.'

Ia hung on to the starboard. 'It int goin anywhere.' She lifted herself up on to the cracked gunwale let her full weight drop into the boat. She heard the girl cheer and she lay on her back and smiled took a minute to catch her breath.

'I'm goin to row to you,' she shouted, she sat up and with knife in hand she leant into the briar and cut until the boat tilted free.

'I'm waitin,' said Geeva.

'Stay put.'

'Course.'

She picked up the oars and rowed through the thick muck water toward the kid.

'Goin to take a minute to get to the river proper,' she told Geeva when she reached her.

'No problem.' The girl laughed.

Together they pushed and levered their way from out the sucking debris until finally they reached the river they couldn't help but smile. Solitary confinement was where Ia belonged she and the girl alone in the boat nobody could catch them.

'We found a boat,' shouted Geeva. 'We found ourselves a rowin boat!' When she started to laugh Ia joined her it was both infection and remedy it was needed.

THE LANDSCAPE OF SEAS and rivers and streams these things were everywhere. The landscape of dreams nothing seemed real.

Ia settled herself to the drift occasionally sticking an oar into the water a makeshift rudder to keep them on track whilst the river moved at its own speed. Nothing mattered in that moment nothing more to do but sit back relax perhaps.

'We'll be home in no time,' she said.

'No time at all,' said Geeva.

Ia looked at the child flat on her back in the middle of the boat so at ease on the water maybe this was her true home.

'What if you int from land at all?' she said.

'What if?' Geeva repeated.

'Maybe you really is a mermaid.'

'That would explain some things.'

'Like what?'

'Happiest on the water, in the water, by the water.'

'All the time?'

'Safest init? Nobody can get you on the water.'

'Bran did, wrecked your boat dint he?'

The girl sat up and she was slow to nod, it was as if she had forgotten something and then remembered it all in the same moment.

'But here I am.' She smiled and she returned to resting her head in the clouds.

Without the rain the river had become a silent living thing, it crawled around oxbow bends and let the boughs of trees reach down caress one moment and then with a snap and pull the water made light of the living.

'No more rain now, that would be good,' said Ia, 'today at

least.' She saw a heron come in on the wind it laid its wings down on unseen pressure and came close to the boat and she made a note of its span and the muted greys she wished she had a palette more than one shade.

She looked down at Geeva to tell her look but she had fallen asleep and anyway the bird was gone. The days the nights this morning had taken their toll on the child, she thought herself braver wiser stronger than Ia but they were just the same. The difference between them was the kid had mastered the art of illusion; she could hide her emotions wear her face like a mask, magic was where she was at.

Ia directed the boat into the middle of the river closed her eyes a moment to catch the breeze it had gotten cooler and for the second time she hoped for no more rain it was too cold for forest sitting as things stood the wet would make it worse. She lifted up her collar to meet the cold pulled down her hood so she could see her new world she didn't want to miss a thing. She made a list of all the trees, the giant sycamore that pulled their feet from out the water and the oaks so old they knew how to do this they had seen worse seen everything. Some trees strong holding on some stranded in the wash, tiny islands on which to stand dragging them down, bonsai. She felt in the sack for food found some forgotten bread it reminded her of old life she swallowed hard wondered when the time would be right for going in? Where were the mooring places the inlets where they could set up camp?

Ia looked to the sky to try and read it but all movement had gone, no clouds now just flat hoary tar and tile, slatted.

She came to a run of bends in the water and picked up an oar when the boat started to slow she was glad of something to do it kept her mind from wandering back up the river returning to sea and that other home. Hours passed and nature filled Ia with joy, her heart lifted with the things she'd never seen from a lifetime of knowing other water and she wished she had a camera a way of recording more than with memory and eyes.

When Geeva woke she told her what she had seen and they ate a little of the dried fruit saw a collapsed bridge sailed over it nothing could stop them now. To the left of them the bank burst with forest firs they coloured the stretch with every shade of green and Ia thought it an ocean of trees.

'Could make a good camp in there,' she said, 'if we could get close, would have timber for shelter and fire.'

'No way,' said Geeva. 'No way in.'

Ia looked at the girl and told her they couldn't stay on the river when night fell. 'We need to sleep.'

'I can row.'

'We need to light a fire and eat and shit.'

The girl leant out of the boat and looked into the water.

'And you can forget about that.'

'What?'

'I int shittin off the side of the boat.'

Geeva smiled. 'You read my mind.'

'It int hard.' She told her to turn around face forward and keep watch, the next drift of low-lying land was where they would head, dusk was closing around them they were going in.

Where the riverbanks widened the boat grew small, a piece of thrown driftwood it bobbed from side to side, if once it had known how to go straight it had forgotten now. Ia kept her eyes on the morphing mudscape and the thicket reeds that gathered and grabbed from the crooks and turns. The more they looked the more no path seemed available to them and Ia wondered if the river had claimed them without their knowledge. What little light of day remained it was fading fast, the forest playing its part shuttering the sky and securing it with heavy weight.

To the left of them Ia could see the shadow of a chimney stack and she told the girl it was an engine house; tin, copper, silver, lead and arsenic were all mined here maybe some still was. Old days returned she could see smoke the pillars of people overlooking standing stone. Something about those strangers pricked the hairs at the back of her neck they watched their boat pass without concern no words of hello good evening and Ia saw some of them had guns strapped against their backs.

'Don't like it round here,' said Geeva.

'Me neither.'

'We int stoppin is we?'

'Can't get to land in any case.'

They continued down the river and Ia lit the lamp told the girl to hold it up so they could see about them but there was nothing but space, the black water the sky crushed the earth gone to gravy. Not one sound bar lapping water and the hunting call of a barn owl somewhere above their heads, searching for a field to feed between the plains of flash water. Time moved slowly minutes seemed like miles maybe they were but when finally the girl shouted jetty Ia was determined to row through the thick bog water.

'You got somethin to tie up the boat?' Geeva asked.

'I'll use this.' Ia undid the rope from the sack and she knotted it to the cleat and looked for someplace to secure the mooring.

'Over there,' said the girl. 'There's an old post.'

Ia stabbed an oar into the mud and stretched to pull them forward. 'Well spotted.' She bound the rope to the post and tied it twice. 'That'll have to do.'

She picked up the sack and carried it in her arms and she told the kid to go forward with the lamp.

'We won't go far,' she told her. 'Just a little way so we can put the coats down, stretch out a little.'

They went slow through the undergrowth, careful where they put their feet the earth had a habit of sucking. All around them the foliage pressed tight clung to them, if once a path ran down to the jetty it was long gone long forgotten. This was the place Ia dreamt up as a child the setting of her horror stories it was her favourite but in reality she knew she had never quite got the level of fear exact. She put her hand into her pocket made a fist around the empty pill bottle, it was something.

'Where we goin?' asked Geeva.

'Just keep on.'

'How I know when to stop?'

'When it int so wet and it's clear enough for sittin.' She heard the girl sigh nothing was ever so bad inconvenience was all.

'What bout over there?'

Ia looked to where she stretched the lamp its light catching in the round and returning brighter.

'It's a quarry,' said Ia.

'Is it OK?'

'It's perfect.'

'We can light a fire,' said Geeva and Ia agreed. Together they found driftwood that had journeyed in and out of the river and they carried it to their pit camp and set about assembling and lighting, it was usual routine.

'You gotten good lightin the fire,' said Geeva and Ia agreed but still she would have been happier with the stove from home.

'Can't take nothin with you on the road,' said the girl.

'Well that's true.'

'Can't take nothin in the end either.'

Ia told her to shut it with that kind of talk and eat the bit of fish she'd saved from yesterday.

'Tastes funny today.'

'It's fine, just eat it.'

They pulled up close to the fire so cold was this new night. Ia wondered which was worse wet or cold and she settled on cold it fingered in there was no way of ousting even with fire it slumped across her shoulders. She pulled the blanket from out the sack and stretched it across the girl's lap and she told her to try for sleep, tomorrow would be their longest day.

She took off the coat and put it over her own legs and she added more wood to the fire and lay back.

'Do you think we'll get there tomorrow?' asked Geeva. 'To the waterwheel I mean; day seven you said.'

'Int day seven yet.'

'It int?'

'Not yet, don't reckon.' Ia scratched her head, wondered.

She had hoped to get to the waterwheel sooner rather than later but knew the river was tidal it had its own plans. If it was coming in then at some point they would hit it that wall would be hard to push through.

She took out her journal and pencil and waited for something to come to her and she drew the heron from memory but it came out garish, a cartoon.

'That for your sister?' asked the girl.

'When I see her.'

'At the chalet or whatever you call it.'

'Chalet is right.'

'And everythin the same, you hopin anyway.'

Ia put down the book. 'What you askin?'

'How you know she's goin to be there?'

Ia sighed. 'Cus that's where she is.'

'But how you know?'

'Cus it's our home.' Ia heard the girl tut and blow air and she told her she liked her better when she was optimistic.

'Funny what family means to some and not others,' the girl continued.

'What's this now?'

'If you got em you love and miss em and if you don't you don't.'

'You had a dad.'

'Don't remember much about that.'

'And a mum, you had to come from somewhere.'

Ia lay down stretched her legs toward the fire and she put her hands to her belly they had gotten used to travelling there. She thought she felt the baby move imagined it turn its face toward warmth.

'Girl or boy?' asked Geeva, she had been watching her.

Ia didn't know, some days it was a boy and others a girl she didn't mind.

'I int choosy; my own kid, healthy and hearty, I'd be happy with that.' She closed her eyes to keep the mood in it was good it reminded her of before Bran, the creek, before childhood had abandoned her. If she concentrated she could imagine the amity that came from unsullied thought, time spent unaware of the demons and dissolute things that were everywhere.

'You gotta stay alert,' she said and she looked across at Geeva saw that she was part-way toward dream. 'Night girl, night baby, got to get you home get born to a better life.' She pulled the hem of the coat over her eyes and listened to the bustle of horseshoe bats prepare for the night's hunt in the crag behind them, their guard reassuring; in the woods you were never alone.

'YOU ON YOUR OWN?' asked a man's voice.

Ia pulled the coat from her face looked toward where she heard the smack of boot in bogland she rubbed her eyes for the all clear.

'Who's that?' She sat up and shielded her eyes from the torchlight saw the gun barrel pointing through the trees.

'You know it int safe for a young woman to be out in the woods on her own.'

'I reckon I know that.' She put a hand on Geeva to wake her.

'All sorts taken to roamin just recent, all em gangs and mercenaries on the loose, you hear bout what's bin goin on?'

Ia nodded and her stomach grabbed at the baby. She watched as two men stepped from out the bushes and she knew they were the men from the mine she'd seen upriver. They stood either side of the dying fire and Ia waited for them to tell her what they wanted, they told her to come on.

Ia looked at the girl awake now sitting beside her and she

wanted to tell her that if she was thinking it this was not the time for cheek, maybe Geeva knew this she was a rough-winged bird same as herself.

'Where we goin?' asked Ia.

'Back to the mine,' said the younger of the two they looked like brothers.

'Why?'

'You're trespassin.'

'You saw me, I was on my way; what you want with me?'

The older brother started to laugh.

'Whoever you think I am, I int; I'm headin down the river just.'

'Int that a surprise?' He grinned.

'It's true.'

'Course it's true, cus someplace you got a boat and there's the river so what you reckon? Now pick up your fuckin shit, let's go.'

They did what they were told and Ia pushed Geeva to walk behind her, as far as these men were concerned she was her daughter she would protect her as so. The youngest brother went out in front he'd not yet fired a gun Ia could tell by the way he petted the weapon held it like a stuffed pup in his arms. She knew by Geeva's poking at her back that she wanted her to ask them questions but Ia knew men like these they were one-thought rigid she would not get any kind of level answer from them. All she had in her was small talk it was what she gave the men who came fucking but this was not the time.

She watched their boots sink into the marshland and looked at her own going the same way the light of their lamp throwing shapes between them pushing up against the trunks of trees like a thug. In her arms she carried the sack she wished she had the rope to tie and swing it was heavy despite its nothing much.

Behind her she heard the girl whisper how much longer and Ia looked to see if the men had heard but nothing they went on. She tried to remember how far back they had seen the mine but they had been on a boat the river it was too hard to call.

They arrived at the quarry camp a half hour's walk by Ia's reckoning, crossing cart tracks and pathways where miners had once hauled rock and mineral from deep under ground, some of the slag could still be seen in heaps around the place, another thing blasted from the earth another thing rejected.

They stood in the clearing a stamp of ground in the trees and Ia saw ruins they were all around, some she could see were occupied saw rags for curtains corrugated iron sheets propped for doors.

'Why are we here?' she asked again.

'Told you,' said the other lad. 'You was trespassin.' He grabbed her by the arm and pulled her into the yard and into full light. 'Got em,' he shouted as they approached the fire, he told her to sit.

'Int good to go sneakin bout others' land.'

Ia turned to see an older man hitched high on a rubble wall behind her.

'I dint know it was your land, I'm sorry.' She looked at Geeva slow to cross the scrub she indicated for her to come here, sit.

'River int no place for a young woman like you.' He slid from the wall came scuttling close a wide-eyed raven his sights moving toward Geeva and Ia coughed for attention.

'I int so young,' she said. 'Was twenty-five last birthday.'

The man nodded and he looked at the younger lad and they laughed. 'Where you from exactly?' he asked.

'South coast then north, but now I'm goin home.'

'Cus the floods?'

'Cus a lot of things,' she said.

'I can guess some of em things; seen some action int you, girl?'

Ia put her hand to her face and her fingers traced the claw marks, the crescent scar from Bran's sovereign ring. 'No more un what's usual.'

'Had a whippin I'd say.' The man nodded, his lank black hair fell into his face he beat it back. 'And why you goin by the river? Only get convicts and crazies comin this way.'

Ia wanted to say about the compass and her escape but he wasn't bothered in any case there was something else on his mind. In the end she said she was just passing through she was sorry for the intrusion.

He nodded winged closer had the air pushed so hard Ia could feel it press into her lap it tightened around her throat.

'I'm headin home to my sister, she's expectin me so . . .' Ia haunched ready to leave but he grabbed her and shouted for food called her their guest and waved people over to the fire to join them.

'I wish I had my tablets,' she whispered to Geeva. 'Int just escaped to be captured again.'

'We could escape,' said Geeva.

Ia shook her head and nodded toward the gun in the younger brother's arms. 'We'll sit and eat and abide, gain their trust, and then when the night's fully sunk we'll make a move.' She looked at Geeva to see if she understood, she'd barely whispered. The girl nodded.

They sat and watched the men tend the fire the skinny women mad-mustelid dancing round about the way trash women did they were drunk they were up for it anything anytime.

Ia watched the older man stir the pot in the embers he tossed the flatbread on a hot-stone shelf he had done this a million times before and Ia thought of something to say she always appreciated the gift of food she said just that.

The man turned and smiled. 'We found oats stored in the shed over there, untouched, dry as bones, good for most things they is.'

When the food was ready the gang gathered on the granite plinths that circled the fire pit and some of the men glanced her way maybe they knew what she was perhaps she showed giveaway signs she looked at the younger brother and he was the last to look away.

Ia ate the stew and the oat bread she stuffed to keep from talking this wasn't the place for anything other than enduring.

Out beyond the treeline of the forest she could hear the cry of others and occasionally one or two clan kids returned the call it was a savage sound meant something, these people were a different kind of wild breed from what she knew they were organized and civil despite their pheromone stink. They unnerved her and she pulled the girl close.

'You got family more un a sister?' the man asked.

Ia nodded said about the campsite kin their whereabouts asked if he knew them.

'I know em.' He took Ia's hand and said he wouldn't bite pulled her nearer to the fire and some of the men joined them, some joined the women beat kerosene cans to accompany their dance.

'I know of em well enough, got a good thing goin int they? Sellin candy cross a few towns up north-coast way, I heard, and all in between; long as em stay up there we're good.'

'I don't know much bout any of that.'

'Course you don't.'

Ia wanted to add that she was a loner a solitary creature grown accustomed to the quiet but it would have only made him laugh.

'Good bit of land em gathered this past year, so rumour goes.'

Ia nodded this was something she did know.

'You drink?'

'Course.'

He shouted for the bottle to hurry up be passed and took a tight-lipped slug told Ia to help herself.

'Sugar beet,' he told her.

Ia put the bottle to her lips she took too much. 'Could get used to that,' she said.

The man smiled. 'Half these here said that and here we are now, a collective.'

Ia returned the bottle. 'Thought you was a gang like all else is a gang.'

The man started to laugh. 'You always just say what's in your head?'

'Do, but mostly I'm alone when I say it. Thought you was family too.'

'Just my two boys, came across this place few months back and int left since.'

Ia looked into the fire the bottle was back in her lap and the car seat she'd been pushed into had a way of rocking when she leant it was homely enough. She watched the night clouds hang themselves in the trees and listened out for the river but it had been silenced with noise.

'Don't drop nothin,' Geeva whispered in her ear.

Ia looked at her and shrugged.

'Your guard.'

She shook her head of course not, the girl reckoned her stupid and Ia wanted to say she'd survived all these years without her.

'Lucky we found you,' he continued. 'Lucky us and not any of em others.'

Ia looked at the lad with the gun across from the fire there was no luck about it.

'Headin south coast you say?'

Ia dropped the bottle from her mouth and said yes.

'Floodin worse downriver.'

'That's where I'm goin.' She passed him the bottle and took off her coat her hoodie she was getting hot.

'South int the place for flashin that tattoo either.'

'My old man had the same, he lived south.'

'Backalong was it? Things have changed since backalong.'

'Not everyone's fightin, wantin to fight.'

'Girl, you got a lot to learn; int no civilians left.'

Ia shrugged and took back the bottle, she had Mum's blood was born south she would be fine.

'Shame we int got many young birds in this nest, all bucks and broads past breedin age.'

Ia ignored him, these people were a hundred times more cult than crew. She finished the bottle and pushed the chair from the heat when she cooled down she pulled on her top and returned her coat closed her eyes and hoped the man would leave her be.

'Tired bird,' she heard him say; she put her hand to the feather in her pocket wished she was a buzzard she would fly them away.

When it was time to turn in Ia told the old man that she preferred the fire, for this one night she knew they would let her. She lay close to the girl both facing heat their coats and boots buttoned and tied nothing taken from the sack not even the blanket or the lamp. She watched the others crawl into the buildings everybody merry addled if Ia were stupid she would have believed this some kind of saving place but the two brothers lying across from them told her otherwise.

'Don't sleep,' Ia whispered to the girl. She had a habit of drifting when things got tough it was her way of hiding from threat.

She checked her buttons and pulled the collar tight and when the fire calmed she watched the brothers' fingers unfurl from the gunstocks their duty forgotten and she waited for the light to fade complete.

Somewhere above their heads hung the moon it settled in the trees like a night bird a little light thing it sat sideways but still Ia was grateful.

'OK,' she whispered.

'OK,' said the girl.

They got to their feet. So slow it was as if there was no go left in them at all. Ia held the sack tight she could see white knuckle-bone knots this night this escape was everything.

They disappeared from the clearing and climbed into the forest she wished she prayed for no sound no sound no sound.

Without lamp or light Ia found the path that would return them to the boat she told Geeva to stay close it would not be long half an hour was all.

'Keep the river to your right,' she whispered, 'no matter what.' It was to herself that she said this.

'Int got options anyhow,' said Geeva.

'And don't get cheeky and don't go wanderin: those are my rules.'

'You int doin too badly,' said a low voice.

Ia slid her hand into the sack and found the pocketknife. 'Who's that?' she asked.

'Over here.'

She squinted into the gloom and stepped closer saw a low wooden structure nestled in the brambles.

'Who the fuck?' she said.

'Come closer.'

'Don't,' said Geeva.

'I int.'

'Won't hurt you,' said the man. 'Come closer.'

'This some kind of ambush?' asked Ia.

'If it was you'd be got already.'

Ia thought this a good point. She stepped again.

'Ia,' said the girl.

'Just lookin.' She took the lighter from her hip pocket and

flicked it and crouched to the wooden box. 'You in there?' She held the light to the wire mesh.

The first thing she saw was the whites of his eyes he was a badger a fox a deer all animals captured all beasts that got slit easily.

'You're a man,' she said.

'You got it.'

She knelt closer. 'That's a chicken coop init?'

'By the mount of shit in it I'd say you're probably right.'

'Why you in a chicken coop?'

'Well now, that's a long story, but seein we int got all day, I'll tell you simply: them men in that camp over there, them think I'm some kind of monster needs cagin, think I done somethin to one of em. I int done nothin.'

'Murderer,' said Geeva.

Ia nodded. 'OK.' She let the flame go she stood in darkness the stranger at her feet. 'Sounds like things is messy.' She felt the girl tug at her sleeve it wasn't like Geeva to want to go from danger.

'You could help me,' he said. 'You know how things are, you could let me out.'

Ia didn't know what to say said nothing she put her ear toward the mine.

'Please, I int done bad, saw you pass by, them nabbed you dint they?'

'Them just bein friendly.'

'You know that int true.'

'I'm fed and watered.'

'Like a sow for eatin.'

Ia let his comment go. 'What's it you want?'

'Girl, can you get me out of here or no?'

'Why they botherin you say?'

'Who?'

'Them lot, why don't they just kill you?'

'Penance.'

'Cus they think you killed one of em?'

'Amongst other things.'

'What things?'

'Dispute; come on girl, what's it goin to be?'

'Seems both sides is shady.' She heard him sigh and it made her think of life back at the van.

'You goin to help me?' he asked. 'I know you're mullin it.'

'I can barely help myself.'

'Just let me out, you won't see me again.' The moon came through the trees she could see his face it was old struck down stuck in desperation.

'You'll make things worse for yourself if you get caught, must be a reason you're in there.'

'Don't you worry girl, I've learnt to make fuel from the heat of burnin bridges, bin doin it my whole life.'

'And you int no murderer?' She heard Geeva tut it was a stupid question.

'If I was I wouldn't be interested in a short-ass girl.'

'I'm a woman.'

'Well, OK then.'

Ia passed the knife from hand to hand what harm would it do to set him free he might shout hell and high if she didn't.

'OK.' She bent to the lock and prised it open felt for the bonded rope arms and legs she cut them free.

'You int got no boots,' she said.

'That's somethin I know.'

'What happened to em?'

'Them bastards took a fancy.'

'That int right, int right to take a man's boots.' She saw Geeva tap her boots together and she ignored her.

'Good luck anyway.' She watched him grow from the cage it took him a moment to put himself back together he was bear big.

'Thank you,' he said.

Ia nodded and she gripped the neck of the sack and swung it over her shoulder grabbed Geeva's hand and together they continued down the path.

They went as fast as they could through the trees and Ia told the girl to keep her eyes peeled if she saw the quarry say they would know where they were. Walking in opposite direction it was hard to make sense of anything the river the only thing of note it mocked them was a snake in the grass.

'Lost int we,' said Geeva, it wasn't a question.

Ia took the lamp from the sack and lit it and she stretched it out in front of her the path transformed into a stream at their feet. 'Nothin,' she said.

'Nothin,' repeated the girl.

They went on. It felt like another night but it was the same night. One strange hour going forward falling back when would it end? Up ahead the girl had stopped she had taken the lamp without Ia noticing and was looking at something close to the riverbank.

'Don't go no further,' said Ia.

'I found the jetty, the rope, where's the boat?'

Ia caught up and she told her to hold the lamp out toward the water.

'Nothin,' said Geeva.

'Shit.' She picked up the rope and tied the sack corner to corner and put it to her shoulder it was light relief.

'Easy come, easy go,' she said, she hated that phrase it was Branner's he didn't like it either.

'Them bastards took it,' said Geeva. 'What they want with us, Ia?'

Ia didn't know but she could guess. 'Sit down.' She sat on a broken branch and hitched her feet out of the suckling mud.

'Them want us to take their side on things?' Geeva asked.

'Maybe.'

'And what side we on?'

Ia looked at the girl beside her. 'Survivin just.'

Geeva nodded. 'And we int got no boat.'

They sat for a time and listened to the surge of the river the current strong its capacity stretched full to bursting.

'Back to walkin,' said Ia, she hoped the words would sound better out loud they didn't. 'Back to walkin; goin to take longer to get to that waterwheel.' She thought about Jenna her forbidden fruit dangling amongst thorns.

'That int good.' The girl got up and set herself for doing.

'Where you goin?'

'I'm goin to find the boat.'

When Geeva started to walk Ia followed and she told her this was silly the boat had been taken downriver was probably burning as firewood as they spoke. She waited for the girl to slow she didn't like to see her hungry for hope there was little spirit left to split between them.

They went a little further beyond the jetty the girl with the lamp outstretched her tiny back stiff with expectation and Ia wanted to tell her it didn't work like that. Want was not rewarded with what it was you wanted. Never was that so apparent the night was like the end of days.

'That's enough now,' she said.

The girl stopped tracks.

'We'll try for sleep and at first light we'll go on.'

Geeva turned her face wet with tears she had returned to the sea.

'It's OK.' Ia coughed these were not her words they sounded strange in her mouth.

The girl nodded, speechless.

They took off their coats and laid them on the wet and lay down and pulled the fabric over. The sudden winter nights were too long, where had the golden autumn days gone when she had first found the child?

Ia closed her eyes and thought of seashells and she lined up her favourites she could remember every one; the smell of salt and weed some sounding waves inside their ears the touch of silk on her tongue. That life gone but in time she would reclaim the best bits her life returned to better.

Out in the forest on higher ground she could hear gunfire, the muzzle-blast and bang the sound of silence ripping she imagined the hit.

'It int no concern of ours,' she said.

'What bout that man?'

'What man?'

'The old man in the cage.'

'He'll be all right.'

'They found em and shot em dint they?'

'Don't reckon; I'd say he got a head start and got away.'

'You sure?'

'Course.'

'You believe that?'

'I do.' Ia said this but not at all did she believe it. The old man was dead or dying and the gang with the guns were gathering, the land on which they roamed they stamped their claim it was good hunting ground the season had just begun.

'You asleep?' she asked.

'Tryin.'

'OK then. Tomorrow we're goin to find ourselves another way of gettin down, gettin cross the river; know this, if nothin else, know this.'

THE MORNING RAIN WAS a surprise even though Ia had been waiting for it. She listened to the soft pat of water felt it tap her hip her cheek beneath the coat it wouldn't be long until the flood followed. She put out a hand to touch the girl outstretched her arm to find her to know she hadn't disappeared completely yesterday's tears were enough.

'It's mornin,' said Geeva.

'Thank God.'

'Gotta get goin int we?'

Ia pushed to get up and she shuffled the coat on to her shoulders and buttoned up.

'Night went quick,' said Geeva.

'That's cus we were up for most of it.'

'I forgot.'

'What?'

'We int got the boat.' Geeva sat up and looked at Ia. 'What day is it?' she asked.

Ia thought for a minute. 'Five,' she said. 'No, six.'

'Tomorrow then.'

'Tomorrow.'

They pulled together and went slow toward the river. Every sinew in their bodies taut every bone rubbed and worn, brittle thin.

'If there's a boat, any boat, it would be moored in the reeds,' said Ia, 'or on the bank; only a fool would take a boat from water.' She looked at the child and she agreed. 'It won't be long till the rain gets a grip again,' she continued. 'All em fields like sponges, can't hold no more.'

Geeva dared them to go close to the river their hems dragging their boots half taken in the mire the mud soup inside and still no boat. As quick as it had been gifted it had been taken away that was what happened to good things it just was.

'Wish there was a ferryman someplace,' said Geeva. 'Is there such a thing?'

'Used to be, backalong.'

'Why not now?'

When gunfire blasted out Ia said that was why.

Occasionally they stopped to eat a little and empty their boots and Ia said they shouldn't worry it was probably pheasants they were shooting.

'Most folk too worn to fight.'

Geeva looked at her with disapproval she did not believe her. 'Those that int, what they fightin over?'

'Food, fuel, good huntin land.'

'That Jenna said killin weren't the way.'

'Did he say that?'

'Somethin like it, you said.'

Ia smiled she closed her eyes she wanted to cry, scream, erase the tears that brimmed in her eyes. She tried to remember his face his eyes he was all the colours that were absent from her life.

They went on and the only thing to pass them by was time. Not one single bird or boat or body seen or saw them but still Ia could not help but sense they were being watched eyes were on her she could feel it. It had always been with her this sixth sense, back at the van she knew without looking if somebody stood out on the track or came too far on the coastal path, she could see them in her mind before they had chance to spot the trespass signs and run.

She looked at the girl knew she had this feeling too.

'Maybe it's a deer?'

'Maybe,' said Ia.

'You reckon?'

Ia knew the girl still looked at her she said yes it was probably a deer, footsteps and funny feelings maybe it was.

'Cus fightin or no, there's all weird folk round int there?'

'Always has been.'

They went on watching their feet looking for safe places and missing sinking under. Every step put down with hope every stride going on toward a memory an ideal she could see it through the tunnelling trees it was a light and it drew her in like a moth.

'Ia,' whispered Geeva suddenly, 'over there.'

Ia looked to where the girl was pointing it was the boat it had been caught by the reeds.

'Stay there,' she said. 'Don't move.' She gave the girl the sack and snapped herself a tall branch for steadying and moved on toward the vessel. The closer she got the more the creepers clung to the soft rubber of her boots with each step she felt them skip out slide in again she stabbed the branch out in front of her.

'Fuckin boat,' she said. To have a thing and then to lose it before you could get used to it was typical it always happened. Ia wondered if she could ever hold on to something worthy or was her life destined to collect the flotsam they struck hard swung heavy.

She heard the girl shout her name and she told her shush she was happy to wallow sometimes it was the safest place.

'Ia.' Her name again a funny voice what was wrong with this child? She stretched out to the side of the boat. 'I'm nearly there,' she shouted.

'Don't know why you're botherin.' That voice again.

Ia held on to the boat and she strained to look behind her.

'Geeva?' she called. 'This int the time for messin; where you at?' She could feel the boat pull away and then her boots, the river had a tide all of its own.

'I'm goin under,' she shouted. She felt a rope hit her slap

on the back the mud in her eyes it took everything to get it tied around her waist.

'Hold on,' shouted the man, Ia recognized him from the mine. 'Hold on and I'll pull you in.'

There was nothing Ia could do nothing she could have done no other way of saving herself but hold on allow herself to be pulled free.

'You went after the boat.' He said he was the younger of the brothers.

'It's my boat.' She was quick to untie the rope she threw it at his feet.

'I knew you'd return.'

Ia shrugged.

'I got a fire goin.' He pointed through the trees with his knife. 'Knew you'd come lookin for the boat; my brother said to leave you but I knew.'

'Should have done what he said.'

'Maybe.' He looked at her wet clothes and said she should get warm by the fire.

Ia looked at Geeva she had her eye on the blade. 'OK,' she said.

They went on ahead and Ia could think of only one thing: the boat snagged in the reeds if the water rose higher it would take it away for real this time.

'Sit down,' he told her when they got to the fire. 'You thirsty? I got brandy.'

Ia nodded and she sat on the sacking he'd laid and watched him climb into a fire-bombed car the space where the seat used to be.

'You in the shit, back at the mine,' he continued. 'That bloke you set free is a murderin fuck; int wise what you did.'

'Don't know what you're talkin bout.' She patted the ground to her left made Geeva sit down.

'Is that right?'

Ia picked up the bottle he'd placed beside her. 'That's right.' She moved closer to the fire and reached out a hand to the heat saw the flames coil like wire about the wet-spit wood and wondered how they would get away this time. She pulled on the bottle it tasted good it always did.

'These is dangerous times, got bad folk everywhere you look.' Ia noticed he slurred his words he was days drunk his hands kept going to the steering wheel the knife a heavy weight he kept dropping it.

'Times always bin dangerous,' she said. 'Always bin somethin or someone waitin to screw things up.'

'Past year got worse for some, better for others. You know, you bin round I reckon.'

Ia ignored him.

'Travelin alone a long time too, no man nor nothin?'

Ia wanted to say she had two but each one incomplete.

'Who do that to your face, a john? You runnin from em?'

She ignored him and he beeped the car horn.

'I'm meetin someone,' she said, 'downriver; if I int there by tomorrow they'll come lookin.'

'Don't reckon.'

'Next village along.'

'Calstock?'

'That's it,' she lied.

'Calstock's flooded and gutted, int nothin in Calstock no more.'

'Well, anyway, that's where I'm headin.' Ia pulled her knees to her chest he was looking at her without the usual ask this man was all about the take.

'I should get my boat,' she said.

'Don't reckon.' He climbed out of the car.

She put down the bottle and got to her feet. 'I'm headin.' She bent to her sack and that was when she felt it, the knife-shank bolster heavy it hit her temple within seconds the man had her floored.

IA LAY IN THE dirt her hands to her head heard the fire crack smelt the acrid stench of the river she kept her eyes shut tight. If she had been got at she couldn't tell, everything ached in any case. She thought she heard a noise a sparrowhawk letting out its hunt's call desperate for meat; the rain had most animals starved they were all in it together.

'Geeva,' she whispered felt a hand go to her arm she opened

her eyes. 'He get you?' she asked and the girl shook her head looked across the fading fire at the old man sitting in the back of the gutted car his legs too long they hung where the door used to be.

'You're alive,' he said.

Ia sat up and her good hand went around her head to find the wound, the other lay limp in her lap her shoulder heavy and raw with torn pain.

'You int goin to die, don't worry; you was passed out mornin through.'

'You int the boy with the knife,' said Ia. 'You're the old man from the cage.'

The man shrugged and he unclipped the canteen that hung from his belt flipped the lid and came and knelt beside her.

'Drink,' he said.

Ia took the bottle and drank the water she kept her eyes on him his white curls falling everywhere wrong and his eyes sunken spit-lines looking.

'Where's the lad?' she asked.

'Gone.'

'Em comin back?'

The man ignored her and looked about the fire.

'Any of this yours?'

'That's mine.'

'The sack?'

'It serves a use.'

He picked up the burlap and threw it toward her.

'Anythin you want here?'

Ia glanced around the fire and saw the half-bottle of sugar-beet brandy. 'That's mine,' she said.

'The drink?'

Ia nodded and tried to put her hands out to catch but the pain in her left arm was too much she let the bottle land at her feet.

'Is that the lad's knife?' she asked, it hung from a scabbard at his belt.

'Was mine; the fucker stole it; I got it back, and the canteen.'

'It's a good big knife,' she said.

'Works well enough.'

'I don't like him,' whispered Geeva and then she shouted it, the old man ignored her.

'You should head soon,' he said. 'That lad won't be long wakin; them ropes tied good, but still.'

'I'm plannin.' She put the bottle into the sack and said she had a boat she was long gone.

'That rower in the bushes?'

'Is mine.' She was careful to hook the sack on to her shoulder.

'Spose it does the job.' He rubbed his red stubble was thinking something.

'That boat's mine,' Ia repeated.

The man looked at her and folded his arms. 'This all I get for helpin you?'

'I helped you backalong; we're equal.'

'Where you headin?'

'Downriver.'

'No more un that?'

Ia shook her head.

'Suspicious thing int you?'

'I got my reasons.'

'How old you, girl?'

'I int no girl, I'm twenty-five.'

'You seem younger.'

'Fuck you, it's a good age.'

'For a dog.'

'What you call me?' She stepped forward wondered what had got into her how brave this new day. She looked down at the girl she was glaring up a storm kicking stones the same.

'Good age if you're a dog, nothin meant. Where you from?'

'North coast; I'm headin south.'

'Fuckin hate north coast.'

'Me too. Why you?'

'That's where most my baggage lays strewn; it's a long story.'

'Well then.' Ia took one last look about the fire pit there wasn't much light never was daylight had a hard time splitting the woods.

'I'll be seein you,' she said.

'Downriver.'

'Dint I just say that?'

'You goin Plymouth way?'

'Int in Cornwall, so no.'

'But you're headin downriver.'

'What you gettin at? Just spit it would you?'

The man thought for a minute. 'You know if they still got ferries crossin the river?'

'Bin told the train bridge come down and people livin on the other one. Why don't you just walk? You're on the right side of the water.'

The man sighed; he was losing patience Ia could tell just by looking. 'You know I got folk after me?'

'Know that; whatever you done int nothin to do with me, it's your business.'

'And you got a duff arm; how you spose you'll row?'

'He's got a point,' said Geeva.

'I'll work somethin out.'

'You seen the river?'

Ia looked at the rapid water it sped past she imagined it was what traffic used to look like.

'Who are you?' she asked.

'Harper.'

'Harper what?'

'Just Harper.'

'What you do?'

'Was army backalong.'

Ia nodded. 'You know a lad called Jenna?'

Harper looked to be thinking, something had him stopped a minute. 'No,' he said.

'AWOL is you?'

'Not in years.'

'Why em after you? I mean really.'

'It's a long story.'

'We got time int we?'

'Depends on whether you'll spare me room in your rower.'

'My boat.'

'Your boat.'

Ia looked at Geeva the kid's instinct was better than hers.

'Did save you,' she said. 'Plus, time's runnin out.'

Ia nodded. 'OK then.' She started toward the boat. 'But we gotta stop when I say, there's somethin I gotta do, won't take long.'

DOWN AT THE RIVERBANK Ia watched him wade toward the vessel, his legs stamping forward his huge fists punching the branches out of his way. A man to be feared but Ia did not fear him.

'Don't do nothin stupid,' she said.

'Could have done that already,' he shouted. 'You gotta learn some trust.'

Ia stood at the water's edge and watched the strands of silver light take flight above their heads they fell between the branches and staked themselves to the river. Shards of white going under and coming up colour such beauty in their revelation she nearly shouted for him to look.

'You think he's all right?' she asked Geeva.

The girl looked at the man as if seeing him for the first time. 'He's like a beast,' she said. 'An old beast, a beast without bite.'

'I know what you mean.'

'And he still int got no shoes.'

'Poor beggar.'

'He should nick that lad's.'

'Too late now cus I int goin back.'

'You reckon he'll sink the boat? He's a biggun.'

'If he don't, he'll be good for rowin.'

'Shall we trust him Ia?'

Ia shrugged, she didn't trust anyone but recently she couldn't stop. 'Maybe,' she said. 'Enough for now.'

When Harper reached the boat he found the boy's rope in the mud he tied it and readied himself to throw told Ia not to let it fall into the water.

'I int no fool.' She caught the coil in one hand tied it tight around her waist swung the sack to the front and told the girl to climb on to her back hang on best she could and the child's arms were a comfort around her neck.

'Water's deeper than before,' she said to herself. 'Shame we dint get gone yesterday when the water was down and nobody to bring along.'

'Still got me to bring along,' Geeva whispered in her ear.

'You int no burden.'

'Say if ever.'

'Couldn't think of me without you, cut from the same cloth we is.'

'True?'

'Shut up, I'm tryin not to go under.' She was careful to steady herself with each foot down, the weight of water pushed past her put the boat out of reach and she told Geeva to tighten her legs she could feel her slipping.

'Pull the rope,' shouted Harper. 'Pull the boat in a little.'

Ia did what she was told and when the vessel was close enough to catch she lunged forward threw the kid head first and then herself.

'Shit.' She lay on her back and waited for her breathing to calm.

'You're all right,' said Harper. 'You're in safe.' He dragged her to sitting and then toward the seat.

'Thank you,' she said.

He nodded and took up the oars.

'I'll tell you when we got to stop.'

The old man ignored her he wasn't used to taking orders.

'You hear me?' She waved to get his attention.

'When will that be?' he asked.

'When we see the waterwheel.'

'What waterwheel?'

'I'll know it when I see it.'

'What you got goin there?'

'I'm meetin someone.'

'Friend?'

'Maybe.'

'We'll be lucky to get to the middle of this damn river, let alone anywhere else.'

Ia ignored him she had her days counted out there were none spare.

They crossed the river in silence, the boat half animal it thrashed against the tide like something below had it tethered to stone.

'Goin to take forever,' said Ia, she looked at Geeva and said this was the seventh day she was sure it was. She turned forward in her seat and looked to anchor her sights on something solid but everything moved even the dark crawl clouds were speeding up speeding in.

'Won't be long till rain,' said Geeva, her back against Ia's her eye on the man.

'That's a shame,' said Ia. This was her life, a place where the shit kept hauling and hitting she realized that back at the caravan she had too much time on her hands, those days before the storm when the girl had come to her somebody else's child but still she had given Ia so much hope.

'Funny how things change.'

'What's that?' asked Geeva.

'How things change so fast you don't realize em gone at first.' She thought about her parents her sister her childhood that time would never return.

'Don't be sad.'

Tiny hands slid on to the seat and rested against her hips.

'I int sad,' said Ia, 'just hankerin after somethin I dint long have.'

She watched the bow hitch up against the river waves the murky splash spitting at their faces could smell its breath it smelt of too many days on the drink.

'You'll see Evie soon enough,' continued Geeva, 'and maybe that Jenna's somewhere close.'

Ia smiled.

'And you got the baby to look forward to.'

Ia slid her good hand on to her belly and asked the baby to flag itself up, time was a cruel cleaver it fell where it wanted was heavy and heartless and slow.

An hour passed maybe it was two the clouds filling in the blanks between trees the boat companions sick and worn and thrashed Ia thought she saw the waterwheel but it was a push-bike come down to the river to die she felt shrunken, Geeva said she felt the same.

'I could curl up and sleep for a long time.' She looked down at the girl creeping into her lap held her belly close. What she wouldn't give for a cut of that, a slice of childhood a little time to make fresh what she couldn't remember.

She watched a murder of crows scoop low above their heads sensed they were not long up but already they were looking to roost. Ia imagined their eyes on her as they settled in the buckled trees the wind in their feathers the mizzle-rain rinsing the ink from the down.

'Them birds bin followin us,' she said. 'All along em bin followin us.' She turned to the man and asked if he thought it were true.

'You askin me a question?'

Ia sensed his anger, sweat ringed his eyes his neck flashed chicken red.

She nodded.

'Birds don't follow cept if you got grain; you got any?'

Ia shook her head.

'Any bread or such?'

'Not no more.'

The man went back to ignoring her his arms connected to the water the oars like picks in snow.

'Got nothin at all.' Ia turned forward in the seat and when they passed the crows she took a handful of grit from the floor of the boat and pitched it their way.

'HEY,' SHOUTED HARPER, HE made the boat tilt with his outburst.

'What the fuck?' Ia pushed the girl away and turned in her seat.

'Over there, is that it? That's it init?'

Ia leant back she saw the old tall ship first it had taken a battering more shadow than actual and beside it the waterwheel, its shaft welded to a stop the water fell furious it was in a hurry to get to the river. She smiled said yes this was it.

They hauled up to the quay like they were day trippers come to see the attractions Ia tried to imagine it filled with people the tourists from not so long ago and the folk plucked from history she and he and the girl more like them than anyone passing since.

She watched the old man drag the oars through the clay-pit stalks swing the rope and loop the spoil she stood to help and with her good arm she grabbed the stubble-straw to pull them closer.

'Bet people used to pay good money to come here,' said Harper when they reached the jetty. 'Fuck knows why.'

'Rememberin backalong,' said Ia. 'Only nobody needs to bother so much now, we're livin it int we?' She liked these words it sounded like she was a part of the world now she had begun to experience it.

They stood where they dropped and looked up at the buildings the black eyes empty mouths it had been a long time since that place had seen strangers everything suspicious everything jarred jaw-dropped fallen into a gape.

'You reckon your friend's here?' asked Harper. 'Only we int got much time before the past catches up.'

Ia shook her head. 'He'd be standin right there waitin for me if he was.' She watched Geeva run toward the waterwheel the hat the coat off and then the boots. The immovable wheel made a waterfall, a new way of seeing water the child couldn't contain her joy she stood in the spray it had her lifted.

'What now?' he asked.

'We wait,' said Ia. 'This is day seven on my clock; we wait, see the new day in.'

'And then?'

Ia sighed.

'You know I got guns comin for me don't you?'

Ia ignored him she went on toward the buildings the houses and the shops paused in time which way forward from there they had forgotten. She stood and looked up at the signs still swinging advertising blacksmith, wheelwright, baker's. There was even a shop.

'I int never been near a shop,' she said. 'Sounds stupid I know but it's true, and here we are: a shop from the past how many years?'

'Hundreds,' said Harper; he asked if she had escaped a cult that was why she was on the run.

'Maybe.'

'You see any tobacco in there, you grab it, it's mine.'

'Will do.' She push-jarred the door and a little bell made a go at duty something from memory it failed and fell from the frame landed at Ia's feet.

'Or anythin to eat to go with the drink,' he shouted behind her.

'That's my drink,' she said to herself. This now, what was this? She wanted to savour the moment she was all girl again like Geeva all experiences were good ones. She pulled down her hood and unbuttoned the coat whatever was offered she needed to breathe in she stepped toward the counter imagined this real this moment it was outside of time the universe didn't exist.

So many tins and cartons on the shelves Ia had never eaten from a packet just out the ground or what Bran brought home in his bag. He told her everything at the campsite store was scooped up from floor-standing containers no prices you paid by weight Ia didn't like the sound of that she liked this. She thought of Evie, Evie would have loved it. She wrote her name in the dust on the counter felt bad for the intrusion wiped it clear and she went behind to lift the tins all empty she knew this already.

Still it was something. This place was where she belonged with all her old-fashioned ways the past suited her perfectly. She wished Jenna were here right now to see her in these time-worn surroundings they transformed her into something new. If he were there they could hide in that ancient time build themselves an alternative future from this greatest find.

She went full circle around the room left nothing unturned nothing left behind except fingerprints tiny footsteps flitting from one object to the next she walked them over everything.

'What you find?' asked Harper when she returned to the quay, she could see he was trying on shoes.

'Nothin. Where you get them?'

'Mannequin over at the blacksmith's.'

'What's a mannequin?'

'Kind of a doll.'

'Big fuckin doll; they fit?'

'They'll do.'

'Why dint you take that lad's backalong?'

'He was wearin wellies, me un wellies don't get on, big calves.'

She watched him take out his knife and cut the leather from the tips and they both laughed at his toes sticking out.

'They'll do,' he said, smiling.

Ia sat down beside him and shared out a little of the dried fish and she watched Geeva climb the wheel toward the sluice above she waved and the girl waved back.

'You see your lad?' asked Harper.

'No.'

'You plannin stoppin through the night?'

Ia shrugged and then she said yes she would stay the night. If Jenna hadn't arrived by light up then she would find a way to hate him long enough to get away. 'I int hangin round longer un that,' she added.

'Good, cus I don't like this place, int from any time I know.'

'It'll do.'

'That's it, for now and up until all the bigger-picture things that need workin out get worked out all over again.'

'What you mean?' she asked.

'The country, when it gets back on track.'

'If it does.'

They both knew there were more causal factors to the crash than they could imagine they didn't say them it was a long list.

'Spose there int nothin out there for me tonight,' he said, he'd been weighing up his options Ia knew. 'All's quiet and there's roofs here; it would be daft to head in the dark in the storm.'

Ia nodded. 'River's risin up, we should drag the boat up some.'

Harper agreed and he got up tried out his new shoes went down to the water's edge.

'I'll find us a dry den, put the lamp in the window, in case.' Those two words they stuck to her tongue held no weight had no shape for picturing. Everything was in case, why was that? What was anything for?

She stood and went toward the waterwheel picking up Geeva's things as she went she told her to come down.

'I love it,' the girl shouted.

'It's close to pitch, we're beddin down.'

She watched her use the wheel like a ladder it barely moved so bent by habit and use and years Ia knew exactly how it felt.

'That Jenna here yet?' asked Geeva, she dropped down beside her.

'You know he int.'

'Other one gone?'

'Not yet.'

The girl lifted her face to the falling hill water dared herself to stay there.

'Put on your coat,' said Ia, 'you'll catch your death.' She passed her the huge leather coat pulled on her hat gave her the boots.

'You hear that?' asked Geeva.

Ia bent to the girl's ear. 'Music,' she said.

'Let's dance.' Geeva pulled Ia's hands from out her pockets and stood on her tippy-toes she swung Ia around made her laugh with the spin.

'Harmonica,' shouted Harper. He came closer lifted up the pace with a reeling jig.

'I can't,' said Ia, she struggled to catch her breath felt stupid for the laughter the letting go.

'You can dance,' he said.

'Fuck off, I can't.'

'I reckon you can.'

'Don't shame me, I'm goin to find shelter.' She took Geeva by the scruff and together they looked over the cottages and buildings everything gutted but with roofs still intact they chose the one closest to the quay it had a windowsill and Ia put the lamp where glass used to be.

'Int much of a room,' said Geeva.

Ia rubbed her hand over the hoary wall her hand sticking to the damp surface when she moved it the plaster fell to the floor.

'Stinks too,' said the child.

'That's the mould.' Ia rubbed her nose, she could smell animal piss too. 'It'll do.'

When the old man Harper joined them they staked their corners in the fetid building and rolled the bottle between them it wasn't long gone.

'How you learn to play that thing?' Ia asked.

'Int hard.'

'How you know what tune?'

'By ear, I only know one, can teach you if you want.'

Ia shook her head. 'We should light a fire.' She looked at him and he sighed and yawned and she did the same.

'You know him long, this lad you're waitin on?' he asked.

'Not long.' Ia went to sit beneath the lamplight the window seat wide enough to lean back bring her feet up get comfy. From the window she watched the wind catch in the trees a little rain carried with it. She could barely make out the jetty through the black of the dock she told herself if he was coming that was where he would be.

'And he's a good un you say?'

Ia nodded.

'Know more un that?'

Ia shook her head she felt stupid waiting on a near-stranger.

'We all got to hold on to somethin. He dint do that did he?' Harper pointed at her face.

'No he dint; this is from another place, another time. What bout you? What's your story?'

'I'll get back to you on that one.'

'So soldier is you?'

'Was, but int nothin worth doin in regards to abidin by rules, not now.'

'All em got attacked on the streets by gangs, most AWOL now.'

'Say so.'

Ia kept her eye on him. 'You done some shit, I can see it.'

Harper sighed. 'So don't look.'

'My husband who int my husband, he had that look, recently it come in worse.'

'I see that, and now you're on the run, you me both, rene-gades we is.'

Ia asked what he had done that had people want to put him in a cage.

'You ask too many questions; a girl could get herself in a lot of trouble askin too many questions.'

'I int afraid of you.'

'You should be.'

'If you don't like me wonderin, you know where to pick up the track.'

'It's the boat I'm after; shit int likely to catch me up on the river.'

'You int havin my boat.'

'I got standards kid, dint used to but now I do, that's why I'm sittin here waitin; I int goin to steal from a young girl.'

'I'm a woman; I'm twenty-five.'

'I think you told me that already. Anyhow, if you're worried bout the way things are in the world, don't; it's a rocky route we're walkin if it's a route to anythin at all.'

'I int worried.'

'Just if you are, I'm still here and I'm an old un if you int noticed; you're lucky to have youth on your side. You got to keep your head up, don't go round scorchin the earth if you can help it.'

Ia shook her head; most men barely spoke this man was all mouth.

'You got time too,' he said.

'For what?'

'Time to plan for the future, make good, make amends.'

'This you we're talkin bout?'

'Int much future left for me I'm sure.'

'What bout shit you done you can't change, can't go back on?'

'Old sins cast long shadows I know, but you still got to find a way to ask for forgiveness.' He looked at Ia and shook his head. 'I'm sure you int erred too much, a girl your age.'

'What you say bout forgiveness, from who?'

'Good question.'

'It's the only one I got.' She wrote Jenna's name in the damp on the wall when Harper saw it she rubbed it clean.

'So this new lad of yours, love is it?'

'Fuck no, it int that; I dunno, dunno what it is.'

'OK, leave it grandpa, I know, back away.'

Ia wondered what it was, there was no word for it this thing that was similar to hope but not hope, maybe it was love what did she know?

'The thought of somethin better,' she said, 'somethin without fault.' She looked at him and shrugged. 'Sounds stupid.'

'Sounds fine to me.'

'Does?' She settled her head in the dip where plaster had pulled and fallen away and her eyes returned to the night. 'Somethin better, but on shit days I know I don't deserve much more.'

'Guilt,' said Harper, 'is that it?'

Ia nodded she looked at Geeva was glad to see she had fallen asleep she didn't like her to hear this kind of talk.

'Girl, you int got nothin to worry bout.'

'How you know? You don't know me.'

'Cus I'm here and I done untold bad shit and the world int done with me yet.'

Ia pulled up her hood to keep the wind out of her ears, she wanted to listen.

'What?' she asked.

'I had a wife, a kid; I dint deserve em, should've walked out at the start.' He felt in his pockets for cigarettes he didn't have he sighed made himself comfortable on the dirt floor. 'Bottom line is we int no way to know the future.'

'Wish I knew more of everythin.'

'Future is down to fate I reckon.'

'Your wife and kid, you kill em?'

'Fuck no.'

'You beat em? Make em worthless?'

Harper looked at Ia told her she asked too many questions she saw the look in his eye he was a wounded bear had no teeth no claws if ever he were a threat it was a long time ago.

'Let me teach you my tune.' He pulled out his harmonica and started to play.

'Int much teachin involved in you just playin.'

'Listen just, I'm tellin you a story.'

'What about?'

'Love and loss and life.'

'Int that everythin?'

'Perhaps.'

Ia rested her head and closed her eyes to the familiar tune she thought about the good in bad people and the bad in good. She forgave him for whatever he had done it was easy he was a stranger. She thought about Bran. She would never let him off, his every sin she could feel, his every kind of mean was in her it dragged her down.

'Leavin home,' she whispered along to the music, 'never to return.'

'You see the music?' asked Harper when he had finished.

'I see it,' said Ia. 'Throw me that thing.'

IA SAT AND WATCHED the trees split rip open and be light felt Geeva's hand push into hers and she smiled and said all right then.

'You don't know,' said the girl. 'Bout what you're thinkin, if it's true or no.'

Ia looked down at her. 'If I believed he was comin and nothin was goin to stop him, then I believe he either bin got or come to his senses.' She had hoped for something but in the end it was just another thing to be let down Ia wasn't used to high expectation.

They left the tumble of buildings and walked down to the jetty three unlikely cohorts going on going forward because they could not go back and they pulled the boat into the water and climbed in without one word more than morning.

High tide had come in the night, Ia knew it was due but still it was a surprise, the river had gone in amongst the trees in search of loose limbs and roots it had found them dragged the biggest down.

Ia and Harper decided to take one oar each they sat in pews and worked the oars in constant motion and Geeva up front shouting everything into view.

'Dint reckon on this,' shouted Ia, pushing against the current. 'I did not reckon on any of this.'

She heard Geeva laugh and the old man behind her say something about last night's high winds Ia must have been dead to it all. She kept her head down to the graft her eyes tired from constant watching her shoulder stiff with new pain she told herself to think of other things besides misery she could not.

That morning they made little headway on the river. The broken trees leapt like feral dogs into their path and between the fallen boughs barely any space remained for them to manoeuvre through the reed beds. So many trees, living yesterday today dead in the water, their trunks going under coming up mortis; Ia wondered if they would ever get further than sitting in the boat. The scene was set for melancholy she could not stop thinking about Jenna, each thought worse than before they dropped into her lap like stones each one heavier than the last. She took the feather he had given her from out her pocket put it against her lips something to lighten the mood something to kiss his lips on hers. She thought about their first last night together on the beach his fire in her everywhere she closed her eyes to remember the burn she could not. She tried to keep busy with the oar pushed the branches from the boat made a laneway in the river, going on going forward because there was no way back. She imagined retracing her tracks returning to the creek she didn't want to she had found freedom would rather die than give it up.

The further they went the harder the journey became. It was as if all the taken trees had ended up here a graveyard of stiffs a dam there was no way around, when a jetty came into view they went toward it anything was better than wood and black water.

'This a village?' asked Ia, she looked up at the buildings on her right saw the viaduct in the distance and answered her own question with yes, she had seen this photo.

'Looks like it,' said Harper. 'There's a path there, we can pull the boat around, maybe we'll find food, some baccy, God knows I could do with both.'

Ia put down her oar and hung from the boat to find a gap between the jetty planks her better hand beneath the water the river undulating, splashing mad. She thought about her baby bundled inside and the future she had set for them, every day it ebbed a little further out of reach why didn't joy step closer, show itself? The battle should have eased by now where were the breaks? Just then her fingers found a split in the wood and she was quick to pass the rope and knot it.

'We can pull it up when we're out,' she said, 'hide it over there in the brambles until we know what's what.' She jumped from the boat and stood in the suck and looked up at the hillside village in the distance.

'If you're meant to be hidin, this might not be the place for you,' she said.

'How's that?' asked Harper. 'What you hear?'

'Nothin, but the place is full of buildins, I'd say there's folk about.'

They stood looking a moment more and Harper told Ia to go on, see if she could find food they were in desperate need.

'What you goin to do?' she asked.

'I'll hide out, mind the boat.'

When Ia didn't speak he said on his life he promised.

'That int much.'

'Int likely I can get far is it? The river's blocked.'

Ia nodded. 'OK then.'

The quay was a smashed plate of hard bitter bricks and concrete corners, things that had washed there or been dumped perhaps to keep the water from coming, it hadn't worked. Where tiny cracks existed the river had found them had divided the car park into two it was on that ridge of scree that Ia walked with the girl tailing behind.

'You should go back,' she told her.

'Why?'

'Cus this place is unknown more un the woods and the water; we int done well with others so far have we?'

Truth was she wanted to be alone, it was a gut thing, something was brewing taking shape.

When the girl didn't speak she told her to sit in the reeds and keep an eye on Harper.

Across the quay Ia saw an uphill path and she took it went on climbing toward higher ground. In the valley below she watched the tidal water push the river in the wrong direction she could smell the sea it smelt like home.

Across the creek wading egrets made the short journey from nest to marsh, oblivious to the clawing currents their legs like twigs sticking and bending in the wet clay. From this vantage Ia could see the quay she searched the reeds the manmade defences saw that the child was gone and she shrugged the girl was strong-willed like the tide, once upon a time Ia had been the same.

Everywhere she looked the remains of journeys made lay strewn; on the roofs of buildings and in the branches of trees broken boats hung like carcasses they would never be repaired. This was the detritus of giving up. All the world's fallen had tripped up here, all windows smashed all doors swinging every inhabitant put out, bin day, and all this had happened in an instant.

Ia had thought her plight special in some way, stupid girl, they were all the same all running from disaster running toward hope. The bare bones of existence were built from this, not quite skeletal but an X-ray of the shape of things to come, map ready.

If anybody existed in this place they did not want to be found, but still, the first threshold she stumbled upon she stepped across called out said that she was harmless but the crack in her voice told whoever this already.

Ia had never been in another's home, her parents' her own was all. She imagined something better, a little cosy coming at her the scent of seasoned firewood the smell of cooking, everything was missing, maybe it was people was all, or the ache in her gut that pierced her thinking. Was this fear she felt?

In the hallway she stood and shouted up the stairs then into every downstairs room her voice bird-brittle full of funny hope then hoping not.

In the kitchen she opened the cupboards and stretched her arm to the corners not even crumbs and she climbed the stairs just to see new things. She imagined the people who lived here wondered how long gone and she sat on the bed and wished she hadn't for the pull of another life it wasn't hers. She got up, in the corner of the room a wardrobe not built into the wall like in the van but standing free a proud man its skin the colour of pine bark. Ia put her fingers into the hole where the handle used to be and pulled perhaps she'd find something warm something to barter, casting out her net despite nothing always nothing. She moved on. Other rooms the bathroom and the shitter she sat down to relieve herself closed her eyes to enjoy the humdrum moment, be stopped. That was when she felt it. More than a feeling it was a noise the sound of her world crashing. She looked down and saw red.

Ia supposed she made her way back to the quay, she couldn't remember. She stood where the pub still declared itself free and leant against the wall and wondered if inner hurt had ever presented itself like this before. If it had it was something forgotten, a forbidden memory.

She saw the girl come toward her she'd found stepping stones she walked on water, her eyes on Ia, knowing. Nothing to say, neither of them speaking they went into the pub like a million lost souls before them.

The first door and then the second door gone they went to the bar and stood in the river water that pooled on the floor looked things over all familiarity wiped clean.

'This what a pub looks like,' said Ia, she didn't know what else to say.

'Don't look worth it,' said Geeva.

'Reckon it int.'

'Just a big old room.'

'That bout sums it up.' She went to the window and saw Harper heading their way he'd seen them enter he looked like all his hopes and dreams were where they stood he had simple needs.

'Any drink?' he shouted.

Ia shrugged shook her head she didn't care.

'Any food?'

'I int looked.' She linked her hands where the baby used to be and looked to the sky it had darkened the rain sucked ready for the spit.

'We should shelter here,' she said; the weather was an excuse, she didn't want to go on.

'You sure?' asked Harper. 'Cus I've had a gander and I reckon we can float the boat through the car park there, get around em fallen trees in the river.'

'Just for a while; there int nobody here, all that have been have gone again.'

Harper nodded, maybe he sensed a change in her she didn't know what showed.

'You go on if you want to go on,' she said. 'Take the boat, it int no use to me now.' She saw Geeva look at her and she looked away.

'OK,' said Harper. 'I see where things are goin here.'

'Where's that?'

'You're worn down from the storm and your man int comin and, well, maybe an hour or two for restin and then we'll see where we are.'

'You can take the boat, I'm sick of the fuckin boat.'

'Look at that, there's a grate and hearth,' he said. 'Anythin worth burnin lyin round?'

Ia sighed, she wanted to hide find the place for daydreaming forgetting, she wished she had her things her shells and bones the box of sea-glass collected over time.

'I'll go see.' She went around the back of the bar and took out her knife didn't waste time pulling wood panelling from the walls and she bundled it and carried it to the fire. 'There.'

She stood and watched Harper light a little dry-thing kindling slowly add the wood and when the flame took hold she sat on one of the bottle crates he'd pushed close.

'You got kids you said.' Ia looked at Harper when he sat down.

'One; should've stuck at none at all.' He looked at her. 'I don't mean that with any menace, would've saved em soul a lot of heartache is all.'

'Cus you was a fucker?'

'Well, yes, but that int why; I was never meant for any of it, got a girl pregnant, she weren't even mine to fuck, was from another community complete.'

'Then what?'

'Did the right thing, stuck by her, married her, joined the army cus of her, that only made things worse. Settlin down was never meant for me.'

'Why dint you just leave her?'

'Weren't the right thing.'

'Sounds like it was.'

'Know that now don't I?'

'I don't get why folk stick round when they int happy.' She thought about Bran, tried to understand his sense of duty tried to understand her own.

'Stubbornness,' said Harper. 'Some people can't accept em wrong.'

'So you stuck round, made all lives a misery?'

'All right girl, I int proud.' He got up and added more wood to the fire and stood with his back to her she listened to him fumble for the harmonica and start up his tune.

'Int stubbornness,' said Ia, 'it's cowardice, craven.' She watched him think a way around her words, waited for him to finish playing.

'I feel like I've known that tune forever,' she said.

'If it's in your head all you gotta do is practise.' He stepped forward and hit the spit on to his thigh. 'Have it, I'm thinkin of takin up the fiddle.'

Ia took it from him wiped it in her own jeans and blew a few notes to start the song.

'Practise,' said Harper.

'If you say so.'

'That lad you was waitin on.'

'What bout him?'

'Good lad, you say?'

Ia nodded. 'Everythin he's been through recently, I reckon he is.' She looked at Harper and saw that he wanted to know more.

'His mum got killed,' she said, 'murdered.'

Harper cleared his throat, about to speak, he put a hand over his mouth and held it tight.

'And you wouldn't think he had a care in the world to look

at him,' she continued, 'all warm fire glow and sparks and red, red hair.'

Harper came close to her, stopped, he had something to say but couldn't find the right words and he returned to the fire.

'Don't matter now,' she said.

'Things don't always fall right time, right place.'

'I think I learnt that thirteen years back and every day since.'

'But then again, sometimes fate falls, has a hand.' He sat and looked at Ia to see if she knew what he was talking about.

'And where em now?' she asked. 'Where's your family?' She wanted to keep talking keep from thinking.

'I had a farm before the army; it was me dad's, I hated it, left it to em.'

'That's somethin.'

'It were nothin, probably more trouble than it was worth. You got any food left? I'm starved.'

'Got a little of the dried fish.' She split what she had and they ate slowly, all eyes on the heat.

'You cured this yourself?' he asked.

Ia nodded.

'Self-sufficient spose, like most this last year.'

'Int so bad; there's sometimes food on the land and in the sea always.'

'You barter?'

Ia looked at him with suspicion.

'You trade ever?'

'Only when needs must. Why you ask?'

'Askin is all.' He kicked off his shoes and stretched his shit-stick feet to the fire and Geeva did the same. 'Flood came right in here, would you look at that, halfway up the wall is the tidemark.'

Ia looked to where he was pointing it was hard to see in the dim.

'One good day,' he continued, 'one good day and no more land, we'll all be at the coast just about.' He stretched on to the floor spread out and closed his eyes to the heat.

'One good day,' said Ia. She watched the child take a thin splinter of wood and poke it into the fire and the circus of animals that lived there jumped and circled and set themselves free.

One good day was all she asked for what had she done so wrong in her past life that she be punished over and over? Each day worse than before each day clogged with more wreckage to endure.

She fingered the compass from out her collar and opened it, to see it moving would have been sufficient a little beat movement but no it laid still a dead thing in her hand dead to her now.

FRAILTY DID NOT BELONG to Ia it was a looked-at thing perhaps a thing to be picked up and toyed but never had she felt it never more than that night. She woke without the usual start and watched the last remaining eye of fire wink out she grappled for good thought and heard the child say her sister's name.

'I know,' she said.

Across the room she saw Harper turn on the floor heard his knees grind his hip click she felt the same her bones smashed and grabbed back wrong.

'Mornin or night?' she said.

Harper sat up and his hands went looking for a cigarette it was instinct.

'Mornin,' said Geeva, standing at the window.

'Fire's out.' Harper pointed at the smouldering grate. 'I put wood on bout an hour ago, fucksake.'

Ia sat up and looked around the room for bearings, the pain

still plucked at her insides the rag she'd stuffed between her legs stiff with night-old blood she got to her feet and went and stood behind the girl and put her arms around. Something to hold on to something to hold her if she fell.

'Tis mornin,' she agreed. The smell of dew hung in the air its scent caught in her throat like a gob of fish roe she could taste it.

'River's still up,' she said. 'Fuckin river.' She turned and told Harper he could have the boat told him she meant it.

'Girl, I told you I int stealin your boat.'

'It int stealin if someone gives it you.'

Harper sighed. 'If you're sure.'

'I'm sure, take it, int bin nothin but trouble.'

They said their goodbyes at the edge of the car park, Harper said he would try to get the boat past the trees in the river if nothing worked and he couldn't set it free he would catch her up.

'Whatever you want; I'm headin downriver, goin to walk the rest of the way.' She caught Geeva's eye her outrage visible she ignored it.

When they were alone she told the girl that the river was a bully and she was sick of those.

'Goin to take us forever,' said the child.

'What's the rush? Jenna's gone, the baby dead before it had chance to birth, I bin waitin to get back to Evie thirteen years, I don't even know if she's there, I don't know what I'm doin.'

'You done what needed doin already,' said Geeva.

'I have?'

The girl nodded. 'You escaped.'

SLOWLY THEY CLIMBED TOWARD higher ground, their boots jabbing into the pock-scarred lane their heads bowed to the rain their hearts hidden it was best. To keep moving forward was to keep from thinking back. They passed the overgrown yards and garden walls stolen by green and the tiny cottages, the beginnings of her baby sunk in one, and up toward the treeline of a new wood. All the while the upper valley subsidence washed past them the skim-bits of slate that hit their shins like knapper flint. The higher they went the more the river took over below it was a fat pig stuffed with all it could find of life and death and all the other-world ferrymen who drifted between. They stopped to watch a herd of Friesian cows float on their backs, a bunch of balloons colliding, giving themselves up to the half-starved crows a tableau of life and death played out in black and white. Nature in all its glory the gory detail left in.

So captivating was the view so snagged in moment Ia did not bother with the voice she heard in the distance she thought it was the girl dallying behind.

'What?' she shouted.

'Int me,' said Geeva.

They stood in the river road and waited.

'You hear anythin?' asked Ia. 'See anythin?'

The girl held up one finger. 'Maybe, if the fog cleared,' she said.

The cloud bagged low in the sky it draped itself across rooftops like cobwebs.

'Somethin in the lane,' said Geeva. 'Shadow or maybe more un shadow.'

'Who's that?' shouted Ia and her good hand went to the knife.

'It's him,' said Geeva. 'It's the old bear.'

'Boat's gone,' said Harper; he bent to his knees to catch his breath and Ia waited. 'Disappeared completely this time.'

'Well then,' said Ia, 'spose that's what folk call fate.'

'And that int all.' He pulled up straight. 'Them that captured me is after me still.'

Ia stopped and narrowed her eyes. 'The brothers?' she asked.

Harper nodded. 'Reckon so.'

'You see em?'

'Heard em just, but I know it's em; they think I killed one of em, I dint, wrong time and place is all.'

Ia folded her arms. 'I reckon there's more to it for all that botherin.' She kept her eyes on him for signs what kind she didn't know. 'What type of work you say you was in?'

'You don't want to know.'

'Try me, I int delicate.'

'Grave robbin.'

'Really?'

He nodded.

'That's a dirty job, what you get out of it?'

'Jewellery, medals, gold sovereigns off em eyes.'

'And then you killed someone?'

'That was a misunderstandin.'

Ia shook her head. 'Let's go, higher ground.'

They went on toward the highest flank of trees and Ia was thankful for the shelter and the tempered land she looked for Geeva to wave her back but the girl had seen or heard something preferable up ahead had started up the other side of the track. Ia tried to imagine the paths below the bridleway they were on, the laneways and tracks meant as short cuts, cut off complete. A long time ago money had paid for seedling in that part of Cornwall, there were foreign trees all around her she could not name them, their peeling bark like cigarette paper, delicate wrappers against her callused hand. Such beautiful things she had not seen enough in her lifetime.

'Worked all my life,' she said suddenly. 'My whole life, guttin, curin fish, since childhood; that int right.' Ia stopped and put a hand to her stomach to catch the pain, it crept up on her in waves clawed at her insides like a cast of hermit crabs.

She pulled the lip of bark free and put it to her own it was so soft what she thought lace might feel like. A pretty thing a found object hidden amongst the dirt and grit and she thought about the van the cove and all the world's shells collected there and still she could not make that place pretty. She kissed the bark and folded it like posh paper put it in her pocket for later.

'Let's go.' She followed Geeva's footprints in the muck said she would not stop walking.

'Before army, used to work the farm, since I was a kid,' said Harper when they got into a rhythm. 'Was born to work the land but I dint take to it.'

'So why you bother?'

'Cus it was my father's land, nothin more un that.'

'And then you joined the army?'

'For a while, easy way providin or so I thought.'

'When you sign up?'

'Twenty-five.'

'My age.'

'Seemed like a good idea at the time, spose it was.'

'Got to see the world? What int worth that?' She wondered what this man knew of heartache he had absolutely nothing to weigh him down he'd erased all burden from his life a long time ago.

'It weren't no holiday,' he said, 'if you was thinkin it.'

'Where you fight?'

'Iraq.'

'Thought you older un that, one em world wars or somethin.'

He ignored her. 'Other wars don't seem so bad when the fightin comes to your door,' he continued. 'I brought half of it back with me.'

'How's that?'

'Some days the past gets to pullin me back there. Memories return, jump out of nowhere.'

'Cus of what you seen?'

Harper shrugged and nodded said yes.

'Some things are best left int they?' Ia said.

'If you can find a way to unsee what you seen.'

Ia looked at him she wanted to tell him there were ways she was well rehearsed in forgetting going under.

The path they clung to cut into the landscape like cliff-face rock it almost was, a hundred feet in the air she felt herself go giddy the track so narrow in places they changed direction found a new way through the woods.

'I need to stop.' Ia could feel the pain increase, her ripped insides bloated putting weight on her legs they dragged behind her tried to dislocate. Never had she experienced this before, never had she gone so long carrying, hoping. 'Just for a while I need to sit down.'

She sat where she stood and waited for a part of herself to return the kernel she had lost; not just from the toll of fall-by moments but from the years that stacked against her where had she gone? A tree shaken taken down Ia had no leaves to shield her no protective bark to wrap around her colour gone to ground but still she told herself to get up, for all the times she had fallen and felt sorry, fucksake Ia, get up keep moving this was not the end.

She watched her companion hide between twin trees his face white, pinned like a sheet between.

'Hear somethin?' she whispered.

'Thought I saw somethin. Fuck.'

'Where?'

Harper put a finger to his lips and pointed through the trees to the path that ran parallel to theirs below.

'Shit.' Ia sat up and looked to see if Geeva had returned. Since leaving the caravan the child had a habit of testing herself, each day she went a little further the girl hoped for better Ia knew one day she would find it find her own freedom.

'If you want to run, then run.' She got to her feet felt the blood surge put her hand to a tree to steady herself.

Harper looked at her and shook his head. 'I int leavin you to fend,' he said.

'I'll be fine, bin fendin my whole life.'

She watched him walk a little way down the track came back said by rights he was a fucker but he couldn't leave her to those men.

'I seen you hammered and prepped for reeve and rape, I int leavin you to em.' He put his arm around her waist and pulled her upright. 'Come on, em getting closer.'

What remained of higher ground they scrambled up they kept to the treeline and found shelter in the ruin of a folly, Ia wondered if she were destined to live amongst the bones of buildings. She sat at ground level her back to the wall her legs loose beneath, her hands hooked in dirt.

'I'm goin to climb up for the lookout,' said Harper, he put a blanket across her lap told her everything was going to be OK.

Ia closed her eyes her mouth her heart to stop the pain the aftershock of internal blast. She sat amid the rubble, dazed. Nothing to grip on to nothing to hold in order to let go, no breath but minute pinpricks stabbing her chest no pulse but the throb in her belly, time moving on, cruel tricks. No words to describe, none needed, it was all the punches all the hits and trips, fracture upon fracture, blood over blood.

Ia felt between her thighs without looking she knew the wet of final purge was everywhere. She had been gutted, fish-stripped, turned inside out.

'I THINK WE'RE IN the clear; int seen or heard since.'

Ia jumped when she heard the male voice for a moment she was back at the van she was quick to open her eyes.

'Bin here an hour and nothin,' said Harper.

'He's right,' said Geeva, she had returned she linked her fingers into Ia's, held tight.

'You hungry?' Harper asked. 'I found some nuts.'

Ia sat up and squeezed the child's hand. The pain had lessened she could feel some strength return.

'What kind of nuts?' she asked.

'Hazel.'

'You pick em?'

Harper nodded and opened his fist. 'Found em on the ground backalong.'

'I'll take some.'

They sat in a circle and cracked the nuts in their teeth spat the shells and ate.

'Dry as bark,' said Ia, she reached for the water.

'How you feelin?' he asked.

'I'm OK.'

'You sure?'

Ia pulled up the blanket. 'Give me a minute.'

'You take your time, we int in no hurry.'

Ia smiled, thanked him.

THEY LEFT THE FOLLY and re-entered the trees, a space to walk, breathe. Occasionally Harper chanced his knife at a squirrel he pinched the tip and threw it spinning and Ia and the girl watched him run.

'I like it here,' said Geeva suddenly.

Ia looked around, apart from the exotic trees it was woodland same as all the rest.

'You do?' she asked.

The girl nodded.

'You got some memory you int tellin me?'

'Peaceful just.'

'You're a good girl,' said Ia. 'Always be that.'

They heard Harper swear up ahead, he'd killed something it spasmed in a slick of mud on the ground.

'Shit,' he repeated.

'What is it?' They caught up to him.

'That int no squirrel,' said Geeva.

'Fuck,' said Ia. 'An owl, you killed an owl.'

Geeva told Ia to look it up in her book.

'I know what type, it's a short-eared owl.'

'Thought owls only come out dusk to dawn,' said Harper.

'Do, cept this one.'

'Ears int so short,' said Geeva, she went close and Ia told her to stop.

'It's dead, it's fine.' Harper lifted it by its legs.

'I int eatin it,' said Geeva, she ran into the trees.

'That's bad luck,' said Ia. 'You kill an owl, you better watch your back.' She lifted a wing and sighed, wished she had the energy to draw it, it was beautiful. She let it drop.

They went on with Harper up ahead his prey swinging he wasn't ready to give it up just yet.

'Hey,' he said suddenly when they arrived at a clearing. 'Look what we stumbled on.'

Ia stood beside him she saw the house and the girl standing dumbstruck at the entrance she waved them over.

'What kind of house is this?' asked Ia.

'It's like the ruin but it int so ruined,' said Geeva. 'More like a castle.'

'I int never seen no castle before.' Ia walked slowly across the gravel she wondered how to draw such finery the arched doorways and neat jewelled windows the towering chimneys wondered how many fires.

'Manor house,' said Harper, he read the sign that swung in the breeze: '*Cotehele.*'

'There's a tree growin through the flagstones.' Geeva took Ia's hand and pulled her through the arch across the courtyard and into the main hall and they stood beside the table it was the size of the van and they looked up at the imprint of weapons that used to adorn the wall.

'What I wouldn't give for one of em huge axe things,' said Harper. 'A spear would make life easier too.'

'Look at this.' Ia stretched to touch the tapestry on the wall a coat of arms perhaps but it was out of reach, she asked Harper to help but still it was too far it was a shame, she couldn't shake the cold it would have done for extra warmth.

'What you seen?' she asked Geeva.

'Rooms with beds and cupboards all empty, nothin warm.'

'Nothin much,' said Harper. 'We should find the kitchen.' He pushed open all the doors picked one and went through and Geeva followed.

Ia let them go on ahead she wanted to absorb this moment

create some memory of feet silently stepping her hands touching the walls the security of the corridor. She pictured the paintings either side imagined the snapshots of summer and nature all in place this was how life should have been.

'There's a hearth big as a cave,' shouted Harper, 'and stoves as big as I don't know what.'

Ia stood against the door jamb. 'Not much cookin goes on in here, this is a museum we found ourselves.'

'Look.' Harper put a barrel of rotting apples on to the table. 'Food.'

Ia turned away. 'Maybe later,' she said. 'I need to lie down.' Apples replacing oranges nothing else had changed.

'I'll look for somethin to light the fire,' said Harper. 'Give me em jeans and I'll rinse em in cold water, hang em up to dry.'

Ia covered her face looked away for the shame.

'Seen worse in the army, girl; come on, let's clean you up a little.'

Ia looked at Geeva and the child went whistling away.

'OK.' Boots off Ia peeled the damp sticky fabric from her legs the skin puckered pink and stinging, rape raw.

She left the kitchen and went to lie down on a stranger's bed her own blanket wrapped tight. She watched some hidden breeze pet the rank cloth canopy above her head and imagined the four corner posts filled with rot and fucking insects it turned her stomach this house was worse than woods.

She lay like a flat stone sunk after skimming. Her baby had

been the thrust the propulsion without it Ia could barely keep her head above water she was doing circles, spinning.

The worst of things had happened, she'd pissed the blood and the baby away the one good thing in her life gone in a splash.

Her dead-weight heart her belly barren, a void echoing the heart's ache empty space.

She turned on her side and dropped her arms nothing to protect except herself she had never been good at that.

Down the hall she could hear Geeva in her chosen room singing some song a lullaby Ia remembered it from her own childhood. A song Evie used to sing. She closed her eyes.

A FULL MOON CAUGHT in the window it opened the curtains and let itself in. Ia watched it cross the room and help itself to the bed, something in its arms a baby laid it at her feet told her to take a moment take time to remember this.

Ia sat up. What to do with the white slither it was so small a fillet in the moonlight. Every part of it accounted for, a dug diamond, perfect.

She slid from the bed in one stretch put on her coat her boots and the scarf she wore around her neck she cut with the knife and made a little purse to put the baby inside.

'Little thing,' she said.

One hand beneath one hand was all she needed. Ia lifted the baby and placed it in the rag turned the corners and folded it cradled it to her the face of an angel its wet body like thin air.

'Tiny thing.' She kissed the head made a wish that she could return it put it back, hope that it would re-root and start over.

She carried the baby through the house and despite knowing this was a dream Ia had to see it through, she went into the garden found a spade dug a shaft beneath a cherry blossom and closed the infant's swaddling one last goodbye and stretched to put it deep into the ground. Somehow it had been gifted from the earth it was right that she should return it and she watched the hole fill again and the vines and creepers go over. A beautiful garden hidden beneath the weeds Ia knew come spring it would again bear fruit become reborn.

I A WOKE AND SAW Geeva standing starfish at the door the worry was in her she looked startled.

'What is it?' Ia sat up and wondered what was coming in on the horizon worse than what had been before.

'Harper,' said the girl. 'I can hear him shoutin; can you?'

'Where are your clothes?' asked Ia.

'In the bedroom.'

'Put them on, we gotta go.' Ia watched the naked child disappear down the hall and she got up and pulled on her hoodie her fire-dried jeans she found folded by the door she packed her meagre belongings into the sack and tied it tight to her back everything run ready.

'I like this house,' said Geeva when they met on the stairs.

'I know.' Ia took her hand to keep her close. 'You got all your clothes on, not just the coat?'

'Have.'

'OK then, let's go.'

They found Harper in the front courtyard he stood at the gate and told them to go on for fucksake hurry the men were coming through the back fields he had seen them.

'Em be in the orchard now,' he shouted. 'Go on girl.'

'You int comin?'

'Best we split, this int your shit em throwin anyhow.'

Ia told him she'd wait at the river someplace she told him to be careful. Whoever he was whatever he had done he had helped her for the sake of going on he was worthy of good luck.

They watched him return to the house and Ia told the girl to remember this moment when things broke gave up on hope there was hope and Geeva said she knew this these were her words.

The house and its buildings they left behind headed long into a tunnel and down through a garden it was the garden from her dream. The dovecote with the blather-bent jackdaws squatting and the pond thick with marsh weed and fairy moss it was then she saw her baby's tree.

In the silver light of dawn the night garden was a charcoal sketch of what it might be come morning, no depth no colour the first thing on Ia's journey to come straight from her journal.

She closed her eyes and painted the tree into full cherry-pink blossom and she smiled and looked toward it saw the girl standing there the compass in her hand.

'Kid, come on,' she shouted. 'What you doin? This int a game.'

Ia could hear voices punch the courtyard walls their pitch sharp and bitter bitching like the birds the place filling with disagreement and she turned back to see the coat heaped on the ground knew the boots the hat the girl was gone.

'Geeva,' she shouted. 'I int done with healin, you gotta help me mend.'

All this all that for nothing a child that was forever fading always on the brink of going gone now, to ground to the trees to the moon and back to water.

'Perhaps again,' said Ia, but her words were optimistic they weren't hers they belonged to Geeva.

She hurried through the garden and down into the woodland the roots of trees coming at her limbs from beneath the earth they tripped her running and Ia kicked back until finally she fell. She lay flat out and watched the arching canopy above grapple with the wind saw crows come to laugh at her kick pine needles into her hair. She sat up and took stock a moment to catch her breath. South through the weave of branches hove and fallen Ia could see water it flashed flicker-book through the black weed. So much had she wanted to find the river how had that tributary become such burden, a barrier last hurdle? She was so close to home but still she could not jump it.

'How many more miles?' she shouted. How many more miles of busted road and rapid river and alone now she always ended at the blunt bashed dented tip of alone.

Ia stood and shook the mud-water from the tail of her coat

panicked for the sack and found it where it had plunged in the slide.

Down then, down toward the water maybe it was all she knew but God she missed the sea. What she wouldn't have given for one more minute of long-stretch looking the horizon the distance of everything.

The proximity of valley dug at her like an open wound the bulging banks and thin-stick skyline the water world heaped upon her she could not see beyond. She stood at the treeline where their boughs bent to swim and listened for noise other than water looked for familiarity but drew a blank these were impregnable shores.

'Geeva,' she called. 'Where you at? We had such plans dint we?' She clambered up to a high-ledge wall that looked down upon work buildings and the stagnant mire that creamed thick with every kind of dead. The moment made more miserable than any when she thought she saw something white in the woods those water-wanting eyes. Perhaps the girl had found home maybe she wanted this place to be so.

'OK then.' Ia knew she would wait a little longer she had to. One hour, two hours, it didn't matter time at the river did as it pleased if it existed at all.

She watched the tide retreat and the large plateau of water splinter into smaller plains and when gaps wide enough for walking stretched between she jumped from the wall, the curiosity that she might find something in her still, scavenger she supposed.

Archways crabbed low beside the quay and Ia tried the wooden doors for pull, she peeked and found nothing of any significance, she returned to the first arch and swung the doors wide and amongst the hemp rope and offcuts she sat and pushed herself against the wall where the wind wasn't so much bother.

'I'll wait,' she said, her heart drubbing in her ears her mouth her tongue gone numb with bite. Wait for Geeva to come on now wait for Harper to pull up and tell her what to do.

No boat no motivation for anything it was like she'd been struck down. So many times had she lain upon the ground perhaps it was her fate, this abysmal damp hole as good as any she had ever known. She undid the top buttons of her coat let the cooler air in she was nothing much more than bones and skin in any case, all the softness callused, all her corners knuckled and scabbed.

From her hide she could see a gull scoop down to land at the water's edge it caught in the wind hung motionless like a bag blown and pegged in mid-air. Ia watched it attempt to get a wing on things but when three bullets blasted it unhooked itself dropped into a current and was gone.

'Geeva.' Ia ran out into the open afraid for the child a moment, mother after all. She stood with her back to the river looked up into the scrub of trees wished for white please, the dress the tangle of hair the wide eyes searching why weren't they looking for her?

'Geeva,' she shouted, 'I can't do this without you, you without me.'

It had been the start of things. Ia finding the child, in turn the girl helping her to find herself, the bond between them could not be severed there was no knife sharp enough that was what she had believed. And now the bullets, hitting the earth like meteorites the water like skimmers, the air around her shattered, sulphuric, everything smashed eggs.

She thought she saw something flash at the top end of the closest path the blur of somebody running they shouted her name told her for fucksake hide.

'Harper,' she said.

She watched him fall pick up keep running and shouted for him to follow, beneath the towering arch and into the cavern she pushed the doors shut and dragged what she could to barricade.

'You gotta be quiet,' she told him.

In the dark Ia found her sack bundled on the floor and she told Harper hang on let her put a light to this.

'They got me,' he coughed.

Ia took her lighter from out her pocket and she lit the lamp its glass smashed but wick intact and she carried it to him put colour into his face where there was none.

'You look like shit,' she said.

'Bet I do.'

She sat on a spool of rope too heavy to pull to the door and set the lamp on the ground.

'They got me,' he said again.

'Let me see.'

'It's too late.'

'Probably just a scratch.' Ia helped him with his coat his belly bloodshot through she wondered if there was anything she could do.

'It's my luck they int got nothin vital; it's a slow death marked on my card.'

'I'll stay with you.'

'This int your fight,' he said. 'They're after me; if they see you helpin, they won't think twice, they'll bullet you the same.'

'I won't leave you,' she said.

'For your future, babies to be, don't give up.'

Ia put her hand to her stomach, it still felt right to go there it was a settling place.

'I can't leave you to die,' she said.

'I know that.'

'They'll draw this out.' She looked at him and saw terror in his eyes it was the first time she'd witnessed it, it looked misplaced something fallen into wrong hands. His eyes were mostly kind she had seen them before.

'Here,' he said, he reached for his belt.

'What is it?'

'My knife, I seen you lookin.' He unclipped the sheath and passed it to her.

'What about it?'

'I've drawn enough blood with that thing, it's only right what I'm goin to ask.'

'No.' Ia dropped the blade and stood and her shadow doubled and stood beside her in solidarity.

'Em out there—'

'Don't ask me.'

'—will torture me, you know they will.'

'Fuck no.' Ia went to the door and bent to a shard of light. She turned her ear for voices and heard them.

'Girl,' he said and Ia turned to look at him.

'I int no girl.' She had tears in her eyes.

'I'm a bad man.'

'No you int.'

'I int done right by nobody but myself.'

'You did all right by me.'

'I don't deserve mercy but it's the best I can ask.'

Ia returned to the door she could hear them kicking up stones the splash of water they were getting close.

'Fuck.' She turned and looked at him in the dullard light a huge man with a hundred swollen stories to him gone small got wasted only one tale left to tell. She saw the knife return to his hand it turned and held the light, winked, told her the decision was hers she knew this.

'Never killed nothin more un fish,' she said. She crouched beside him took the knife and felt the weight of a well-made blade.

'You take care of yourself, Ia.'

She nodded wiped the tears there was nothing she wasn't crying for. 'All right then.' She leant forward and went as if to hug a moment calm she held him close.

'Tell Jenna I'm sorry,' he whispered.

The knife went in it was that easy, of course it was. The line between life and death was a lie there was nothing there a forever ocean in which to drown. Ia heard the splash, the brief flail and then the final gasp for air, the choking going under. Blood-red river.

Ia held him until he became himself again the weight lifted the stories at float telling in every line on his face.

'If I see him I'll tell him you was a good man,' she said. 'I'll tell him that; what I know of his father I'll tell him.'

Despite what he'd said and done he had shown her otherwise, forgiveness was his final call it would also be Ia's.

She returned him to the rope and lay back a moment and that was when she saw it: a canoe bolted and roped into the high-arch eaves.

I A WIPED THE BLOOD the knife into her jeans and she slid it into the sheath clipped it to her belt and climbed the ladder that stood against the rear wall, she cut the rope and felled the boat. She went to the door and made a space for running and listened to the rampage another door kicked she could hear them arguing their boots scuffing in the wet, the click of a lighter smell of cigarettes the scent brought her back down to earth.

It didn't take long for Ia to get to the river, compared to the rest of her journey it didn't take long at all.

First the door jarred for looking and then the canoe dragged ready she pushed her sack into the bow, this was it this was all she had left, she grabbed the vessel and lifted it above her head counted down some number and then she ran.

Her arm still hurt and the weight of the boat had it twisted wrong took all her strength to get it into the water. The paddle in her hands as she pushed from off the quay wall, when she hit the bight the men shouted what the fuck called her a bitch, a whore, too late. She paddled fast toward the current in the centre of the river and joined the debris in its last-ditch attempt at freedom.

Ia's law the weather had choked on its own greed it had become dumbstruck the water laid flat and wide a long lake beneath. Something unused to came over her some peace despite the one distant gunshot fired and wasted, the birds taking off the birds returned.

She rested the paddle across her legs and closed her eyes allowed what was left of herself to float downstream there wasn't much to her, empty belly no baby empty heart no girl.

A silent drift of light blew in and became morning and perhaps the sun joined Ia briefly it showed up as colour in the flanking fields made a muddle of the clouds.

'Geeva,' she said.

There was nothing to do but sit and wait the tiny boat the river widening out she missed the girl's constant chatter missed her just. The loneliest place on earth was in that moment going home; all that it had meant at the start of her grand journey was almost forgotten in the detail of slog. There had been four things positive only one remained but the thought of Evie had slipped from view it looked smaller, a half thing dangling. Half of one was almost nothing but still it was something if she could find the pieces she could fix it. She pulled the harmonica from her pocket and practised Harper's tune let the river dictate her course whilst she filled the silence with sobs and something similar to music.

Time moved meandered lifted its momentum. The river pinned itself between the two counties a sheet flapped and badly ironed and Ia so small upon it she passed unseen a discreet ghost, a stain.

She passed a warehouse on her right the windows gone the glass replaced with flash faces they threw their voices at her told her they were stranded she could tell the water went up to the winch in the wall. She went on. There was nothing she could do she doubted she would even if she could. They were all stranded every life an island just different kinds was all.

Ia let the current navigate this last leg of her journey it traced the Cornish bank as she watched the greater world pass by the stretch of water flooded so far there was nothing to distinguish between river and field the tracks of hedges and trees splitting the water like strung-out beads.

The small canoe found a spur a fold in the land and when it drifted toward a cottage Ia let it. She took up the paddle and pushed against the granite wall and walked the boat between the windows she could not help but spy to get a feel of real lives. The boat pressed up against the glass extension and Ia cupped a hand for looking she wished she hadn't there were too many images branded at the back of her mind already. The old-dear couple sitting everyday normal their hands held tight holding on to something, one thing good it didn't matter now they had departed.

Ia jabbed the oar into the plastic window frame and returned to the deep the bulk of water dragging behind threatening to pull her under. If she had lain down it would have been easy to stop dead, river coffin, watch the clouds be clouds without wondering about rain waiting for a sun that might never come again. If she died wouldn't she see all of life's loved folk? She wished she could see all the kin gone by to stop her remembering wrong the fine-line detail of their deaths. Hadn't Mum and Dad been hand-hold tight? She thought so; if she closed her eyes she could see it clearly. Imagination didn't matter Ia had improved things with embellishment. Every painting looked better with colour, each picture told a beautiful, brilliant story. It was what made Ia what propelled her forward, this was the reason for her demise the reason for her rise again.

She heard an explosion downriver toward the dockyard and saw fire charge the sky.

'Phoenix.' She took up the paddle and continued toward the confluence where all rivers collided. Up ahead she could see what was left of the bridges, the Tamar Bridge urbanized with static vans and trailers they had been going someplace had forgotten where.

Ia paddled beneath the laddered steel structure unnoticed and she listened to the echo of argument of fight heard a baby yell and took a moment to erase all trace of that which she could not change.

'Be a phoenix,' she told herself and she followed a family of sculling egrets as they navigated the fallen joists of the second bridge the train-track spears and girders rising like fins from the deep.

Further down the river Ia could see the fire that had taken hold of the dockyard, the flush of flame welcome against the grey it flashed between buildings and lit up the cranes and the dead ships she wanted to join the bridge community behind her in cheer.

How wide the river how long the rhythm the ride going home. Ia recognized the landed car ferries on the Torpoint slipway stripped of their panels the guts of them gone only the giant rusted chains remained.

At times she thought she saw the sun come on now carve up the clouds but it was nothing, more likely her eyes playing tricks she had not slept well in weeks if she had slept at all. The river so wide getting wider Ia wondered how much of it was sea where one body of water ended where the other began.

So close to the south coast; she could smell the salt air it clung to the rain and fell at her feet home from home she could paddle in the boat her boots immersed in inch water.

'Evie.' She hunkered down and put her back into rowing no rain would weigh her down no wind could push her back no matter how hard it tried Ia Pendilly was coming home. In that moment she realized she was not running away but going toward.

She watched the city on her left retreat within a fog of fumes and smoke and the green of higher hills roll in to the right, the nub of Drake's Island rising up from nothing no more than a shingle dump, erosion in the estuary had taken its toll. The surrounding cliffs had been eaten by the fresh- and salt-water mix, gobfuls of earth bitten out of the landscape this place almost unrecognizable.

So many things had changed the headland that led to home somehow shrunken taken down. If the land was like this the people would be worse. The storms that hammered here had hit heartless, this was no place for new arrival only return.

When the tide came in to greet her the waves recognized the girl that used to be and made themselves known, Ia told herself she was coming home a hundred times it was the one thing the only thing that kept her from the dark. The bright childhood light returning it led to the courage to believe in a better version of herself.

Ia paddled on, the river becoming ocean wide. There were moments when the familiarity of things past unnoticed hooked her eye, Kingsand and the clock tower still standing the waves hitting the bedrock, spitting surf into the village; Ia wondered if anybody still lived there but it was too close to the shore most of it gone under, she doubted it. She kept the canoe from the hidden rocks that skulked the headland like snares she remembered them from childhood. When she saw the hermit's hut perched on the summit it was so sudden Ia jumped made the boat sway, she had not prepared for this, home. Whitsand

Bay, Rame Head and the tangled Freathy cliffs this was where she had been born where she would find the thread and pull it right. With every row forward Ia could feel the last thirteen years unravelling so much had been wasted so much could be fashioned new.

She kept her eye on the cliff edge and trawled it for signs of home some of the structures had been picked apart by wind, as she powered closer she saw most were scattered fallen to ground some trusses and roofs lay dumped in the sand. She looked for chimney smoke but nothing only gobby seagulls remained on the standing flues. The birds shouted down to her warned her to steer clear of the debris it was everywhere things that had fallen into the sea turned the tide into threat but it was too late no going back she stabbed the paddle into the surf she was going on going forward going home.

I A FELT THE UNDERSIDE of the canoe hit the rocks the cut-through passage blocked for a moment she went under held her breath felt the waves pushing she pushed back.

'Not today,' she shouted, she coughed the salt water from her lungs hung on to the side of a rock, waves in waves out. Breathe, get up, get free of water.

She went slowly across the wide stretch of foam and sand looking for their cave she had forgotten how many hollows and crags and dead ends there were more than she remembered. If things were still standing she would have found it in an instant but so many signs and markers had vanished it wasn't until she walked the main beach end to end that she saw it.

Ia stood at the mouth of the cave and let it speak to her say her name. So many years lost she barely recognized it wondered who had passed through had sat there since. She took a deep pull of sea air ducked her head and entered, it never used to be this small; the tide had gifted a little shell-sand it scooped into the corners made an ovum of the floor and walls everything peachy, blond, safe.

Instinct was to put her hands out to touch the sides, the things the cave had seen the things that it had heard Ia knew it was laughter that it remembered most. She looked for hanging shells and found none all trace of them tide taken. The slate walls wet with tiny rivulet water the land above veined through with natural springs the cliffs had been a good place to live.

When her eyes adjusted to the gloom she moved on to the rear of the cave their secret hiding place. More memory than ever before, she put out her hand and saw that she was shaking.

She hoped the message jar was still in the nook. She hadn't seen it since a long time ago, she imagined it far flung floating perhaps it found itself settled on another shore its message meant for Ia lost in translation.

'Where you at?' she asked and she thought she heard Evie giggle. She stretched into the crevice with her good arm tried to remember the left or the right of the thing it wasn't where it was supposed. That was a good sign, it meant Evie was the last to return the jar she never put it right and Ia reached again she pushed a stick into the split and heard the ping of glass and rolled it toward her. She lifted the jar and held it in both hands a new message folded within, the blunt pencil beneath in need of sharpening that was Ia's job.

She tried to unscrew the rusty lid hit it with her pocketknife and took out the note.

Such silence. Ia couldn't breathe. She recognized the paper it was all coming back to her; she wished she could stem the flow the cut of memory she didn't want to bleed out.

Her name Evie's name five lines between she traced her fingers over the words reading was not enough; each letter written perfectly despite.

Ia,

Promise me you will do all the things we said we would do don't forget to do them for me and you. I know I'm not going to make it I have to leave you leave this life I know you won't let me so I'm going while you go for help. Don't blame yourself Ia I don't blame you I love you.

Evie

Ia said her sister's name signed it off with this one word. Numb hands returned the letter to the jar, the jar to the gash in the rock. She sat down on the flat rock it was where she always sat she pulled the coat around her dug her heels into the sand. She didn't want to remember, the past was better left selected the best bits keepsaked that was all.

'Fucksake Evie.' She watched the band of sea retreat, the entrance to the cave a screen on which to view the world in all the years it had not changed so much. Still there was no part of Ia that could bear to remember all she knew of that night of their parents' suicide.

Ia had wanted to stay in the cave, that was all. One night and then two perhaps, she needed time to work things out make sense of circumstance. Except she couldn't and they hid in the cave until too late; no food so cold too late.

'It was my fault,' she said. 'It's my cross my fault my burden why did I let you die?'

Guilt and grief combined it was the worst kind of weight. Ia looked across to where her sister had lain so consumed by cold, Evie had returned to warm this failing moment the instant Ia had run, the sorry paring from her in layers she had climbed the path gone close to the chalets but she knew it was too late. Her sister was gone she had felt it had known it when she returned to the cave she found her half undressed face down in the sand, gone for good.

'And still you wrote me.' Ia opened the sack and found the journal she wiped it dry and stood and reached and put it with the jar. 'I drew for you.'

She stood outside the cave and caught the last of daylight sat with the mess of reminisce strewn; she had come home to Evie to her memory, what now?

Ia watched the gulls land on the wet sand to peck at lugworms and she caught their eye and told them she was no bother they believed her.

'All that for this,' she said. 'Evie, how could I have forgotten?' She heard laughter and turned toward the rocks saw something maybe a little seraph light catching in the creases of a white dress.

'Geeva,' she said.

Ia put her hand over her eyes and stood the sky had brightened behind the cloud it was hard to see through the haze. She shouted the girl's name went toward her waited for her to stop playing games come into focus become familiar face. The girl turned and smiled and put up her hand to wave.

In that moment, in that child Ia saw the best of herself the part that she had lost. All those years she had been looking to find herself again so she could return to innocence.

She watched the girl throw off her coat and start to run toward the sea the hat gone and then the boots the white dress skin-thin against her the fade was sudden.

Ia stood in the entangling surf and watched it take the dress away and in its place one final memory: a lone girl carrying the body of her twin into the waves, lifting her sister's locket to her lips one final kiss to seal their faces their fate like delicate wings, a beautiful butterfly set free she knelt into the water, let go.

'I never let you go,' said Ia and she repeated her words it was as if she never understood the reason why until now. It all came down to loss, an unbounded cavern that no matter how stuffed with imagination it never did fill never did heal complete. Ia's life was built from the loss of those she loved, it was a story of parts that would not connect she would never be whole. With Evie gone she was half a person even though she blocked the guilt it had always been with her. Nothing forward nothing back nothing to hold on to or to hope for, hollow cave hollow heart.

She threw off her coat the boots traced her childhood footsteps in the surf her bare bruised and blistered feet at home in the spray so much water endured and yet never enough she asked it one final question shouted it ran it into the sinking silt: 'What now what now what now?'

IA LAY ON HER back, breathless. Clouds in clouds out, the rain finally stopped. She felt the waves beneath her, holding hands, carrying her to the sand, fingers to her belly, putting her down. One final gift, an exchange for all the lost souls, little creatures. She sat up and lifted her sodden top put her hands skin on skin she felt her insides move the beginnings of new life, budding.

'Twins,' she said. Two flowers growing from the same stem one weak one strong like she and Evie, split. The frailer fallen, Ia would keep this one afloat hold it heaven high she promised this. The baby's life would be guarded by her life.

She turned to face the cliffs found the path and went to it the climb no longer a bother in Ia's mind she had walked the earth in her break for freedom.

'Somewhere here,' she told herself, somewhere buried beneath her feet was the rub of concrete the foundation of home smelt jasmine knew this was the place. She kicked at the last remaining pile of clapboard that someone had collected for firewood and told herself it would do for one night warm. She saw the swing the tree on which she and Evie used to play free-falling its roots put out to air nothing to hold on to.

Everything Ia thought she knew had slipped past, what she would relearn would be love and hope, veracity. She sat amongst the wreckage and pulled the harmonica from her hip pocket played the one song she knew. From the corner of her eye she saw a shadow smear up against the horizon it reminded her of the painting in her journal that came from spilt ink the river of black that ran the page without direction. A bird an animal creeping toward her with one hand she kept playing with the other she pulled out the knife. She watched the form move freely a river widening coming to her heard a voice it was humming Harper's song.

Ia stopped playing and stood.

'Jenna?' She dropped the instrument the knife and her hands went to her belly.

'I bin waitin for you,' he said.

'I thought you was dead.'

'Close.' He stepped forward and smiled. 'I waited for you at the waterwheel, dint know if you been or gone.'

'I lost track, int never bin good at time.' There was so much to tell him her mouth filled with words, jumbled: Harper, Evie, their baby's beating heart inside. She kept silent and put her hands into his took his time and gave him hers, no need to hurry, they had plenty. Their lives stretched so far ahead of them the horizon did not exist, forever sky.

Ia smiled when he pulled her to him, one kiss, the love in his eyes reflecting in her own, firelight.

'Don't leave me.' She pulled closer.

'I promise.'

She turned her face into his neck saw the sudden flash of gold at his chest. 'That's my locket.' She stepped back. 'It is int it?'

Jenna took a moment to unclasp the chain he handed it to her.

'Evie.' Ia wiped her tears so she could see inside the locket. 'I int seen your face in so long.'

'Let me do that.' Jenna took the chain from her and fastened it around her neck. He told her not to ask how he had got it from Branner.

'I don't want to know; the creek and all em are dead to me already.' She took his hand and kissed it told him to never let go.

'Never.'

'Cus we're family now int we? We're all each other got.'

Jenna smiled. 'You're all I want.'

They returned to the beach to walk the shore hand in hand it was what they did a thing they would always do.

'Int so bad here,' said Jenna, and Ia agreed all things considered it was the best place on earth.

'We'll build a house from scratch, won't stop till it's perfect,' he added.

'And a garden,' said Ia. 'Fruit trees and vines, maybe grow an orange tree. Start over.'

'This coast is perfect,' said Jenna, 'and not one soul about.'

He looked across the beach and down at Ia and she smiled, if only he knew how many stood in the sand beside them, they were river running, freedom found.

A NOTE ON THE TYPE

In 1924, Monotype based this face on types cut by Pierre Simon Fournier c. 1742. These types were some of the most influential designs of the eighteenth century, being among the earliest of the transitional style of typeface, and were a stepping stone to the more severe modern style made popular by Bodoni later in the century. They had more vertical stress than the old-style types, greater contrast between thick and thin strokes and little or no bracketing on the serifs.